THE

Bell at
Sealey Head

Ace Books by Patricia A. McKillip

THE FORGOTTEN BEASTS OF ELD
THE SORCERESS AND THE CYGNET
THE CYGNET AND THE FIREBIRD
THE BOOK OF ATRIX WOLFE
WINTER ROSE
SONG FOR THE BASILISK
RIDDLE-MASTER: THE COMPLETE TRILOGY
THE TOWER AT STONY WOOD
OMBRIA IN SHADOW
IN THE FORESTS OF SERRE
ALPHABET OF THORN
OD MAGIC
HARROWING THE DRAGON
SOLSTICE WOOD
THE BELL AT SEALEY HEAD

Collected Works
CYGNET

THE
Bell at Sealey Head

Patricia A. McKillip

ACE BOOKS, NEW YORK

THE BERKLEY PUBLISHING GROUP
Published by the Penguin Group
Penguin Group (USA) Inc.
375 Hudson Street, New York, New York 10014, USA
Penguin Group (Canada), 90 Eglinton Avenue East, Suite 700, Toronto, Ontario M4P 2Y3, Canada
(a division of Pearson Penguin Canada Inc.)
Penguin Books Ltd., 80 Strand, London WC2R 0RL, England
Penguin Group Ireland, 25 St. Stephen's Green, Dublin 2, Ireland (a division of Penguin Books Ltd.)
Penguin Group (Australia), 250 Camberwell Road, Camberwell, Victoria 3124, Australia
(a division of Pearson Australia Group Pty. Ltd.)
Penguin Books India Pvt. Ltd., 11 Community Centre, Panchsheel Park, New Delhi—110 017, India
Penguin Group (NZ), 67 Apollo Drive, Rosedale, North Shore 0632, New Zealand
(a division of Pearson New Zealand Ltd.)
Penguin Books (South Africa) (Pty.) Ltd., 24 Sturdee Avenue, Rosebank, Johannesburg 2196,
South Africa

Penguin Books Ltd., Registered Offices: 80 Strand, London WC2R 0RL, England

This is an original publication of The Berkley Publishing Group.

This is a work of fiction. Names, characters, places, and incidents either are the product of the author's imagination or are used fictitiously, and any resemblance to actual persons, living or dead, business establishments, events, or locales is entirely coincidental. The publisher does not have any control over and does not assume any responsibility for author or third-party websites or their content.

First edition: September 2008

Library of Congress Cataloging-in-Publication Data

McKillip, Patricia A.
   The bell at Sealey Head / Patricia A. McKillip.—1st ed.
      p. cm.
   ISBN 978-0-441-01630-3
   I. Title.

PS3563.C38B45 2008
813'.54—dc22

                                          2008021614

PRINTED IN THE UNITED STATES OF AMERICA

10 9 8 7 6 5 4 3 2 1

THE
Bell at
Sealey Head

One

J udd Cauley stood in his father's rooms in the Inn at Sealey
Head, looking out the back window at the magnificent
struggle between dark and light as the sun fought its way
into the sea. Dugold Cauley seemed to be watching, too, his
gray head cocked toward the battle in the sky as though he
could see the great, billowing purple clouds swelled to over-
whelm the sun striving against them, sending sudden shafts
of light out of every ragged tear in the cloud to spill across
the tide and turn the spindrift gold. His pale eyes seemed
to reflect stray colors in the sky. But they had already lost
their fight, Judd, glancing at him, thought with sudden pity:
those old eyes overcast with mist. Slowly the wild light faded
outside as well. Twilight smothered one last burning ember
of sun. The bell rang then, as always, and Dugold, groping

his way into the rocker behind him, turned his face toward his son.

"Was that a carriage I heard in the yard?" he asked, predictable as the bell.

Judd murmured absently, still watching the cliff behind the inn, where the waves were breaking so hard they sent spume high in the air that turned again and fell as a gentle rain onto the rocks. Gulls hung in the wind, white as froth, so neatly balanced they were motionless in all that roil before they dropped a wing, caught a current, and cried out as they flew over the sea. Another bell was sounding: the channel marker tumbling about in the tide, jangling to guide one last fishing boat toward the harbor on the north side of the headland.

"Judd—"

"I know, I know," he said mildly. "They're fetching up in droves for the night."

"I'm sure I heard—"

"Mr. Quinn will call me if someone stops. Stiven Dale's boat is wallowing up the channel like a cow trying to swim. His hold must be full of something."

"Water," his father said dourly. "That tub is as old as I am."

"Fish, I'll bet you. I'll send Mrs. Quinn down in the morning to see what he's got."

"Water."

"You hope." Judd dropped his hand lightly on Dugold's shoulder. "I know Mrs. Quinn has trouble with fish."

"She thinks they're not dead unless she drowns them in boiling water for an hour."

"I'll have a word with her."

"Why bother?" Dugold set the chair going on its rockers with a restless push. "I'll be in my grave before Mrs. Quinn learns how to cook."

"So will I," Judd breathed, having a sudden, mouth-watering memory of his mother's cooking.

"Her chowder," his father said wistfully, reading Judd's mind as he sometimes could. "Butter and cream and the clams so tender they melted between your teeth. Her leek-and-crab pie. You've got to find a better cook. Then we'd have them coming."

"I'd have to pay a better cook," Judd reminded him. "Mrs. Quinn works for as close to nothing as we can afford." He was still then, his eyes caught by an unexpected bit of color among the rocks.

"Marry somebody," Dugold suggested, again predictably. "Then she'd cook for free. Only make sure she can cook before you ask."

"There's a proposal sure to charm a woman into my life."

"Well, it's a thought to think about, isn't it? Last time I looked, you had a few charms of your own. All from me, of course. Have you changed so much since I went dark inside?"

"How would I know?" Judd asked absently, peering through the thick whorls of glass at the odd bobble and flut-ter beneath the soft rain of tide. "Somebody's out there."

"Who?"

"I can't tell..." He narrowed his eyes, picked out the sky-blue lining on a black cloak flapping like bats' wings, a matching blue scarf streaming down the wind, a gold band on the hat the wearer clapped firmly to his head with one hand. "A stranger, I think. But what's he doing out there?"

3

"A guest," his father exclaimed, slapping the rocker arm with his palm. "Go and catch him before he gets away."

"Before he gets swept away, more likely."

"Whatever. Go on—" He was squinting at the window, too, as though he could see the elegant idiot wandering at the edge of the cliff with the tide thundering and breaking over his head, the hard rain of a sudden squall mingling with it now, streaking the glass. "Reel him in before you lose him."

But the stranger was gone when Judd went out to look for him.

Judd lingered on the cliff. The squall passed overhead and away, blown inland by the fierce wind. He watched the world around him melt into twilight. He was a sturdy young man with pale, curly hair and fair-weather eyes, unshaken by the wind trying to buffet him into the sea. He went just close enough to the edge to make sure that the stranger wasn't clinging desperately to a rock below, or floating like some exotic bird in the water. Accidents happened along that rough headland, where the bluff sloped down toward the deep channel the fishing boats and the occasional merchant ship used to reach the calmer waters of Sealey Head harbor. The town clung like a colony of barnacles to the rocky shore and the hillsides, bracketed at one end by the inn and at the other by Sproule Manor, on its lofty perch overlooking the harbor and the inhabitants. Judd could see its broad, mullioned windows glazed with firelight, lamplight. On the wooded hill above the inmost curve of the harbor, the ancient, stately façade of Aislinn House stood fading like a ghost of itself into the dusk, fires flickering randomly, frail as moth wings within the dark windows.

Judd knew every face born between those juts of land.

He had drawn his first breath on Sealey Head, sent his first piping cry back at the seagulls. The inn had been built by his great-grandfather at that point along the rugged cliffs of west Rurex, where a traveler watching the sun sink into the sea from his horse or carriage window might decide that the broad stone building, with its thick walls, bright windows, clean, cobbled yard, might be a good place to stop for the night. For half a century there wasn't much choice in the matter: it was either the inn, or the frumpy tavern beds in town that you reeled into drunk so not to care who pushed in beside you and snored in your ear all night.

The town had grown more prosperous since then. Some days over half a dozen merchant ships shifted their spiky profiles near Toland Blair's warehouses, as dockworkers unloaded goods that would travel overland to the cities. Now the traveler had choices: a newer tavern along the docks or another inn at the back of the harbor, far from the exuberant winds and the cliff that shook under the tide on a stormy night.

All that Judd explained more than once to his father. But Dugold still blamed himself: his failed eyes, his failure to follow his own father's footsteps into prosperity. Judd, he decided, must restore the inn to its former glory. It was in his blood. His destiny. Judd had no particular ambitions beyond reading every book in the world and taking care of his father. He had grown up making beds and fires, cleaning stables and scorched pots, carrying baggage to and fro, filling tankards in the dining room, chopping carrots in the kitchen. It was no hardship to stand in the doorway under the inn sign, welcoming travelers. These days, he handed them over to the care of Mr. Quinn, who brought up their baggage and stabled their horses, and Mrs. Quinn, who cooked. Their daughter, Lily, washed the sheets, dusted the mantels, swept the grates. They stayed on even as business dwindled. A bed was a bed, Mrs. Quinn said forthrightly, and better the one under your back than the one you left behind when you left to look for better than you had. Judd would never have to fear she would want to leave. No indeed.

He gave up hoping, resigned himself to her watery chowders, her rubbery fish, her bread so dense he could have bricked a wall with it. When there were no guests, he ate with his father, hunched over a table, turning pages with one hand and shoveling in whatever it was Mrs. Quinn called supper that night. After Lily took their plates away, he continued reading aloud while Dugold rocked and drank ale. When he started snoring in his chair, Judd called in Mr. Quinn and went to read in his room under the eaves, where the books along the walls stoppered the chinks in the mortar. He read anything that came his way: histories, romances, speculations about the nature of things, journals of travels to far-flung places, folklore, even the odd book about an elusive, unwieldy, nine-legged, hundred-eyed beast that sang like a swan and burned words like paper when it spoke. Magic, it was called. Sorcery. Enchantment. It was everywhere just beyond eyesight; it was yours for the making of a wish. So he read, not quite believing, not knowing enough to disbelieve. Inevitably his thoughts would turn to the bell that tolled each day, exactly when the last burning shard of sunlight vanished beneath the waves.

As though someone in an invisible world watched, and in that precise, ephemeral moment, the dying sun and the single toll bridged one another's worlds.

That night he fell asleep on his bed with a book some-one had left at the inn: *The Lives of Beetles in Their Habitats.* Abandoned, mostly likely. Fled as from a tome of evil sorcery. The fussily detailed sketches of the Blue Wood Beetle and the Green-Winged Black Beetle fell over his face, a beetle on each eye. For a while the wind and tide, the passing squall, sighed and murmured about him; window ledges creaked; the fire burrowed noisily into itself; flames hissed and gut-tered into ash.

A tap on the window woke him. Another. Then a hand-ful, as though bony fingers had drummed themselves on the glass. Judd sat up abruptly, the book sliding to the floor. Hail? he wondered. Then: Why am I dressed? Another spo-radic run of taps hit the glass, and an improbable vision came into his head, that the merchant's daughter, Gwyneth Blair, had wandered over the cliffs on a whim to stand under his window and throw pebbles at it.

"Right," he grunted, and reached for the lamp.

It nearly lost its chimney when he swung a casement open and held the light into the wind to see what was going on. He pulled it in hastily, but not before it had revealed a face.

It was the colorful stranger, holding his hat on his head with both hands now, the cloak luffing against him like a sail. The lamp had produced an odd flash of fire coming from the stranger's eyes. Magic, Judd thought, still befuddled. Then he amended that: spectacles.

"Good evening," the man called politely. "Sorry to bother, but yours was the only window lit. I need a room. Do you know which window I should pitch pebbles at next?"

Judd blinked. His mouth was open and full of air, he

realized; he forced it to move. "Welcome, sir. Of course I have a room for you. If you'll meet me at the front door, I'll be happy to show you in."

"Thank you," the stranger said, after Judd had taken his lamp downstairs and opened the door. Judd stepped back abruptly to dodge a voluminous sneeze. "I beg your pardon. I've been out on the cliffs since this afternoon."

"I know. I saw you earlier." Two horses stood patiently behind the man, one saddled, the other carrying a bulky assortment of baggage. Judd lifted his head, shouted up through the floorboards. "Mr. Quinn!" There was an answering thump: Mr. Quinn falling out of bed.

"My books," the stranger explained. "I should get them inside."

"Books."

"I packed them very carefully, but they may have picked up some damp from the rain."

"How?"

"How—"

"How could you leave your books out in this weather?" Judd demanded. "You should have come in earlier."

The man gazed at him, then smiled suddenly, very pleased about something inexplicable. He looked slight but vigorous beneath his cloak. His lean face seemed colorless in the lamplight, perhaps from reading all the books he carried. Beneath the spectacles, his eyes were very dark; his long black hair was damp and tangled from the briny air.

"You like to read, then?" he guessed. "That's rare among proprietors of wayside inns. I'll let you borrow my books if you like."

Judd's eyes went to the bulging leather bags tied to the packhorse. "You'd leave them here?" he asked huskily.

"No. I'm staying here. I don't know how long. If you can accommodate me. I'd prefer a room at the top of the inn for now, a corner room, if you have such, overlooking the harbor and the town."

Mr. Quinn appeared in the lamplight, yawning, buttoning his vest with one hand and carrying a lantern with the other. He was an affable man, thin as an eel, with a great gray mustache and one eye swiveled outward, as though he were perpetually thinking of two things at once.

"Sorry, sir," he said, for no discernible reason to Judd, and to the stranger: "Good evening, sir. You have horses to stable, I see."

"Books first."

"And then the horses. Yes, sir. Is the gentleman hungry? Should I wake Mrs. Quinn?"

"Yes," said the gentleman.

"No," Judd said hastily, remembering supper that night. "I'll fix him something."

"Some bread and cheese will do me," the stranger suggested. Judd gazed at him worriedly. "Just cheese?" he amended tentatively.

"I'll see what I can find," Judd promised. "And I have the perfect room for you upstairs, very large and comfortable, with views of the town and the hills. I'll show you."

"This seems a quiet place," the man said, stepping at last across the threshold. "I didn't notice a great deal of activity this evening. Very little. In fact—"

"None at all," Judd finished wryly.

"Is that unusual?"

"These days, no." He paused, added despite feeling his father's eyes pop open in the dark, "There is another inn on Sealey Head harbor. If you dislike the sound of the sea."

"No, no. I don't dislike it at all. In fact, I may need another view later, facing the cliffs, if there is room."

"Good," Judd said, bemused. "Follow me, then, Mr.—Ah?"

"Dow. Ridley Dow. Traveling scholar." He held out his hand. "Mr. Dugold Cauley, I assume from your sign."

"My father. Retired to his rocking chair. I'm Judd Cauley."

"I'll start on the baggage," Mr. Quinn said, the waxed twists of his mustache beaming happily upon them.

They all staggered upstairs with the baggage. The wide room, with its bed and desk and wardrobe, looked suddenly a great deal smaller, with various cases and sacks littering the floor like debris washed ashore after a shipwreck. Ridley pronounced himself satisfied. Mr. Quinn left to see to the horses. Judd hesitated over the fee; Ridley proposed an amount so generous for room and board and stable that he took Judd's astonished silence for reluctance.

"Being a scholar, a traveler, and a book collector is unkind to the income. Fortunately most of mine is inherited. Perhaps, though—"

"No, no—"

"Perhaps I will find some trifling way to repay you for putting up with my eccentricities."

"If you can put up with our cook's eccentricities, which most have to bear only one night, we can tolerate any number of yours."

The dark eyes regarded him shrewdly behind the lenses. "I suppose she has been here for some time?"

"It seems like most of my life."

Ridley nodded. He tossed his hat and cloak on the chair, unwound the blue scarf. Judd, accustomed to a schoolmaster's rusty black, was surprised by Ridley's variations: the tiny gray birds on his black vest, the satin collar on his jacket, the silk piping along seams and sleeves. The scholar indeed had money, he realized. He had come deliberately to the wild shores of west Rurex. To Sealey Head. To stay indefinitely.

"Why?"

Again the lenses flashed at him, signaling a swift comprehension of matters at hand. "Why did I come here to this rough place at the edge of the land?"

"Yes."

"Because I was reading one afternoon in my study in the middle of the great noisy city of Landringham on the other side of Rurex, and I heard the bell toll the sun down on Sealey Head." Judd stared at him; he nudged a bag gently with his boot. "In one of my books. Among my eccentricities is the pursuit of things mysterious, otherworldly, magical. There is magic in this place. I want to find it."

Judd found his voice after a moment. "Can I borrow the book?"

"I hoped you'd ask. You would recognize names mentioned."

"I never recognized anything magic around here."

"You live in it."

"People say the bell's just an echo of something that happened a long time ago. Live here long enough, you don't hear it anymore."

"Did you? Stop hearing it?"

He shook his head. "No. I always wondered . . . It's just a

sound, though. Vanishes the moment you hear it. It comes out of nowhere. How do you go about finding nowhere?"

"I have no idea," Ridley said simply. "But I'm here, and I intend to find a way. If you have time to spare, perhaps you'll help me?"

"I think I could eke out the odd hour here and there," Judd answered dazedly.

"Good," Ridley said, with his quick, pleased smile. He added, "Does Mrs. Quinn brew the ale here, too?"

"No. You're in luck there. Come downstairs. I'll put some supper together for you."

"There's more magic in a tankard of ale than in most of the world, some days," the scholar mused as he followed Judd through the quiet inn to the kitchen. "Along with transforming memory and a very rugged road, it's usually there under your nose when you need it. You must only recognize the magic. That's what the books say, anyway. In the raw ends of the earth, in a tankard of ale. Perhaps, one day, even in Mrs. Quinn's cooking."

"Never," Judd said flatly, and went for the eggs and sausage in the larder instead.

Two

Gwyneth Blair heard the bell as the last, dying ember of light guttered into the cloud bank over the sea, and put down her pen.

She looked over the cobbled street, her father's warehouses, and the bobbing masts in the harbor from the highest room in the house, just below the peaked roof, where the sharply slanting walls made the place unfit for anything but brooms or a writer. She had wedged a tiny writing table under the single window, a rickety affair from the schoolroom, whose surface her older brother had riddled with a penknife when he was bored. An ugly cushion, covered with lime ribbons and liver-colored velvet, that she had purloined from the parlor protected her from the split in the scullery stool she had rescued from the trashman's wagon. There was just room enough in the angle between the table legs and the roof for a small tin chest into which she dropped the pages of unfinished stories. When they were completed, various things happened to them. Some she read to the twins; others she took to the bookseller, Mr. Trent, for comment. Most were consigned to the dark under her bed, to be considered when she was in a better mood. A few she took down to the garden and burned.

It grew dark quickly in the tiny room after the sun went down. She dried her pen, capped her ink, dropped a half-covered page into the chest. She sat a moment longer, following the ebb tide out of the harbor, through the rocky channel where a fishing boat foundered, invariably, once a year, and out to the restless deeps, already growing shadowy with dusk.

The bell had haunted her as long as she could remember.

It was the first thing she had written about, years earlier, the most exciting, the most dreadful piece of writing she had ever done. That had gone under her bed and never come out. Since then, her written explanations of the mystery of the bell had grown more sophisticated, more complex. Most still ended up under the bed. Some she showed to Mr. Trent, who held the common local belief about the phenomenon but enjoyed what he called her excursions into the imagination.

The makeshift latch on the peaked door rattled up and down. Gwyneth, who had heard no footsteps on the steep, narrow stairs, moved quickly, dodging the ceiling as she stood from long practice, and opened the door.

The baby of the family grinned at her toothily. She was not yet three, a plump, golden-haired, violet-eyed armful. Of all of the siblings, she most resembled their mother, who had died a few months after her birth. No wonder Gwyneth had heard no steps; Dulcie had done away with her shoes again, and who knew where this time?

"Tantie says come down."

"I'm coming. Where, you miserable child, have you hidden your shoes?"

"Guess."

"Indeed." Gwyneth hoisted Dulcie up into her arms. "Do you think our father has nothing better to do than send his ships out to exotic lands to bring you back new shoes?"

"The bird is here for tea," Dulcie said complacently, knocking Gwyneth's spectacles askew with her dimpled elbow. "And Dary."

Gwyneth stifled a sigh, as well as a few thoughts unwise to express around the chatterbox Dulcie. "How wonderful," she said flatly. "How extremely pleasant for all of us to be favored by the magnificent presence of the bird."

She started carefully down the stairs, keeping an eye out for stray shoes. She, too, had inherited their mother's curly gold hair, but her eyes were practically colorless, gray as a fogbank with no storm in sight, and she had somehow grown nearly as tall as their father. That this did not discourage Raven Sproule, the bird, from seeking her out over his cup of tea never ceased to amaze her.

What ails the man? she wondered, putting Dulcie down to walk at the bottom of the stairs. I'm a merchant's daughter who wears spectacles and spends a good deal of her life in an attic. Has his father run through the family fortune already?

She remembered to plant a smile on her face as she opened the parlor door.

Their mother, who had rarely used the dark, windowless

room, had furnished it with her least favored items, hence the lime-and-liver cushion. Curiosities their father had gleaned from his ships wound up there: lamps made of seashells, animal-skin carpets complete with eyes and teeth, a huge round brass table, a folding screen painted with a snake coiling among jungle plants and flicking its tongue toward a squawking fledgling in its nest, an entire collection, in various sizes and styles, of ships in bottles. The more interesting oddments had been pilfered by the twins: the strange drums and rattles, the deeply bellowing conch shells, the peculiar games with polished stones for counters, the curtain made of strands of beads and minute stuffed hummingbirds. What was left was uncomfortable, ugly, or too bizarre even for the twins.

Aunt Phoebe considered the room an educational gift to the inhabitants of Sealey Head, a sort of museum, and opened it to guests as often as she could. She sometimes wore the thin shawls with their bright, glinting threads while she poured tea, though the pinks and oranges rarely matched her habitual somber shades. She had come to live with her brother and care for his children after his wife died. It was, Gwyneth had thought at the time, like continually tripping over, or having to avoid, some cumbersome foreign object her father had brought home and constantly shifted into inconvenient places. But they gradually learned to live around her, for, despite her stodginess, she had a good heart.

"There you are," she purred in her deep voice, as Gwyneth entered. Raven Sproule, trying to smile with his mouth full, was having his customary effect on Phoebe. Daria was there, too, his younger sister, all flutterings and lace, doing that thing with her gooseberry eyes. Her long lashes went winking and blinking up and down a few times at Gwyneth;

she complained of weak vision, even to total strangers, as she peered confidingly at them.

"Gwyneth!" she exclaimed, as though the gloom had cast some doubt upon the matter.

"Daria. How lovely," Gwyneth exclaimed back, trying to remember exactly when the Sproules had somehow become a fixture around the tea table. "And Raven. What a surprise. How are you?"

"Much better now," he said meaningfully, having worked his bite into a less obtrusive position. Like his sister, he was fair and stocky, with a beak like a jungle bird and practically no chin. It was an odd combination, she thought. But what would he care what anybody thought? His father was Sir Weldon Sproule; his family had lived at Sproule Manor for two hundred years, and owned most of the pastures and small farms in the protected river valley east of Sealey Head. Raven was heir to the lot. Except for Aislinn House, which had begun crumbling while Sproule Manor was only a wish in an ambitious farmer's heart, nothing in Sealey Head was more stately than Raven's pedigree.

"Now," he added, in case Gwyneth hadn't quite understood him, "that you're here. Your aunt said you must have been upstairs writing your stories for the children."

"Bad, bad for the complexion." Daria waggled a finger chidingly, then bit into a tart with the other hand. Her eyes widened again; she looked reproachfully at Aunt Phoebe, who had pulled Dulcie onto her knee and was being charmed by her. Rhubarb, Gwyneth guessed. She plucked the tart from Daria's fingers before Daria dropped it into the umbrella stand made from some unfortunate pachyderm's foot.

"Never mind that. Have a seed cake instead."

"What are your stories about?" Raven asked. "I hope there are horses in them."

"Or pirates," Daria added with enthusiasm. "Great, hairy pirates with gold in their ears who are tamed and civilized by love. I read one like that just last week."

"Oh, novels," Raven said restively, glancing under the lid of an oddly hairy wooden box. "I can't bear to read novels. Why sit still in a chair reading about somebody else's life when you could be living your own?"

"Good question," Gwyneth said, licking jam off her finger. Her aunt swiveled an eye at her; she lowered her hand hastily. "I think—"

"I mean, I'd rather ride," Raven went on, encouraged. "Or you could sit around a good fire with your companions and talk. Why do something so solitary?"

"How else could I meet a pirate?" Daria demanded.

"Why would you want to? I'm sure they never bathe, and they wouldn't know what to do with a cup of tea. Pour rum into the teapot and drink through the spout, no doubt."

"Not my pirates," Daria said firmly. "Mine would be the well–brought up, sensitive types, who were driven to the sea through no fault of their own, and welcome any chance to escape from their debauchery."

"Bauchery," Dulcie echoed happily from her aunt's knee, and Phoebe's spine straightened abruptly against the wicker.

"However did we get on such a subject?" she wondered to Gwyneth, as though her niece was the one who had invited pirates into their tea party.

"Not a clue," Gwyneth murmured, and groped for a subject. "How are your horses?" she asked Raven, and he was off into knees and hocks and hoof infections. Daria put her hand to her mouth, yawned delicately, and shifted closer to Gwyneth, while Raven, beamed at by both Phoebe and Dulcie, wandered toward the warmth.

"We came to ask you to ride with us tomorrow," Daria said softly. "We must pay a visit to Aislinn House. My mother is sending Lady Eglantyne some novels to read in bed, and an herbal pillow. She finds them very comforting when she can't sleep." She lowered her voice even further. "Dr. Grantham says Lady Eglantyne may not live much longer. She's old and very frail."

"But what—" Gwyneth said incoherently, thinking of the huge, quiet, melancholy house, the few servants left in it, most of them as old as Lady Eglantyne.

"The doctor advised her to summon her heir from Land-ringham." Daria gave Gwyneth the full force of her round, green stare. "It is immeasurably exciting."

Gwyneth opened her mouth again, was distracted by Dulcie's laughter. The sight of Raven on his hands and knees, his hair in his eyes like a pony's, arms and legs pumping rhythmically up and down, rendered her speechless.

"Raven, whatever are you doing?" his sister cried.

"I'm being a perfect trotter."

Dulcie crowed again; even Phoebe had begun to laugh. Gwyneth closed her mouth. No, she told herself adamantly. I can't like him just because he makes the baby laugh.

"What a girl it is," Daria sighed fondly. "Your tiny sister is already turning heads. So, tomorrow. Will you come with us?"

"Of course she will," Aunt Phoebe said briskly, keeping

one eye firmly on priorities, even in the midst of revelry, and that, the speechless Gwyneth thought, was that.

Later that evening, after Dulcie had been put to bed, she read the beginning of her new story to the twins.

" 'The Bell at Sealey Head.' "

"Not the bell again," Crispin groaned, and Pandora clouted him lightly with her knuckles.

"Be quiet. Go on," she encouraged her sister. "I'm sure it will be wonderful."

They were both thirteen. A spiky age, Gwyneth remembered. Crispin was growing gawky, and Pandora moody, inclined to bursting into a temper or tears for no articulated reason. For the first time in his life, Crispin was taller than his twin, and already talking of following their older brother, Rufus, to sea. They had their father's chestnut hair and their mother's purple-blue eyes, a striking combination of woodland colors that Gwyneth suspected would survive the season of gracelessness, the fits and starts of temperament, the readjustments of the bones, and bloom overnight into beauty.

"Thank you," she said gravely.

They were in the spacious library, the most comfortable room in the house, with its thick layers of carpets, the broad, ample chairs and sofas, the wide fireplace, the potted palms behind which their father had screened himself to pore over some papers. Gwyneth sat on a peculiar hourglass-shaped leather seat with arched wooden legs that her father said was a yak saddle, or some such. The twins sprawled on the green velvet sofa, Pandora hugging an embroidered pillow in her arms in anticipation.

Gwyneth cleared her throat and began.

Suppose.

Suppose one day long ago the little fishing town of Sealey Head had come to very dire straits. Great storms all winter kept the boats in the harbor, and in the spring, the fish, driven southward down the coast, or far out to sea, forgot to come back to be caught and eaten. Suppose, in spring, the boats went out and came back with nothing, and the rain, having fallen with all its might all winter, had simply grown depleted in the clouds. It was renewing itself busily within the floating vapors above, but could not yet fall. So the seedlings in the fields of Sir Magnus Sproule's magnificent farm were drooped and wilting.

Suppose the disasters did not end there.

Suppose the Inn at Sealey Head, exposed on its bluff facing the tumultuous waves, had begun, over the winter, to melt away. Its walls, battered by briny spindrift and rain, grew swollen and soft; its stones cracked under the lash of water and salt. Rooms leaked; travelers left in high dudgeon, complaining of water dripping into their beds as they slept. The stable roof fell in; all the feed moldered in the wet. To make matters much, much worse, a portion of the coast road just south of Sealey Head had been buried under boulders when the towering cliff it passed under collapsed in all the rain. The boulders had torn a portion of the road away, so there was nothing but a long, dangerous ravine from the top of the cliff to the great rocks in the sea below. Those traveling along the coast were advised to make a wide circle around Sealey Head. The town suffered from the lack of business, as did, very keenly, the innkeeper, Anscom Cauley, and his family. He was forced to let his stableman go, then his housekeeper, then, unfortunate man, his cook; Mrs. Cauley had to do all the work herself.

But that is not all.

Two more prominent and influential men in Sealey Head were also suffering from the harsh turn of Fortune. The shipping merchant,

Mr. Blair, had lost three out of four of his ships in the terrible seas, and the fourth had been driven so far out of its charted path that no one knew where it had gone. Rumor sighted it far to the north, trapped in a perpetually frozen sea among the icebergs. Or in dry dock on an island in the tropics, whose people spoke no familiar language, so could not tell the sailors where they were in the world. Mr. Blair expended the last of his fortune to send a fifth ship out to search for the missing.

And all was equally unwell at Aislinn House. Lord Aislinn's profligate ways had so depleted the family fortune that his daughter, Eloise, became his only hope. But a slender one at that: with no fortune, and a face like a vole, all small dull eyes and teeth, she had no prospects whatsoever. Not even the ambitious young Master Tibald Sproule, who had his eye on Aislinn House, would make an offer for her.

In such hideously difficult times, it seemed only a fortuitous stroke of luck would save the town. As luck would have it, it came, though not in any shape anyone could have expected.

Gwyneth stopped. The twins stared at her expectantly. Even their father had shifted a palm frond aside to gaze at her in wonder.

"Go on," Crispin grunted.

"That's all I have."

"But the bell!" He bounced a little, impatiently, on the sofa. "You said it was about the bell."

"I haven't figured that part out yet. Not in this story. Nothing seems right."

"I like all the catastrophes," Pandora commented. "I hope there are more of them before you put everything aright."

"I believe there will be. I haven't yet made up my mind about which of its faces Luck will be wearing." She laughed at their twin expressions, both of them astonished and annoyed at once. "I'm sorry. I was hoping you might have some suggestions for me."

"I cannot imagine how you will rescue your poor characters," Toland Blair told his daughter over the palm frond. "You've certainly made them wretched enough. I hope you'll at least show mercy to your beleaguered merchant. But why the bell? Why do you keep going back to it?"

He was a big, weathered man with gray streaks in his hair and broad mustache. After his wife had died, he took to sea on his own merchant ships for long, wearying periods, returning briefly now and then to comment on his children's heights and give them carved ivory animals, or wooden-soled sandals, or stranger things that Aunt Phoebe locked into a cupboard as soon as he had gone again. He was beginning to linger longer now on land; his seafaring eyes, wide and distant, were noticing again the wonders growing under his roof.

"It's a mystery," Gwyneth said simply.

He shook his papers straight on his desk and came out from behind the palms to poke at the fire.

"It's nothing more than the ghostly echo of the bell on a ship that foundered off the headlands long ago. It tolled its last as it was dragged under the waves, just as the sun vanished into the sea. That's what everyone says."

"Do you believe that?"

He looked surprised. "I never thought about it."

"I have."

"I know you have." He chuckled. "I've listened to your stories. The sea bell that the mermaid rings in vain every sunset to summon her long-dead lover. The bell tied around the neck of a gigantic hound let out only at sundown."

23

Gwyneth flushed. "You heard that one?"

"That was my favorite," Crispin said enthusiastically. "When it ate all the evil highwaymen."

"I liked the bell on the path into fairyland," Pandora said, "that signals the gate between worlds to open only at sunset."

"Well," Gwyneth sighed. "Nothing ever seems right to me."

"Perhaps because the truth of the matter is that simple," her father suggested. "That sad."

She looked at him doubtfully. Aunt Phoebe opened the library door then, sent the twins up to bed. She came to stand next to her brother in a rare, contemplative moment. Both heads bent, her white hair in a bun, his gray and brown tied at his neck; they gazed silently together into the fire. Gwyneth swallowed a sudden, flaring ember of memory.

Then Phoebe raised her head, said briskly to him, "Gwyneth has been invited to go riding tomorrow with Raven Sproule and his sister to visit Lady Eglantyne."

"Really." Her father glanced at Gwyneth. His mustache twitched at the expression on her face.

"He seems quite interested in our Gwyneth."

"Really," he said again, still gazing at his daughter. She widened her eyes abruptly, crossed them. He looked away, clearing his throat noisily.

"Well," he said only, "there is another tale in the making. Let's see what she does with this one."

Three

Emma found Ysabo in the closet under the grand staircase, where she kept the cloths and the brass polish for the carpet rods on the stairs.

From long experience, she kept one foot stuck out to hold the door open, and a good grip on the polish, while the vast hall shimmered into shape far beneath her. Ysabo was standing on a narrow stone landing, from which steps zigzagged forever, it seemed, down the wall. She smiled quickly, while Emma, her head reeling, stared down at knights in their black leather and armor and bright surcoats, so far below that the words in their deep voices echoed and bounced across the walls, became distorted, incoherent, voices in a dream. They had grown up together, the princess and the housemaid; they had known each other nearly all their lives.

"Sorry," Emma whispered, an ear cocked for footsteps on the worn floorboards on her side. "I was just putting things away."

"It's all right. I'm always happy to see you."

"Yes." She allowed herself a rare smile, wondering that she remembered how in those sad, quiet days. "It's good to see you, too. You look beautiful. Is it some special day?"

The princess was dressed in sage green, old lace, pearls as yellow as the foam that piled up on the shore sometimes in winter. The mass of her red, tightly curling hair had been pulled back into a cone of lace and gold wire. Amber the strange, speckled green-gold of her eyes hung from her earlobes and her neck. She made a little wry face at Emma's words, a twist to too-thin lips, an arch of carroty brow in her colorless skin.

"My mother says I'm a goblin-child," she had told Emma long ago, when they were both very small. She had added something that even now Emma wasn't sure she understood. "Well, she would know."

That day Ysabo answered, "It's my birthday. Aveline says something wonderful will happen at supper tonight. All the knights will be celebrating with me." The noise was increasing, crashing upward in waves against the stone walls. "I must go. The bell will ring soon, and, for one night in my life, instead of doing my usual supper rituals, I must go down in the company of Maeve and Aveline. I hope next time we will be able to talk."

"Oh, so do I. It's been too long."

Ysabo smiled again, her face so bright that surely, Emma thought, in some other world it would be considered rare and hauntingly beautiful. She closed the door carefully. When

26

she opened it again a moment later, she put the polish and the cloths on the shelf, hardly starting at all when the unexpected steps creaked across the floor toward her.

It was Mrs. Blakeley, the ancient housekeeper. "Oh, there you are, Emma. The doctor is upstairs with Lady Eglantyne. There is a tea tray ready for him in the kitchen. He'll have it with some brandy in the library when he comes down."

"Yes, Mrs. Blakeley."

The old lady gave a gusty sigh. Her hair and her skin had faded all one color over the years; her face looked like an ivory cameo. Or a cracked and yellowing map, Emma thought, to some wonderful realm that everybody had long forgotten existed. "Sad times, Emma," she murmured. "Sad times . . . And a new mistress at my age."

"Maybe it won't come to that, Mrs. Blakeley," Emma said quickly, stricken by the sorrow in the pale, sunken eyes. "Dr. Grantham will coax her better."

But Mrs. Blakeley only shook her head silently, turned away. Emma closed the closet door and went down to get the tea tray.

In the kitchen, the cook, Mrs. Haw, was weeping silently as she boiled a pot of seafood shells for stock. Crab, shrimp, scallops, and mussels stood in neat little piles, waiting their turn; the kitchen smelled of root vegetables and brine. The cook, a massive mangel-wurzel of a woman, stirred with one hand and dabbed her tears into her apron with the other. She had a long braid of gray-brown hair and expressive hazelnut eyes, which, at the moment, were red and welling over and salting the brine.

"I'm not so much afraid of having nowhere to go," she explained to Emma between sniffs. "Amaryllis Sproule has been trying to steal me away from Lady E for years. But I grew up in this house. It's all I know."

"Maybe——" Emma began helplessly.

"I was scullery maid when my mother was cook, barely old enough to hold a chopping knife, I was. Oh, the size of strawberries, then! Oh, the radishes! And the late suppers among the gold candlesticks and crystal decanters. Now it's enough if a half cup of bisque comes back on her tray with a lowered tide line in the bowl."

Emma murmured something, picked up the doctor's tray, and escaped. The house, as far as she remembered, had been growing quiet and empty for years. Her mother, before she took to the woods, had charge of the stillroom in Aislinn House. Everyone consulted her, from Lady Eglantyne to the townspeople, who came knocking after twilight at the boot room door. Hesper taught her daughter her letters, her numbers, and how to copy the odd scribbles of stillroom doings, the concoctions, the requests, the various success and failures into the records book. When she was four, Emma had opened the pantry to lay a bundle of herbs to dry, and found the wild-haired little princess instead, with her homely face and enchanting smile. Such richness Emma had glimpsed, such space, such bustling, before she had slammed the door so hard the jars rattled on the stillroom walls.

Her mother, measuring some odd purple powder into a bowl, said only, "Don't be afraid. But don't talk about it, either, except to me. It will be our secret."

"But what is it?" Emma whispered.

"I'm not sure yet. I'll tell you when I know."

Emma had begun her training then, learning to care

for the ancient house, and using every door it possessed in the process. Doors opened only one way, she realized soon enough, as she and Ysabo became friends. The princess rarely opened her own doors, for one thing. And even then, she never inadvertently found Emma carrying a mop down the hall or winding a clock. It was always Emma, with an armload of folded linens, or heading in to make a bed, who opened a door and found the princess.

Neither ever crossed a threshold. Ysabo was not permitted to leave her house, though, from what Emma understood, it was all part of Aislinn House. And Emma was wary of the doors that only opened one way. They might let her through, but would they let her back? The noisy, brilliant world she glimpsed through randomly opened doors frightened her with its dizzying walls, the strange rituals she sometimes found Ysabo performing, the gruff voices of the knights, the lovely, passionate voices of the ladies, the echoes of quarrels, booming laughter, the magnificent, outlandish feasts where an entire stuffed deer with flaming tapers and crows among its horns might be paraded, accompanied by hunting horns, through the hall before everyone got down to the business of eating it.

Her Aislinn House only got quieter as Emma grew older. The younger servants left or were let go as rooms were shut up; visitors came more and more rarely. Even Emma's mother left, went to live in a tree in the wood. Someone had built a tiny cottage in a great hollow trunk; Hesper added a hovel here, a lean-to there, and trained some flowering vines from her garden up the walls to give it charm. There she continued her stillroom business, which gave her an income of sorts, mostly in the tender of a cheese or a fish or whatever was ripening in the fields. She encouraged old books, too, as payment, handwritten histories out of people's attics, for choice.

"I'm still puzzling," she told her daughter, when Emma asked about them. "I'll let you know."

By then, Emma had grown into a young woman in a sparse houseful of the aged. Occasionally, the more absentminded among them, like Fitch the butler, or Sophie, Lady Eglantyne's antique maid, confused Emma with her mother. She wore her dark hair in the same tidy braid they remembered down her back; she had the same sloe berry eyes and calm voice. When they called her Hesper, she wanted to laugh, for her neat mother now had frosty hair as wild as Ysabo's, and she only wore shoes when she walked into town. She ran barefoot as an animal in the wood and sometimes slept where she dropped under the stars.

Emma kept an eye on her, leaving a coin on her table now and then, bringing her fresh bread from town and news from Aislinn House. But nothing her mother concocted seemed to help Lady Eglantyne, who spent most of her days in a waking dream.

"She's old," Dr. Grantham said simply, when Emma brought the tea tray into the shadowy library, with its scents of polished oak and leather, and asked after her. "She's not in pain; she only wants to sleep." He poured brandy into his tea, gazed into it a moment before he sipped. He had been a young man when Emma had been born and Lord Aislinn had died; now she was grown, and he was middle-aged, and Lady Eglantyne was dying. "Someone must send for her heir. I've told just about everyone in the house, but nobody really wants the change. I've told her solicitors. Even they seem reluctant." He raised the cup to his lips, eyed Emma speculatively, as though she might take pen to paper and summon the missing heir. "Mrs. Blakeley keeps promising to write, then doesn't. Is there something ominous about this heir?"

"I wouldn't know, sir," Emma said gently. For lack of anyone else in the house to talk to whose wits weren't intermittently woolgathering, Dr. Grantham tended to forget Emma wasn't part of the family.

"What is she? A granddaughter of Lord Aislinn's brother, is that it? Lived in Landringham all her life?"

"I think that's right, sir."

"City girl." He took another sip. "What about your mother? Has she got anything more up her sleeve?"

"Nothing that works any better than what you've got."

"She's old," Dr. Grantham said again, sighing. "None of us has a cure for that. Unless there's some magic your mother stumbles across."

"I know she's still trying."

He set his cup in the saucer, still frowning at it. "Good."

The sundown bell rang. He didn't hear it, Emma guessed. Nobody did, really; it was just another noise they lived among, like wind or tide. But he turned abruptly, reached for his bag, as though someone, somewhere, had called to him. She picked up the tray, listening to Fitch tugging the cranky front door to let him out, while all around her, the vast secret house seemed to reverberate with the dying echoes of the bell.

The next morning they had visitors.

Emma was in the library dusting the windowsills, the

preferred spot for bluebottles to die, it seemed. There was some kind of bulky, colorful flow across the glass; she looked up, saw horses moving past to stop at the broad fan of stone steps in front of the house. The riders waited. Emma, her cloth motionless, watched them. There had been no stable kept for years. No Andrew or Timothy to help them down, take their horses. And no Fitch, either, she realized, to open the door for them. He must be down in the pantry, polishing the corkscrew or some such. One of the ladies laughed at the persistent silence. Emma recognized her then, and the young man as well: nobody else in Sealey Head had quite the parrot profile of the Sproules.

She scrambled out from behind the leather couch, tossed the dead flies into the fireplace, and hurried to the door.

She tussled it open finally, saw that the young master Sproule had dismounted, and was helping his sister down. The other woman had not waited for him; she slid a bit awkwardly to the ground, flashing a length of pretty mauve stocking to the watching trees.

Emma recognized her flighty golden hair, her spectacles. Miss Gwyneth Blair, the merchant's daughter, out riding with Raven and Daria Sproule. She started a curtsy, caught sight of the dust cloth still in her hand, and pushed it into her pocket. Daria Sproule gave her bright laugh again, an unexpected sound around the house those days.

"Good morning," Raven Sproule said affably. "Fine morning it is, too." He surveyed it a moment, complacently, as if he owned it, and then took a closer look at her face. "Emma, isn't it? Your mother lives up a tree or something."

Emma nodded stolidly. "Emma Wood, sir."

Daria rolled her eyes reproachfully at her brother, then

swooped her lashes toward Emma. "Our mother sent a little gift or two for Lady Eglantyne. Trifles, really. A couple of light novels, a scented cushion. Is there any chance we might give them to her ourselves?"

"I'll—"

"Oh." She tugged her tall friend forward. "This is Miss Blair."

"Yes, miss."

Miss Blair was puzzling something out between her brows as she gazed at Emma. They sprang apart abruptly, as she smiled. "That's where I've seen you. You come to my father's warehouses sometimes, for odd things. Plants, rare herbs and teas, dried—" She checked herself, her eyes widening, and ended tactfully, "oddments."

Emma, remembering the monkey paw, swallowed a sudden bubble of laughter. "Things for my mother, miss. Please come in. I'm sorry there's no one to take the horses."

"No matter; we'll just tie them here," Raven said, fixing their reins to some iron rings embedded in the step railing. "We won't be long."

"I can bring you tea in the library. It's a bit dark in there, but the furniture is covered in the parlor and the drawing room; they've gone unused for so long. Then I'll ask upstairs if Lady Eglantyne is receiving."

Their faces sobered at that, the reminders of silence and sadness within. Daria gave an inarticulate coo, and Raven a sort of a reassuring bleat. Gwyneth said more clearly, "Thank you," her spectacles flashing curiously back at the ancient, random assortment of upstairs windows.

Emma got them settled in the library, where Daria began immediately to chatter and Raven sat stunned wordless by all the books. She hurried down to the kitchen, found Fitch sitting in his shirtsleeves, polishing silverware and trading memories with Mrs. Haw.

"There's Sproules in the library, asking to see Lady Eglantyne," she told them. "And Miss Blair. Tea for three, please, Mrs. Haw, while I go up to look in on her ladyship."

"Visitors!" Mrs. Haw exclaimed, astonished. Fitch got up hastily, wrestling himself into his jacket.

"I'll take the tea," he told Emma firmly; no reason she should have all the excitement.

She left it to him and went upstairs, where the shadows clung to the walls like tapestries, and the old boards creaked underfoot as though wind were shaking the house. Most of the upper rooms were locked; only Lady Eglantyne slept there, lived there now in her great canopied bed festooned with lace, and her maid Sophie ensconced in the elegant room adjoining hers.

Emma tapped gently on the door with her fingertips. Perhaps Sophie was in the next room, and Lady Eglantyne asleep, for no one answered. She turned the latch soundlessly and peered in.

The princess stood on top of the highest tower in Aislinn House. Trees, sea, sky sloped dizzyingly around her. Emma could feel the wind blowing the morning scents of salt and earth, wrasse and wrack, newly opened flowers. Ysabo was surrounded by crows, a gathering so thick they covered the tower floor, a living, rustling, muttering pool of dark, consuming what looked like last night's leftovers, the remains of a great feast, crusts and bloody bones, withering greens, the drying seeds and bright torn peels of exotic fruits.

The princess, her bright hair unbound, flying on the wind,

turned her head; a dozen crows raised their heads here and there among the crush, cast black glances at the interloper. Emma put a finger to her lips quickly as the speckled amber eyes met hers. The princess nodded, but without her usual answering smile, only a swift, silent acknowledgment of Emma, as more bird heads turned, eyes catching light, dark-bright, little bones cracking in their beaks. Emma started to close the door. Then the wind pounced into the tower and away, sending Ysabo's hair streaming in its wake, and Emma saw the red blaze on her pale cheek, like a brand, of four thick, blunt fingers.

Emma almost made a sound. But the princess only gazed at her steadily, not moving, while at her feet beaks began to clack. Emma, trembling a little, shut the door.

She stared at the dark, heavy wood a moment, then drew a breath, blinking, and opened it again.

Sophie sat beside Lady Eglantyne's bed. She was dressed as usual in the loose, flowing pastels Lady Eglantyne liked to see, gowns that were decades out of fashion. Her ivory hair was parted and combed with doll-like precision into an hour-glass shape on the back of her head, topped with a little pancake of lace the light blue of her dress.

Beside her, the neatly folded lace-edged sheets and the silken counterpane rose minutely and fell on the breast of the slight figure in the bed. Lady Eglantyne dreamed. The stuff of her dreams, silence, shadows, diffused light, indeterminate shapes behind thin curtains, within mirrors, seemed to crowd the air, fill what could be mistaken for space.

Emma came softly to the bedside; Sophie, who had little enough company besides the sleeper, smiled behind the finger at her lips.

"Good morning, Hesper," she whispered.

"Good morning, Sophie," Emma said, resigned to answering to either name she heard. "Has she been awake this morning?"

"Only long enough to drink a little milk and to allow me to change her nightdress. Then she fell back to sleep."

Emma looked at the thin, distant face, almost lost in the floppy white bed cap.

"She seems peaceful."

"Doesn't she? Perhaps she's getting better. Must I wake her? Is the doctor here?"

"No. Raven and Daria Sproule have come to pay their respects. And Miss Blair."

"Visitors," Sophie murmured, awed. They both studied the dreamer, who was far away in some other world, having unimaginable adventures, or maybe just sitting on a rock and tatting.

"Well," Emma said finally. "We shouldn't wake her."

"No. Dr. Grantham will do that soon enough. He makes her talk if he can."

"Does she?"

"Not if she can help it," Sophie sighed. "She only wants to be left alone."

"Do you need anything?"

Sophie shook her head. "I have all I want. My needle and my novel and my lady." She smiled again at Emma, letting her see the bleakness dwelling beside the hope in her tired blue eyes.

Emma went downstairs again, suggested that the visitors return another time, and went back to work. While she worked, she opened every door she could find: closets, coat cupboards, attics, wine rooms and coal rooms; she even took the household keys from Mrs. Blakeley to unlock the rooms in hibernation. But she didn't find the princess again that day.

Four

The odd thing about people who had many books was how they always wanted more. Judd knew that about himself: just the sight of Ridley Dow's books unpacked and stacked in corners, on the desk and dresser, made him discontent and greedy. Here he was; there they were. Why were he and they not together somewhere private, they falling gently open under his fingers, he exploring their mysteries, they luring him, enthralling him, captivating him with every turn of phrase, every revealing page?

"Is there a bookseller in town?" Ridley asked, shifting a pile or two so that Judd could put down his breakfast. It was a peculiar affair of boiled fish, boiled potatoes, bread, jam, and porridge, Mrs. Quinn being uncertain exactly what meal to aim toward at that hour of the afternoon. Judd maneuvered the tray among the books on the table, unsurprised by the question.

"Yes. O. Trent Stationers, on Water Street. It's been there for over a century."

"O?"

"Osric. The family came from Tyndale, I think. City people. There was a rumor at the time that some domestic scandal forced them to seek a new home."

"Quite a reverberating scandal," Ridley commented, eyeing his meal. "Halfway across Rurex and down an entire century."

Judd smiled. "We in Sealey Head like to keep track of our history. It passes the time."

Ridley poked at the fish, which was strangely bowed down the middle. "What is this?"

"Who knows? Mrs. Quinn is of the opinion that if you can recognize it, it must be underdone." He paused, added tactfully, "I can take your board off your bill if you prefer to eat elsewhere."

"No." Ridley squared his shoulders, poked his fork firmly at the fish. "Let us see if we can get along."

"Mrs. Quinn isn't accustomed to feeding guests a midday meal. Most leave as soon as possible after breakfast."

"I see." Ridley ate a bite of fish, then of porridge. He paused to salt the porridge liberally, added pepper and butter for good measure. "Well, anyway, it's hot. I tend to keep quite irregular hours. Sometimes I'm up all night, sleep half the day."

Judd shrugged. "We can let Mrs. Quinn know what you prefer when."

"Thank you. Will you have time to take me there?"

"To—"

"O. Trent Stationers. I would like to peruse his books."

Judd gave the matter half a thought, then nodded. "I was going to send Mrs. Quinn to see what the fishers brought in yesterday, but I can go myself instead."

"Good!" Ridley said, with his quick, engaging smile. "We might have half a chance of knowing what we're eating."

"I'll just get my father settled first. I told him about you this morning. He was very pleased and would like to meet you at your convenience."

Ridley nodded. "Of course. And I him. He must have some odd tales tucked away of life in Sealey Head."

"He does," Judd said, surprised. "And he loves to tell them, so be warned. He stays pretty close to his rocker now. He can hear the sea from his window, and it comforts him since he lost his sight."

"Ah," Ridley said with sympathy. "An accident?"

"No. Just a slow passing. An ebb tide, he said, that never turned, just faded into black. He enjoys company." He glanced at a pile of books threatened by Ridley's elbow and a pot of coffee. "I'll see what I can find for bookshelves and bring them up. I believe there is one gathering dust in the kitchen."

In the kitchen, he found the wiry, angular Lily taking a scrub brush to the wooden table where Mrs. Quinn had been kneading bread. Judd could smell it baking. He longed to rescue it before it turned into something that could double as a doorknocker. But the damage had been done long before it reached the oven, he suspected, though the nature of the violence eluded him. Lily bobbed her head at him, an intense, serious girl who was growing much like her mother.

"Lily," he said, inspired. "Has your mother begun to teach you to cook?"

She came very close to screwing up her pretty, freckled face, then remembered her dignity. "No, sir. I don't take to cooking at all. Too many things to think about. Pots boiling, how long this, how many that, water or oil, how to chop, what goes in what—You made one bed, you know how to make them all. Or mop one floor. Or clean the ashes out of one fireplace—"

"Yes. I see."

"You don't have to fret about it, just do it. But bread. Well. It never seems to rise the same way twice, does it? Or take an egg. You never know what it's going to come out looking like, and that's even before you start cooking it."

"Yes."

"But cleaning a pot, or beating a carpet—you do, it's done. There. You see, sir?"

"With absolute clarity. Do you think your mother would miss this shelf if I take it away and put the cookbook over here instead?"

"Oh, no, sir. She never uses that old thing. She says the recipes are all out of fashion. And it's filthy with stains."

"With good reason," Judd breathed, putting his mother's cookbook safely on top of a cupboard. He unhooked the shelf from the wall, tucked it under his arm, and continued his ruthless pursuit. He found two more hanging shelves in the taproom, moved the beer mugs off them, and pushed them under his elbow. He came across an entire empty bookcase in the quiet sitting room. He gazed at it, perplexed, then realized what must have happened to the books: he had taken them all upstairs to his room.

41

Mrs. Quinn came at him talking as she walked down the hallway into the sitting room. Her freckled face was leaner, more lined than Lily's, but their neat attire, severe buns, and their expressions were amazingly similar.

"I'll have Lily mop these flagstones regularly now that we have guests, sir. And he might want to sit in here in the evenings among the cushions and the seashells."

"Maybe," Judd said dubiously. "Makes me want to sneeze. Mrs. Quinn—"

"I was at my wit's end as to which to serve him, sir, breakfast or what—I hope it was satisfactory."

"As what it was adequate."

"Thank you, sir," she said, looking pleased. "I do try."

"But I think next time—" He paused, gave up. "I'll have him talk to you about his erratic hours."

"His what, sir?"

"His—his meals."

"Yes, sir," she said, nodding. "Best to begin as we intend to continue, that way we don't forget what we're doing, do we?"

"Yes. No. Mrs. Quinn—"

"Now, sir, about supper—"

"I'm going into town to see to it," he said, seizing the bookcase bodily with his other hand and staggering off with his loot. "I promise you'll be the first to know."

He looked in on his father after adding the shelves to the clutter in Ridley's room. Dugold was napping peacefully in his rocker, a shaft of light along with one of the old stable cats warming his knees. Judd found Ridley outside, talking to Mr. Quinn about his horses. The boisterous and capricious weather had blown itself inland; the sea wallowed lazily against the cliffs, glittered in the distance, where the fishing boats clustered around whatever in the deep was flinging themselves at their bait.

"Mr. Quinn tells me there's a path down to the sand," Ridley said, as Mr. Quinn turned away. "He'll exercise the horses there on days I don't ride. Today, for instance. Do you mind a walk into town?"

"Not at all," Judd said, watching a coin above Mr. Quinn's head spark silver in the light before it fell back into his hand. Ridley had left his cloak behind, but even in sedate black he struck the eye, something sleek and unexpected in the familiar world of Sealey Head, like a red-winged blackbird among a flock of sparrows.

They walked the pleasant mile down the headland, across the steep channel bridge where they watched a ship follow the ebbing tide through the stony narrows safely out to open sea.

"One of Blair's," Judd said, recognizing the figurehead, a dolphin leaping upward out of the wood. "Wonder where it's going . . ."

"Blair?"

"Toland Blair. His family sent the first merchant ship out of Sealey Head harbor. It was gone for three years, during which some fantastic bets were laid. Fortunes were lost when it finally returned. So the tales say. Like fish, the size of a fortune grows in the telling. The Blairs made a genuine fortune from the wares that came in—spices, fabrics, exotic wood, glassware, painted porcelain, jewelry."

"Even then the bell was ringing."

"The bell." Judd paused to pick up that mislaid thread in his head. "Yes," he said slowly. "It must have been. Two hundred years, it has rung, I've heard. Or three hundred. Or a thousand. Every tale changes as it gets passed down. So how are you supposed to know what's true?"

"Ah. That's the question," Ridley said with a great deal of enthusiasm and no answer whatsoever.

Judd pointed out the stationer's shop along Water Street, which curved around the harbor and held all the best shops, the grocers, the bakeries, Blair's Exotica and Other Fine Goods. Ridley went into the expansive shop with its gull-colored walls and its front glass panes neatly framed in black. Judd turned past it and onto the docks.

There on a wooden slab under an awning, he found Stiven Dale's catch of the day before, under the eye of his wife Hazel and their four-year-old daughter, who was dropping a crab net over the dockside. The slosh of water against the pilings, the smell of fish, barnacles in brine, guano, the barking of harbor seals and cries of the gulls diving at the dead fish, filled Judd like words did, left him always wanting more, though these smells, these sounds, he had known all his life.

He chose a stout salmon to smoke, half a dozen perch for supper, some crab and eel for pie, which Mrs. Quinn usually managed without making a total disaster of it. Hazel set them aside for her older son to run up to the inn. That done, he stopped at the grocer's to order a delivery of cheese and coffee, then at the window of Blair's Exotica, hoping for a glimpse of Gwyneth Blair.

He didn't see her. A certain shyness kept him hovering outside. Growing up, they had talked easily and eagerly about everything, above all about books. He would duck into the shop on his way home from school, find her deep in some ornate chair covered with animal skins, stroking the head of a huge, snarling, glass-eyed beast while she ignored the books her governess gave her and devoured the latest novel from the stationer's instead.

Then she went away for a few years to get educated in Landringham. Judd nursed his dying grandfather, then his mother, while his father's sight began to fail and the inn grew quieter and emptier. When Gwyneth finally came home to stay, after her own mother died, she had grown into a tall, fair, willowy young lady whose spectacles hid her expressions. She was suddenly the eligible daughter of a very prosperous merchant. Judd had become the proprietor of the failing inn up the hill who couldn't afford to replace his own lamentable cook.

They rarely met.

He crossed the street, went into the stationer's to find Ridley. And there she was, bracketed by the Sproule siblings, talking to Osric Trent, whose plump face with silky chestnut sideburns framing his intelligent expression Judd could see over Gwyneth's shoulder. Ridley, a book open in his hands, completed the congenial little circle.

Judd almost backed out, closed the door on the elegant company. But Ridley saw him, waved him eagerly over; he was obliged to sidle, redolent with the fish market, through the smartly dressed browsers around the book tables. Seeing him, Gwyneth smiled, but Judd couldn't tell if her eyes, behind the lenses, had added to the welcome.

"Judd!" the bookseller exclaimed. "We see so little of you these days. How is your father?"

"He's well. Happiest when I'm reading to him in the evenings." He paused, nodding diffidently to the others. "Raven, Miss Sproule. Miss Blair. I see you've met my guest."

"So fascinating," Daria breathed. She gripped Gwyneth's

45

wrist in a tremor of emotion. "He's been explaining what brought him here, riding alone all the way across Rurex from his cozy house in Landringham."

"That bell," Raven said, his brows pinched in perplexity. "I haven't really heard it since I was a child. It's fairly meaningless, isn't it?"

"Is it?" Ridley queried encouragingly, his own lenses glinting, full of light.

"I mean, isn't it?" He appealed to Judd. "Do you hear it? Surely you've got more important matters on your mind up at that inn than the ghostly bell on a ship that sank centuries ago." Judd opened his mouth to answer; Raven didn't listen to that, either. He appealed again to Ridley. "Unless it marks a sunken treasure or something, why bother with it?"

"A pirate ship," Daria guessed, blinking with rapture at Ridley. "Is that what you think it is? Weighted with gold and stolen jewels, foundering just off Sealey Head—Oh, Gwyneth, you must write that story! Promise me you will."

"Pirates," Gwyneth answered dubiously, as Judd's voice bumped against hers.

"You write?"

She colored a little as they all gazed at her. "Silly things," she said finally, touching her spectacles. "Scribbles."

"Not all of them," Osric Trent said firmly. "Some of your pieces have a great deal of energy and wonderful detail. Especially," he added with a chuckle, "when you set your tales in Sealey Head."

Daria drew breath audibly. "You write about us?"

"Well, those mostly go under my bed." Her eyes met Judd's, with an odd, wordless appeal.

He foundered a moment, heard himself say, "Yes, I do

remember. You talked about writing when we were children. You were so in love with reading that you imagined going that step farther—writing your own story—must be the pinnacle of bliss."

"Did I?" She had flushed again, deeply, but her smile was quick and generous, warming her face. "I suppose I did think of it that way, then."

"And now?" he said, feeling his own smile suddenly.

"Bliss," Daria interjected firmly. "I think it must be."

"Now, it's a hundred fits and starts, sputtering ink nibs, stray ends going nowhere—like being a spider, most likely, on a windy day, tendrils always sailing off. Mr. Trent is kind enough to make suggestions. I only bring him what I think is my best. And you—"

"Like riding horses," Raven interrupted, illumined. "I see. When you dream about riding, you never fall off. But you can't really learn to ride without actually clambering up a horse's back, which is a completely different kettle of stew."

Gwyneth clung to her question stubbornly. "Do you still read?" she asked Judd. "Or is Raven right? You have more important things to do?"

"Every chance I get," he assured her, and saw again the smile she gave him when they were young: a bit secretive, a bit mischievous, eager to be amused by the world.

He felt his own heart, which he hadn't, he realized then, for some time. It crested to froth like a wave, rode the wind into spindrift. And then fell abruptly, scattering into nothing as Raven, talking again about horses, about continuing their ride back to Sproule Manor, gave a proprietary touch to Gwyneth's arm. Daria still had hold of the other; together they turned her, gracefully and imperceptibly, toward the door. As Judd watched wordlessly, she continued the circling without them, slipping free to look back at him, the little wry smile still on her face, while they stepped forward without her, then stopped, surprised.

"Come to tea," she suggested. "You can tell me what you're reading. And you, Mr. Dow. I still hear that bell at every sunset, and I'm eager to know what you make of it."

"Yes," Judd stammered. "Yes, of course. Thank you."

She turned again, as the Sproules spun back to fetch her, and made her own way to the door.

Judd felt himself under the bright, momentary scrutiny of Ridley's spectacles. Then they flashed elsewhere. The door closed behind the Sproules; they hurried a step or two to catch up with Gwyneth as she moved past the window, breasting the wind as gracefully as a figurehead above the waves.

Then she was gone. Judd blinked, heard voices again.

"Everything," Ridley said passionately. "Everything you have on the history of Sealey Head."

The bookseller scratched the tide line on his balding head. "I can give you a couple now. One is mostly anecdotal, local history; the other is a rather imaginative history of the Sproule family. Written by a Sproule, of course, who tried to link the family to a defunct line of nobility, rather than to the hardworking and very shrewd farmers who made their fortune and achieved their title by turning the rough, rocky Sealey River valley into a large, very fine farm."

"I'll take them," Ridley said promptly.

"I'll have to search my storage room for older works consigned there for lack of interest." He paused, meditatively scratching an eyebrow now. "Except," he pronounced finally, "for Hesper Wood."

"Hesper," Ridley repeated blankly, but with enthusiasm.

"Known locally as a wood witch. She's an herbalist; people come to her with random problems. Even Dr. Grantham consults her sometimes. She lives in a sort of tree house near Aislinn House. For some reason, she collects any kind of family history, memoir, journal, even old letters that have to do with Sealey Head. She takes them in trade, or buys them outright, if she has to. I've been putting such works aside for her for years."

"Interesting," Ridley murmured. His eyes had grown very dark behind his lenses. "Does she say why?"

"Why such an obsession with a rather commonplace coastal town?"

"Yes."

"No. I pressed her about it once; she only looked vague and talked about ancient herbal remedies passed down through generations." Mr. Trent shrugged. "Maybe that's her interest. But I think there's something else..." He gestured toward the window, where a line of wooded hills rose above warehouses, shops, dwellings, and the back lanes of Sealey Head. "She lives up there. She might talk to you about Sealey Head. If you can't find the tree house, ask the young maid at Aislinn House; that's her daughter, Emma."

"Do you know this wood witch?" Ridley asked Judd, after he had paid for the books and they had returned again to the street.

"Of course," Judd said, amused. "I know everyone."

"What's she like? Would she talk to me?"

"She's very kind... I went to her about my father's failing eyes. She tried everything she knew and wouldn't take any form of payment when nothing worked."

"Why did she take to living in a tree?"

"No one knows. She was the stillroom maid at Aislinn House for many years."

"Was she," Ridley breathed. "Was she now."

Judd looked at him, hearing mysteries in his voice, secrets. He knew something about that sad, ancient house that Judd didn't. Something about the bell?

"It was on a ship," he heard himself protest incoherently, he thought, but somehow Ridley knew exactly what he meant.

"Was it?" he only said, and the town that Judd had known all his life changed in his head, transformed by the words of a stranger. Who had also, in that moment, transformed himself under Judd's nose.

A word sprang alive in his head; recognizing it, he began to understand what it meant.

Magic.

Five

Ysabo was on top of the tower, feeding crows again. It was only bread from last night's supper, and a few scraps of meat; the knights had eaten everything else. As always, gulls circled and wove among the crows, crying in their piercing, tormented voices as though they had eaten every fish in the sea, every plump morsel in its shell on the shore, and were on their last breaths with hunger. But they were wary of the crows and rarely snatched a mouthful. Ysabo had seen why the first time she had fed them, when she was a little girl. The gull that had caught a crust out of her bowl had been transformed instantly into a raging tumble of black feathers and beaks. The midair brawl had quickly flown itself over the sea, where, as the black knot had untangled itself into birds again, something ragged, limp, and bloody had dropped into the waves. The crows flew back to the tower, landed peacefully at Ysabo's small, slippered feet. She had stared at them; they had looked back at her, beaks clacking, something knowing, mocking, in their black eyes. She had dumped the rest of the scraps over their heads and fled.

But Maeve had made her go back. "It's your duty," her grandmother said, "from this day. We all have our duties. They must never, ever, ever be neglected. Not one. Don't be afraid of the crows. They are wise and powerful, like the knights. Like the knights, they kill their enemies. But they would die to protect us. All they need is that we never fail our solemn responsibilities."

"Why?" the very small Ysabo asked. "What would happen?"

"We are sworn," Aveline had said in her rich, husky voice, shaking her bright head, her great gray eyes seeming to see, in that moment, all the sorrows of the world in the sunny morning. "That is enough for you to know. Never ask again."

Ysabo had looked to Maeve, who had long hair like cobweb and pale green eyes. Her voice was wavery and frail, no contest for Aveline when she was in a mood, but the right word from her, fragile though it might be, was usually the last word in any argument between them. Then, Ysabo had no concept of age. Maeve looked the way she did because she was Maeve. As years passed, she finally saw Maeve in Aveline's face, and Aveline's in Maeve: the regal bones, certain expressions. But though she searched every mirror in the castle, Ysabo couldn't find her mother's face in hers.

That was one thing she understood now, after more than a decade and a half of growing up Ysabo. She had lost her fear of the crows; they truly needed her, she understood. And she knew why she didn't resemble Aveline. She took after her father, instead. And if she had questions about the rigorous and exacting ritual of their lives, she had learned to keep them to herself.

Three rules were simple, and made very clear to her, very early.

Never leave the house.

She had no idea how. It was enormous, so many halls and stairs and doors, she could get lost for hours just turning a corner. The idea of a door that actually opened to trees, earth, the lairs and paths of animals seemed wildly improbable. Anyway, Maeve explained, everything they needed or might want could be found within the walls.

Never neglect your duties.

If you have to write them down with your own blood to remember them, do it, Aveline had told her passionately. Never forget them. At first, there were only candles to be lit, doors to be locked or unlocked, certain goblets to set at certain places for the nightly feast. Gradually her duties multiplied, became more complex, their exact timing governed by the ringing of the bell. These things must be done, in this order, before it rings; these after. Nothing must be forgotten; the proper order must be rigorously maintained. She did write them down eventually, in ink rather than in blood. She carried the paper with her for years until she realized nothing had been added for a very long time. She had come to the end of learning the ritual, and it was written in her heart.

Don't ask why.

That was the hardest rule. But when she forgot and broke it, punishment was swift: a heart-freezing stare from Aveline, some tedious, endless task from Maeve. Sometimes a blow. So she stopped asking, early, except in her head.

Except two nights ago, on her birthday.

"But why?" she had asked the knight. "Why must I marry anyone? Why must I marry you?"

The bruise his fingers left burned on her cheek like a brand.

Little had been said about it during the feast. Afterwards, in their chambers, Aveline had wept, of course, but not over the knight's behavior.

"How could you?" she stormed at Ysabo. "After all you have been taught?"

"But, Mother—"

"The knights have their rituals, as we do; they dare not deviate. It is immensely dangerous."

"He didn't have to hit me."

"You questioned him. He had no proper recourse but that. No other words."

But why? Ysabo wanted to shout, to weep, to kindle her own storm, set it raging against Aveline. But why but why but why why why?

Maeve, sitting beside the fire, listening, raised her white head as though she felt the silent storm. Or sensed something of it in Ysabo's wide, glittering eyes, her tense face, livid but for the burning shadow of the knight's hand.

"Come here," she said.

For a breath Ysabo stood motionless, staring at her grandmother, fearing another blow. Then she forced herself to move, her mouth tightening so that her thin lips all but disappeared, left a snake's mouth, a toad's mouth in her face.

Maeve only tugged at her wrist gently, until Ysabo sank to her knees on the soft skins under Maeve's chair. Maeve patted her shoulder; Ysabo's brow came to rest finally against her grandmother. Behind them, Aveline opened a casement, let in the wind. Ysabo heard the distant thunder of the sea, a gull's lonely piping in the dark.

"Our world will not come to an end because you asked a question," Maeve said. "But it will, without the ritual. Think of the ritual as something powerful enough to call up the sun, to set the waves in motion, bring down the moon. If you forget, or willfully abandon any part of it, imagine that the sun will not rise out of the sea; the sea itself will stop, lie silent and idle as a puddle in the perpetual black. Imagine that your blood will stop flowing, lie as stagnant in your veins."

"But he does not love me," Ysabo whispered. She heard a sharp sound, very like a snort, from Aveline. But Maeve only stroked her hair a moment, quietly.

"Then look to us for love. Look to the knight for your child. What you do not expect, you won't miss."

Ysabo felt a sudden flash of cold throughout her body, as though she had drunk moonlight or swallowed the icy prick of light that was a star. "My child."

"If it is male, he will become a knight. If female, you will teach her the ritual, as Aveline has taught you."

Ysabo closed her eyes. She felt hot tears well behind her lids, the first she had cried all evening. Poor poppet, she thought numbly. Poor unborn thing.

"Best it be a knight, then," she whispered. Maeve's fingers found her chin, drew up her face to see her eyes.

Before her grandmother could speak, Aveline whirled away from the window, demanded, "Has your life here been so terrible? You have wealth and status; everything is given to you, done for you. All that is asked of you is the ritual, and most of its movements are no more onerous than steps in a dance. You can do this one thing without complaining."

Maeve turned her head, said sharply, "Be merciful to her. You at least were loved."

"Yes." The brittle word made Ysabo turn, too, to look at her. Aveline stared out at the dark again, her jeweled fingers working, tightening and loosening, on the stone ledge. She moved abruptly, went to Ysabo, and leaned over her, drew her so close that Ysabo felt her mother's tears on her cheek. "But," she whispered, "I did not love. I don't know which is harder. Then I had you, and I loved as I had never learned before." Ysabo lifted her arms, groped blindly for Aveline, who dropped a kiss on her brow that burned on her flushed face like the knight's fingers. "Best it be a princess who will never leave your heart."

Ysabo lay awake for a long time that night, watching the moon in its changeless ritual and trying to remember the knight's face. Just before she fell asleep, she realized ruefully: I don't even know his name.

Emma found her the next morning, when Ysabo was returning from the crow tower with the empty bowl. The maid opened a door somewhere in her world and saw the princess in one of the long, empty stone passageways, just about to turn the heavy, iron ring of the latch on her side. Emma said nothing, just gazed at her over the tray in her hands, her eyes as dark and searching as the crows'.

Ysabo gave her a crooked smile, and said, "Can we talk?"

For once, and for a wonder, time and privacy stood with them on both sides of the door. Emma put the heavy silver tray with its ornate handles on the floorboards and sat down beside it. Ysabo hunkered down to the cold stones on her side.

"I'm just bringing Lady Eglantyne's breakfast down. The doctor has already been and gone; nobody else will come up here this morning."

Ysabo studied the remains: a triangle of buttered toast with a crescent moon of a bite missing from two corners, most of an egg congealing in its fine flower-strewn cup, a dab of porridge in a bowl that had not been disturbed, an untouched half of a pear in syrup. A strange, dour thought flashed through her head: the crows would have that eaten in a breath.

"I'm bringing the scrap bowl down," she said. "No one needs me until noon, now. She's still eating, your lady."

"Very little," Emma sighed. "Mostly she just wants to dream." Her soft, chestnut brows were knit in her pretty face, with its bright, full lips and warm, burnished skin that the princess had never thought to envy before. Perhaps, if she had that face instead, the knight might have loved her?

"What happened on your birthday?" Emma asked baldly; she had never been taught to be afraid of questions.

Ysabo's thin mouth twisted wryly. "I got betrothed."

Emma sucked a horrified breath. "Why?" she kept asking, as Ysabo described the supper and its aftermath. "Why?"

"I don't know," Ysabo kept answering. "I must not ask. It's the ritual."

"You don't even know his name?"

"Well, there are so many of them, and they come and go. The faces seem to change so often. Anyway, I never paid much attention to them since they hardly see me when they look at me. I am only there as part of the ritual. I pour wine into some of the cups but not others. I am chosen to escort one, but never the same one twice. They talk among themselves, but not to me. As though I don't really exist."

"It's fantastic," Emma exclaimed, and then, after thought, "It's monstrous."

"Is it?" Ysabo asked, suddenly, intensely curious.

"It would be in my world."

"It doesn't happen there?"

"No. Well, yes. Anything happens here. But even I can choose who I want to marry, and I'm only a housemaid." She paused, her brows peaking again. "I mean, in the best of circumstances. As I said, anything happens here. People marry those they don't know, they're forced into it for money or status, they lie to each other about being in love, they make all kinds of mistakes. Even being obliged to marry someone who hits you before you know his name—I'm sure it does happen here. But why should it happen to you?"

"I don't know. That's the way things are, here."

"But why?"

"I don't know."

Emma's lips tightened; she glanced up and down the wainscoted hallway as though the painted faces along the walls might be listening. "Run away," she said abruptly. "Just walk through this door. Come into my world. I'll find you a place here."

Ysabo felt herself smiling for the first time in days. "You know I can't," she said softly. "I can't abandon the ritual." She lifted her hand, held it in the air above the exact center of the threshold. Emma raised her own hand, frowning and smiling ruefully at the same time. Between doorways, their palms and fingers touched. "This is as close as I can come."

"I know that. But——"

"I may not question. But no one has told me not to think, or look for answers on my own, as long as I break no rules. Maybe there is a way to find out why." She paused, then shrugged lightly. "Maybe, if I can change nothing anyway, it's better not to know why."

Emma started to speak. Ysabo heard a voice, a door opening, somewhere in the dim, quiet house; the maid turned her head toward the sounds.

"I'd best go," she said, getting to her feet. "I have my own rituals to attend to. Our lives won't end if I don't dust, but that's what I'm paid for." She picked up the tray, hesitated, gazing fretfully at Ysabo.

The princess smiled, hiding her own apprehensions. "Maybe next time I can tell you his name."

"I hope so," Emma breathed, and pushed the door shut on her side with one elbow.

Ysabo opened it again, a breath later, and the tidal wave of noises in the great house welled up, echoing against the walls of the hall below with laughter, calls, dogs barking, the clatter of armor against stone, clink of crockery and goblets, distant music. She paused before she gave the bowl to the kitchen maid waiting for it. She could hear, even amid the tumult, the desolate silence on the other side of the door, as though that Aislinn House had already begun to die.

Questions filled her head, crowded like strangers into a room not big enough for them, kept coming, until fear itself, pushed far back against the wall, became scarcely recognizable in the crush.

Six

*L*uck, Gwyneth wrote in her impetuous, untidy hand, *was a ship.*

It sailed into Sealey Head harbor on a fine spring day when another roof beam had fallen into the middle of Anscom Cauley's best guest room, when Lord Aislinn received half a dozen stiff and threatening letters from the lawyers of two wine merchants and a boot maker in Landringham, from a certain Mr. Grimm to whom he owed a substantial gambling debt, and a very private, perfumed letter from a woman with whom we need not acquaint ourselves. On a day when Mr. Blair, receiving no word either of his missing ship or the ship sent out to find her, sank deeper into gloom, and in Magnus Sproule's fields, crows were busy ravening every seed that might possibly have been missed by previous flocks of hungry birds.

The ship, which caused the despondent merchant to sit upright in his chair, was extraordinarily beautiful. It was long and lean, its three tall masts raked back to suggest its speed and power. It was superbly painted in the glossiest of cream, finely trimmed with gold and airy blue. It took the difficult channel into the harbor with a nonchalant roll. A bell sounded as in greeting: a single toll. Mr. Blair was quite relieved to see, as it sailed into the harbor, that it was not armed. Turning his telescope upon it, he was among the first to notice that its crew was most unusual.

Steps pounded up the little stairway: Crispin, she recognized, and glanced out the window. The sun had set already, she saw incredulously; she hadn't heard the bell except in her story.

A palm thumped against the door. "Gwyneth! Come down. You have the most extraordinary visitors."

She must, indeed, if Crispin had bothered to come to tea; the twins usually hid at the sight of Raven and Daria. She called back in answer; the footsteps receded. She put her writing away and hurried after them.

Ridley Dow, in a dove gray vest and a plain black coat whose exquisite cut needed no other adornment, had completely captivated Aunt Phoebe and the twins. Gwyneth, watching him chat eagerly and articulately about nothing—the weather, his dogs in Landringham—blinked suddenly at the gleaming black hair and dark, dark eyes, the warm, vivid smile. She touched her own hair vaguely, wondered if she had ink on her face. Then she caught sight of Judd in the shadows, with a cup and a saucer in one hand and a cake in the other, and not sure what to do with either.

She went to him, smiling. The little, wistful look on his face vanished when he saw her.

"Has Mr. Dow solved the mystery of the bell, yet?" she asked.

"Not even close," Judd answered, glancing around for someplace to put his cup. "He keeps talking about magic."

"Magic," she repeated, astonished. She slid a lantern made of the jaws of some toothy fish to one side on a shelf otherwise cluttered with bone bracelets and strands of tiny colored shells. He looked at the raw mahogany doubtfully; she took his saucer, set it down for him. "What does he mean by magic?"

"I don't know. I haven't figured it out yet."

"Tell me when you do."

He smiled finally, bit into his tea cake. He looked slightly less careworn than he had in the stationer's shop, but not much. His coat was neatly patched at one elbow; the glossy polish on his boots didn't hide the cracks and scars. An image of a roof beam thudding into the guest rooms of her story glanced through her head; she wondered suddenly how close it hit to truth.

"How is your father?" she asked. Never, Aunt Phoebe had told her more than once, ask a personal question at tea for which you are ill prepared to hear the answer. Embarrassment is a distressing sight to others trying to enjoy themselves with cakes and commonplaces. But she and Judd were old friends, and she truly wanted to know which might weigh more heavily on him: his father or his roof.

Not his father, evidently. "He's very cheerful," Judd answered composedly. "Very patient, on the whole, except with our dreadful cook, who stays with us out of the goodness of her heart, though I do fervently wish that she would abandon us and flee."

Gwyneth swallowed tea too quickly, stifled a cough.

"Really? Is she that bad? No wonder she stays: Who else would have her?"

"Exactly."

"Your poor father."

"Yes. Her boiled beef makes him miss my mother sorely." He raised his cup again, still smiling. But the crook of his pale brows, the line above the light, summery blue of his eyes, made her own gaze focus clearly behind her lenses.

She said softly after a moment, "Yes. So do I. Miss my own mother, I mean." He nodded, vanished behind his cup. "We must have lost them both at the same time. How strange."

"You were away at school."

"I was. And missing Sealey Head abominably."

His eyes appeared again, wide with surprise. "You were among all the delights of the great city. How could you spare us a thought?"

"You'd be amazed what sentiments the smell of the Landringham fish market could summon in me."

"Really?" He put his cup down abruptly, ignoring the tremulous rattling as he gazed at her. "Does that mean you'll stay here? But what if your writing makes you famous?"

She opened her mouth, found herself wordless. She could only laugh with delight and longing at the preposterous idea, a sudden, merry peal that brought Dulcie scampering toward her, and, following, Aunt Phoebe.

"My dear," Phoebe said, amazed, "what can Mr. Cauley have been saying to you?"

"He worried that my literary efforts will make me so famous I might leave Sealey Head and wander about the world like my father."

"Litterforts!" Dulcie cried, pushing her face gleefully into Gwyneth's skirt.

"Indeed," Gwyneth said, swooping the child up into her arms. "Say good day to Mr. Judd Cauley, whom you last met, I believe, when you were a bubbling infant. Most days, I do not believe, Mr. Cauley, that my litterforts will find their ways out from under my bed."

"Fortunately," Aunt Phoebe said, her voice abruptly booming like one of the conch shells, "your father will be able to provide for you, in any event, so you needn't—Ah." The door opened behind Gwyneth. She watched, amused, as Phoebe's face rearranged itself into a familiar pleased expression before she remembered the amiable and wealthy Mr. Dow, and her pleasure wavered into sudden confusion.

"The bird," Dulcie announced briefly, chewing a finger thoughtfully over Gwyneth's shoulder. Daria's sprightly laugh preceded them into the company.

Dr. Grantham joined them a little later, on his way back from Aislinn House. Aunt Phoebe summoned her brother and a bottle of sherry, for which the doctor seemed most grateful.

Toland, bypassing commonplaces, asked the question on everyone's mind: "How is Lady Eglantyne?"

Even Daria was silent, blinking moistly at the doctor. He sipped sherry and sighed.

"This is wonderful. It brings out the sun in your veins, even in a windowless room."

"The grapes on the tiny island where it is made have nothing to do all day but grow fat with light."

"Perhaps it might benefit Lady Eglantyne," Daria suggested, herding them back to the topic.

Dr. Grantham sighed again, put down his glass. "Very little change," he said bluntly, "and none for the better. She seems content to dream her life away. I have warned the family solicitors that if they don't send for her heir immediately, I will. An idle threat, since I have no idea where to write. I thought you might know someone, Toland, who knows someone?"

"Indeed I do," Toland said quickly. He plucked the bottle off the tea tray. "Come with me to the library; I have an address there for someone closely acquainted with the young lady. Quite a glitter she sheds in Landringham society, I'm told. I suspect Sealey Head will be a shock to her."

The silence he left behind was broken by Daria's slow, tidal flow of indrawn breath. "Oh," she cried, trembling with the idea, "we must give a party for her!"

"Surely not on such a sad occasion," Aunt Phoebe said doubtfully, and Raven nodded shortly.

"Great-aunt dying in her bed and all that," he murmured.

But their expressions disagreed with them; they were silent again, seeking ways around the unfortunate event.

"A quiet party," Daria said. "To welcome the newcomer to Sealey Head, acquaint her with her neighbors. You shall all be invited, of course. And Mr. Trent, and all the Trevor boys and everyone else who is agreeable, or with whom she might do business. And you must come, Mr. Dow! Being from Landringham yourself, you must know her."

"I know of her," Ridley Dow said, after a tiny, surprising hesitation. He seemed oddly wary, Gwyneth realized, still affable, but choosing his words with care. "As Mr. Blair intimated, she travels in exalted circles, generally unfrequented by dull scholars. Anyway, I am away from the city much of the time."

"Surely not," Daria murmured, smiling and surveying him under her eloquent lashes. "Surely never dull."

"Can you at least tell us her name?" Gwyneth asked. He seemed reluctant to do even that, she saw with sudden, avid interest.

"Miss Beryl," he answered briefly. "Miranda Beryl."

"Soon to be Lady Beryl," Daria breathed, "of Aislinn House. Please tell us you've met her!"

"I believe we have met," Ridley conceded, after a swift, wordless appeal across the room to Judd. "Once. At least once. Very briefly. I doubt she would remember."

"But you do? Tell us, Mr. Dow, is she very beautiful?"

Something hit the floorboards near the mahogany shelves. Glass splintered. A smell of fish oil pervaded the room. Judd, his face scarlet, bent to rescue the fish jaws, and sent strands of seashells clattering off the shelf with his elbow, then bumped a tall wooden shield balanced against the wall. It rapped him back and landed with a bang in the pool of oil.

"Again!" Dulcie instructed with delight. Gwyneth put her down quickly, went to help the besieged innkeeper.

"I'm sorry," he murmured, shaking with what looked like acute embarrassment or an imminent explosion of laughter.

"Never mind," Aunt Phoebe said with unexpected gallantry. "Is it the fish-jaw lantern, I hope? Leave it. We can't stay in here with that dreadful smell. Let's join Toland in the library. Gwyneth, help me with the tea trays. Pandora, you call Ivy to clear it—Pandora? Where is that child? Always vanishing, the pair of them. Gwyneth, you call Ivy, and Mr. Cauley will help me with the tea things."

"Are you sure you trust me with them?" Judd asked, wending his way cautiously around a spiky bamboo chair.

"Of course. You would not dare drop my second-best teapot."

In the library, Dr. Grantham snared Judd to ask about his father; Raven and Daria gravitated toward Toland to question him further about this friend of his who flowed in the bright wake of the heir to Aislinn House. Gwyneth, pouring fresh tea, found herself gazing into Ridley Dow's parched cup.

She refilled it, aware of his dark, speculative gaze behind his spectacles. She set the teapot down and met it, every bit as curious as he.

"Judd told me you think the bell has to do with magic," she said. "When he said the word, I realized I had no idea what it means. Outside of a fairy tale, I mean. What might magic be in the prosaic little world of Sealey Head? When a fishing boat sinks into the deep, not a wish or a word will bring it up again. You'd think if magic were around, that's one of the first things people might do with it."

He nodded. "Bring the dead to life. Surely that would be an enormously powerful impulse." He sipped tea, went on slowly, "I tend to believe that there are varying degrees of power."

"Power."

"Magical ability. When you learn to read, you begin with very simple words, very short sentences. So, I think, magic is learned. One small word at a time."

"What word?" she asked, entranced. "Give me an example."

"Well. For instance, the bell. Suppose it has nothing at all to do with the sea."

"Oh," she said, disconcerted, thinking of her latest tale.

"In theory," he assured her. "In life, anything is possible.

Suppose, in some complex world just beyond our eyesight, the bell is rung by someone very much alive and not at all wet."

"Oh," she said again, disappointed now. "But I've written such things many times, Mr. Dow. The only true magic is in my pen. You can no more find that world within Sealey Head than you can dive headfirst into a piece of paper."

He smiled. "I would like to read those stories, Miss Blair."

"You are changing the subject. Is magic so difficult to define?"

"Perhaps the bell isn't a good place to start. It is subject to all kinds of explanations, none of which can be proven or disproven." He took another sip of tea, meditated a moment. "Think of some action you never think about doing, you just do. Lighting a candle. Shutting a door. Putting your cup down on your saucer."

"Yes," she said, doing it.

"Suppose you could learn to look at a candle and kindle a fire in your mind that will light the wick across the room."

"Well, that's not—How could that be possible?"

"How, indeed? That would be magic."

He smiled, and she saw the reflection of candle fire in his lenses.

She turned swiftly, nearly spilling her tea. One of a pair of candles on her father's desk beyond the potted palms burned in the shadows. He had forgotten to extinguish it, she thought, when he was summoned to tea by Aunt Phoebe. But she did not convince herself; her fingers had gone cold. She looked back at Ridley, blinking; he said nothing, his eyes hidden behind the reflection.

Then the fire was gone, and there was Raven at one of her elbows suddenly, and Daria at the other, intent on the stranger who had come to Sealey Head.

"Tell us what you know of Miranda Beryl," Daria pleaded. "Likes, dislikes, gossip—any scrap at all. We are fascinated. It is the most exciting thing ever to happen in Sealey Head. You will be here for our party, won't you? Judd said he thought you might be staying for some time."

"Judd said he hoped you might be," the innkeeper amended, joining them, and added to Ridley, "I must get back to see to my father, and any stray guests who might have ventured in to alarm Mrs. Quinn."

"I'll bid you good evening, too, then," Ridley said promptly, setting his cup on the table.

"But you were going to tell us tales of Landringham," Daria exclaimed. "You must stay!"

"Don't let me take you away from such agreeable company," Judd protested, at which Ridley cast one of his opaque, light-glazed glances.

"Even I have business to attend to," he answered amiably. "I like to work in the evenings."

"Then you must come to supper at Sproule Manor," Daria said firmly. "Our cook is the second-best along this part of the coast. Our mother will send you an invitation very soon, and you can tell us everything there is to know about life in the city."

"I look forward to it." He met Gwyneth's eyes again. "I hope to explore your thoughts about the bell much further, Miss Blair."

"Yes," she said a trifle dazedly. "Though in the light of—ah—your own reflections, mine seem strangely insubstantial.

Good night, Judd. Please come again soon. We forgot to talk about books."

"Fish oil intruded," he murmured. He hesitated, wanting to say more, she sensed, and she smiled encouragingly. But Raven spoke first, and suddenly she was watching Judd's back, accompanying the astonishing Mr. Dow out the door.

Well, she thought, during a little moment of silence while Raven and Daria bit into tea cakes simultaneously. Well, then. I shall just have to borrow a book.

Seven

Ysabo brought the scrap bowl down from the tower.

No one else was allowed up there, not even the kitchen maid who carried the bowl up the kitchen stairs to the hall every morning and met the princess to give it to her. She waited there while the princess fed the crows, then took the bowl from her with a curtsy and vanished back down into the depths. She kept her eyes and chin lowered, never presumed to speak, and never expected the princess to acknowledge her existence by a word or a glance.

But Ysabo was in a mood to examine everything that had to do with the ritual. Since the moment when she saw herself as part of a pattern, as vital as the ringing of the bell or the daily gathering of the crows, she had been consumed with a strange, desperate need to understand. What exactly was the pattern? And exactly whose pattern was it? Before, filling cups and tossing scraps, she had felt useful but replaceable. Anyone could do what she did every day. Now, seeing her fate in the ritual, she wondered suddenly, intensely: How far back in time did that line of children go who had inherited this piece of the pattern? How far forward into the future would the unborn children go?

What would happen if everything stopped?

So, that morning, she started to scrutinize the details of her days. Beginning with the scrap bowl. It changed daily, she had thought, according to the amount that filled it. For the first time, she realized that the bowl itself never changed; only its size varied. The bowl was silver and copper, always gleaming; it must have been polished daily. Still, it seemed very old, with its odd lumps of uncut jewels decorating the sides, the ribbons of copper wandering randomly over it, the shadow, here and there, of age that no care could remove.

What were these crows that must be fed each day from that magic bowl?

Who had made the magic?

She studied the averted face of the kitchen maid as well, wondering if they changed randomly, or if it had been the same one all Ysabo's life. She had pretty eyelashes, the princess noticed, long, thick, and black as crows' feathers; her pale, thin, milky face looked quite young. But who knew? Maybe she was as ancient as the bowl.

"Do you bring the bowl to me every day?" Ysabo asked. "Or are there others?"

The maid's eyes flew open. The princess's words seemed to bounce off the stones around them, transform into words spoken underwater, words shouted from a distant hill, fraying as they flew. Ysabo glimpsed eyes as green as newborn leaves. Then the maid screwed them up in terror, clapped the scrap bowl over her head as though to hide herself from the princess, and fled.

Ysabo sighed.

Don't ask.

She had no other task until noon. She spent the morning with Aveline and Maeve in Maeve's chambers overlooking the sea. Ysabo, docilely embroidering, kept feeling their eyes on her, swift, wide-eyed glances, as though her silence disturbed them more than if she had raged again, or wept, or dared again to ask a question. She sent her needle in and out of the linen, making yet another length of colorful flowers and vines to hang over the cold stones around them. Through the open casement she could see trees, the distant profile of the headlands, the sparkling blue-green waves bursting into froth against the cliffs. Emma had told her that people lived among the rocks. Fishing boats and ships sailed into the harbor below Aislinn House, which Ysabo could see out a different window: a stretch of blue beyond the wood as placid as a mirror. But no matter which window in all of Aislinn House she looked from, she never saw what Emma saw, only the wood, the cliff, the sea, as though her Aislinn House existed before the human world began.

Why?

Aveline and Maeve, whose silence never lasted long, had listened long enough to hers. Their voices pricked the air with little isolated stitches at first, then longer threads. They drifted into reminiscences; some threads seemed to have no end, just ran into the fabric of memory and disappeared.

Others, unexpectedly colored, snagged themselves on Ysabo's attention.

"No, it was still autumn. The last day of it, I remember, the color of iron, and as cold as. Little flecks of snow in the wind, and the last black bitter leaves falling into the lake, where the cold silver shield and the torn pennant still lay on the tiny island in the middle of the water. The end of a world, it seemed. He said it was important. A sight to haunt this world through the centuries. I didn't understand; I was too young."

What memory? Ysabo thought. What worlds?

"And then he went away." Maeve's voice was thin as frayed thread.

"But he came back. He always did."

"Until then."

"No—he came back again to take us to supper with Queen Hydria in her great court. You must remember, Maeve! The knights' banners hung from the ceiling, all the rich threads of red and blue and gold glittering in the torchlight. Blagdon himself was there beside the queen, an old man as hale as a tree, bearded with moss, tussocks for eyebrows and ears like dried leaves. I was older then." Aveline's voice grew dreamy, rich as cream. "I wore pale green and dark blue, with gossamer over my hair. I remember the queen's eyes, how beautiful they were. The colors of my gown, blue and green together. Do you remember?"

"Yes. Now I do." Ysabo heard Maeve's needle pierce the taut fabric in its frame. It was another mystery, the queen whose name Ysabo had heard every day of her life but who remained invisible except in her mother's and grandmother's stories. "I do remember that wonderful feast. Twelve stuffed swans floating on platters of polished silver and twelve fat salmon on platters of gold... I don't remember eating any of it, though. Did we? Do you remember?"

"No. I remember music, though, but not the musicians; it was as though the music came out of fire and air."

Their voices trailed silent; their threads spoke, pushed and pulled, in and out. Ysabo felt again their little, fretting bird glances. So she turned to the musicians playing old ballads softly on harp and flute near the hearth.

"That was lovely," she told them, though she had scarcely heard what they had just finished. "Play it again."

Their music wove its own thread into the morning. Maeve and Aveline's voices added texture, soft at first, then gaining depth as they misjudged the reasons for Ysabo's abstraction.

"I remember having trouble with that, too," Aveline murmured. "I couldn't wait for supper to begin, so I could see for certain which it was."

"And did you?"

"Not at first. You know how they are. Not one face told me anything. They were lost in their own ritual. Do you remember?"

Ysabo felt Maeve's gray eyes, cold as cloud, drift over her face, away. "Very little. The ones you do remember—"

"Yes," Aveline said instantly. "Yes. The ones you remember are the ones you never meet during the ritual. Those you meet outside of time, in a stray hour, before beginnings, after endings..."

"Who? Tell," Maeve commanded, her hands dropping onto her work, between stitches.

Aveline's voice went very soft. "The one who taught the young knights how to fight. He had the most amazing eyes."

Maeve's hand rose, covered her mouth. "You didn't."

"Didn't I?"

"You went down there? To the training hall?"

"That's where the young men were when I was young. He talked to me, he wrote me poetry. Best of all, he saw me when he looked at me."

"What happened to him?"

"Nothing. For all I know, he's still down there. But I got married."

Maeve's voice leaped out of her like a frog. "You weren't—"

"A virgin? No." Aveline's voice had resumed its normal volume, in case, Ysabo guessed, her daughter needed to hear this. "It didn't seem to matter at all." She added, a bit defensively, "You never told me it might."

"Well, how was I to know—" She rocked forward, laughing suddenly, her hand back over her mouth. "I remember this much: neither was I."

"Tell," Aveline demanded then, and Maeve picked up her needle, her voice going soft again. Ysabo heard Aveline suck breath sharply.

"Nemos himself?"

"Sh," Maeve breathed, softer than smoke from a dying candle. "Sh..."

Ysabo stitched the name into her memory.

At noon the knights rode out. The household gathered in the great hall to watch and pay honor, as two long lines of knights in their silvery mail and white cloaks threaded with red knelt together on the flagstones. They held their unsheathed swords point down on the stones, both hands folded on the hilt. Their heads were bare, bowed. Sun from the high narrow windows crossed them in blades of light.

Ysabo stood between Maeve and Aveline at the head of the lines. The three of them held gold goblets ringed with jewels along the rim. Ysabo's cup held water; Aveline's red wine, and Maeve's a murky, bitter potion that smelled of herbs and dead insects. One by one the knights rose, came forward, chose their cup, drank. They could drink what they liked; if all the knights chose the same cup, it never emptied. Courtiers, old knights, ladies and their ladies, all of whom Ysabo rarely saw except at supper, surrounded the lines, each holding a long, thick, burning candle. Trumpets sounded at each sip. The enormous doors opened wide to the courtyard, where the horses in their caparisons waited restively. The knights mounted as they left the hall. The doors were closed after the last knight had crossed the threshold.

No one saw by what gate they left the yard; there were none when Ysabo looked out. No one saw them ride beyond the walls of Aislinn House; no one saw them return. In the time between those two pieces of ritual, Ysabo had to work her way through a labyrinth of small, strange, and bewilderingly meaningless tasks.

Open this window; light this candle there, though, on such a day, light itself rendered the flame nearly invisible.

Lock the door at the top of the east tower.

Unlock the door on the bottom floor in the west corner of the house that leads to the underground chamber.

Light this candle; place it into the holder. Light this lantern from the taper; carry both into the dark of the subterranean chamber, which was chilly, dusty, and as far as Ysabo could see in the frail, ragged light, entirely empty. The black water that ebbed and flowed silently with the tide in its stone channel caused her some excitement when she first saw it. She finally gathered enough courage to follow it. The water led her not beyond the walls and into the wood around Aislinn House, but to another locked gate. An ornate iron grate was bolted to the sides of the channel; it ran up to the ceiling and down into the water as far as Ysabo could feel. She had been late finishing her tasks that day, and Aveline was furious.

Leave the lantern on the prow of the boat chained to the stake in the stone shore at the water's edge. Return the way you came, and lock the door behind you.

Don't ask who takes the lantern back to its hook beside the door, puts it out, and hangs it up again.

Just do it.

Go to the armory near the practice yard. No one will be there at that time of the day. Take the sword with the single red jewel in the bronze hilt out of its scabbard, and leave it lying across the arms of the wooden chair with the cracked leather seat, the worn back where the figures stamped into the leather and painted have become pallid ghosts of themselves. Rest the scabbard against the wall beside the chair.

Leave the room. Quickly.

Climb up the stairs of the east tower, and unlock the door you locked earlier. Go into the room at the top of the tower. Turn one page of the book on its stand in the middle of the room. That page will be no different from the one you turned the day before, and the day before, and the day before that. A blank book of days. Lock the door when you leave.

Don't ask who unlocks it after you have gone, who reads the blank page.

Cross the parapet walk to the west tower, where, this morning, you fed the crows. Put on the apron someone has left there. Take the bucket of water and the brush. Scrub the leavings of the crows off the stones, their discarded scraps, stray feathers, acrid droppings. Ignore the crows when they line the walls and watch you. They approve. They like a clean house. And with them there, you won't be tempted to lean over the battlements and watch the wood for a flash of armor, a flow of color through the trees, whose lengthening shadows portend the waning of the day, the return of the knights, the bell.

Go to your chambers, take off your soiled clothes, bathe, and dress for supper.

Wait for it, the ringing of the bell.

When you hear it, open your door to the sounds of the knights' voices welling and booming up from the great hall, the sound of stray pieces of armor clanging on stones, dogs barking welcome, musicians beginning to play.

Hurry down to place their chairs, fill this cup but not that, to see which pair of eyes might linger on yours.

Hurry down to meet your fate.

The feast that night began like every other in her life. Four long tables were set end to end down the hall, across the stones where the knights had knelt earlier that day. Cloths of gold and red and blue were spread over the tables. The chairs were lined against the wall, beautiful things with arms and spindles carved of ash and oak and bone, the seats and backs fashioned of brilliant tapestry whose threads never seemed to fade. Goblets as bright and varied as the chairs stood at each place, beside plates round and white as the moon. Sharp, gleaming knives with handles of horn lay across the moons, on napkins red as the blood that would run from the great haunches of meat whose smells of drippings and herbs pervaded the hall. The knights gathered at the two huge hearths, one at either side of the hall. They stood on the hides of deer and soft white sheepskins, telling tales and jesting with one another. Dogs milled around their legs, stirred by the heat and the deep voices as the knights waited for the servants to place their chairs. Ysabo moved among the servants, watching for those they left untouched. The chair with the griffin tapestry she pushed to the place at the table with the goblet whose stem was a griffin rampant, its wings opened to enfold the cup. The chair with the mermaid tapestry matched the mermaid whose uplifted arms carried the cup. The lion tapestry, the unicorn tapestry, the tapestry man with his enigmatic eyes and rack of horns, these she shifted to their proper places. Chairs done, she filled the cups: griffin, lion, mermaid, horned man, with red, spiced wine.

A horn sounded. Ladies entered, Maeve and Aveline among them. The knights moved to greet the ladies, led them to their places, where they would mostly be ignored for the rest of the meal. Ysabo, finished with her ritual chores, looked for her own chair.

Someone took her arm. She started. A knight looked down at her briefly, his eyes as dark and secret as the eyes of the horned man. He was very tall; she could feel the strength in the hard fingers at her elbow. His pale hair was tied back from his young, proud, clean-lined face. His brows were black. She had no idea, she realized with amazement, if he was the knight who had proposed to her, and then left the brand of his fingers on her cheek. She didn't remember him at all.

But he must have been: he led her to her chair, the one with the tapestry turtledoves surrounded by a ring of flowers. The stem of her goblet was a thick silver rose stem with blunted thorns, upon which the gold flower opened to accept the wine. He sat in the fiery salamander chair beside her. She had poured his wine; she remembered that much. She had placed his chair. Someone else had placed hers beside him, where he seemed to think she belonged.

He said nothing to her then. She glanced bewilderedly down the table at Maeve, who was watching her. Maeve's ringed forefinger rose, touched her lips. *Don't ask.* The trumpets cried again; the knights rose to their feet, cups splashing wine in the ritual salute of the woman who never showed her face.

"Queen Hydria!"

A second, unexpected blast of the trumpet made Ysabo jump.

The knight at the head of the table rose again, holding his cup. The chair he sat in changed every evening, Ysabo knew, because she placed it herself. The last chair left along the wall went to the head of the table. That night it was the tapestry wolf, leaping to catch the moon in its jaws; a silver wolf held the ivory wine cup balanced between its teeth.

The knight's voice was very loud in the silence; it echoed as he spoke, bouncing back and forth along the walls. Ysabo understood a word here, two words there. Her own name. *Y-sa-bo-bo-bo.* She blinked, rigid with surprise. The knights lifted their goblets again, shouted something.

Then they gave attention to their plates, which the servants were filling with meat, bread, roots, and greens. They ate as busily and intently as the crows, but far more noisily. The ladies, separated from one another by the men and by the broad tables, never spoke.

At the end of the meal, the knight whose name Ysabo still did not know, turned his eyes again to look at her.

"At the full moon, then," he said. "Princess Ysabo. Attend to it."

He rose amid the clatter of chairs, the music that began to flow more freely, more wildly, the hum of women's voices as they drew together once again and began to leave the hall. Ysabo opened her mouth impulsively, bewilderedly to ask: Attend to what? Aveline, beside her suddenly, pulled her into the drift of women.

"I didn't understand," Ysabo murmured finally, carefully. Aveline knew exactly what she meant.

"Your wedding."

Ysabo received that news numbly. *Why?* turned somehow into *Why not?* in that incomprehensible world.

She said, feeling suddenly insignificant, lost, and very plain, "I still don't know his name."

But Aveline had turned away to greet someone. Ysabo moved with the gentle, inexorable tide of women across the threshold.

Eight

On her rare half-days off of work, Emma went looking for her mother.

That morning, she brought Lady Eglantyne and Sophie their breakfasts. Then she cleaned the grates, laid new fires, and tidied their rooms. Lady Eglantyne, her pink, sunken eyes filmy with sleep as she sat up in bed, murmured a few words now and then to her teacup or to her toast, which she politely refrained from eating. Sophie coaxed a few spoon-fuls of porridge into her and a couple of strawberries. Dr. Grantham was shown up, in time to keep her from nodding off into her poached egg.

"No word yet," Emma heard him tell Sophie before she took the tray back down.

"Nothing yet," she told Mrs. Haw in the kitchen, and "Not yet," to Mrs. Blakeley and Fitch, who were in the butler's pantry polishing silver that hadn't been used in years. Ever since the doctor had sent his letter posthaste to Landringham, Mrs. Blakeley had been obsessively counting things. Bed linens, towels, plates, forks, wineglasses, chairs. She vacillated between tearing the dust covers off the furniture and airing the rooms, or leaving such matters until the heir had given them a definite date of arrival.

"No use undoing what we'll only have to do over again if she doesn't come for months," she kept saying. And, with panic in her eyes: "What will we do with their horses? The stables have been empty for years. To say nothing of the garden."

"Worry when it's time to worry," Mrs. Haw told her, sighing resignedly. "I can't fret over cooking meals single-handedly for guests I can't even count yet. Besides, we don't even know if we'll be kept on." Mrs. Blakeley was rendered speechless at the thought. Mrs. Haw shrugged her massive shoulders, working her way around a potato skin with her knife. "Let's wait to worry until we're told why we need to."

In the midst of such uncertainty, nobody remembered that it was Emma's half-day off. She didn't remind them. Mrs. Blakeley was liable to find a dozen things for Emma to do, and a dozen reasons why she should give up her half-day and do them. At noon, Emma took her apron and cap off, put her walking shoes on, and slipped out the boot room door.

She walked through the woods in the direction of the tree house first, though she had no real expectation of finding Hesper there. She could be anywhere on that sunny, genial day. The trees, maple, elm, birch, busy leafing out among the coastal pine after a weary winter, preened their leaves in the wind like birds flaunting their colors.

Anything—wild ginger, mushrooms, hawthorn, violets, honeysuckle—might have caught her mother's eye, or tantalized her nose, sent her clambering over hill and dale, filling the many pockets of her apron. As well, she might be napping under a bush. Or walking to town in her old clamming boots to buy a fish or a book. Sometimes Emma missed her completely, had to leave a gift and a message on her table in greeting.

That afternoon, Hesper was easy to find. Emma saw her from a distance among the trees, working the debris out of a new patch of garden near her house. Her arms and legs were bare, golden; the hoe wheeled and flashed around her in the light. Her hair, a mass of long, gray-brown curls, streamed in the wind like the tree boughs. She wore an old dress with the sleeves torn out, and the skirt raggedly shortened to her knees. As though she sensed someone's eyes on her, she let the hoe drop abruptly, turned, shading her eyes with her hand. Emma heard her voice, deep and delighted, blown up the hill by the wind.

"Emma!"

"Dr. Grantham has sent for Lady Eglantyne's heir," Emma said breathlessly after they hugged, news tumbling randomly out of her, for she hadn't seen Hesper for nearly a month. "Mrs. Haw thinks we might all be discharged."

"Good," her mother said, washing her hands in a bucket beside the door. "Then you can come and live with me."

"Lady Eglantyne is still alive, though she hardly eats, and

mostly sleeps. The doctor said if you have anything left for
him to try, bring it up to the house."

"I will." She dried her hands on an old apron, smiling at
Emma. The lines were deep around her eyes and mouth in her
lean, sun-browned face. But her smile seemed younger than
ever. "How are you, girl? You look a little shadowy around
the edges. Come in, and I'll make you a tea for that."

She disappeared into the crazed house, the huge, hollowed
tree trunk with a thatched roof, smaller huts and lean-tos
built up around the openings hewn into its bole, the whole
looking like a weird colony of mushrooms burgeoning off
one another and held together by climbing roses and flowering vines. A chimney smoked improbably amid the thatch,
attached to the thick stone hearth within the tree. One of
the lean-tos, Emma knew, was entirely filled with books and
papers.

Emma followed. A thought shook her as she stepped
across the threshold, and she froze. "The princess. What will
happen to her if I leave? If someone else—some stranger wanting towels—finds her behind the linen closet door instead?"

"I'd worry more about the stranger," her mother said cryp-
tically and pulled a stool made of unstripped white birch
saplings out from under an oak door laid on trestles for a
table. "From what I can tell, that's a very dangerous house."

Emma sat down on the stool, staring at Hesper. "For
Ysabo?"

"For any stranger that chances in."

"What have you found out about it?"

"Well, for one thing it's very old magic," Hesper said,
putting this and that from her jars into the teapot. "I don't

know how old, and I don't know whose." She paused, a spoonful of rose hips suspended above the pot; lines rippled across her brow. "There's so little to be found...It's all secrets, between lines, allusions in letters, hints in diaries. But for at least a couple of centuries, if not longer. People writing about stories their children invented, ghosts their servants or some lord in his cups saw. Doors open, they get a glimpse—but nobody sees the whole of it. Ever."

"How much did you see?"

"Enough to astonish me. Enough to make me wonder..." She turned to unhook the steaming kettle hanging above the fire, added water to her mix. She hung it back up, then sat down herself, elbows on the table, gazing at her daughter. "You be careful, girl. Don't even think of crossing into that."

Emma shook her head vehemently, braid bouncing on her shoulder blades. "No. I did invite the princess here, though, after the knight hit her. She said she couldn't abandon the ritual."

"What knight?"

"The one she asked why. Why she had to marry him."

Hesper, absolutely still on her chair, echoed the word silently, "Why?" Then she said abruptly, "Wait. Wait. I have to write this down."

"You didn't know this part?

"Not the part where anybody ever asked why."

Emma told her that part, sipping tea with a dollop of honey in it, holding the warm cup against her cheeks, her forehead, like a soothing hand.

"I guess I wouldn't mind so much," she said, while Hesper scribbled the last of her tale into the end papers of an apothecary's remedy book.

"Mind what?"

"Leaving Aislinn House, after Lady Eglantyne dies. I could get a job in town, take care of us both. Especially if there's nobody I know left in the house after the heir comes and brings her own staff."

Her mother gave her a skewed look above her raised cup. "You don't really think Miss Miranda Beryl of Landringham would settle herself into this backwater."

"How do you know her name?"

"Ah, gossip. It holds the world together. The doctor's been asking around town about her, who might know her." Hesper took another sip. "Strange that even Lady Eglantyne's own solicitors are reluctant to write to Miss Beryl. As though they know she'd never stay, and Lady Eglantyne's death might mean the end of the family affairs in Sealey Head."

"She's Lady Eglantyne's family. She should be here."

"Have you heard Lady Eglantyne talk about her great-niece?"

Emma sighed. "No. She doesn't talk much at all. She mostly dreams. Maybe nobody wants Miranda Beryl here. Nobody wants any changes."

They ate bread and curds and a spicy beef sausage someone had given Hesper in payment. Then Emma took off her shoes and stockings, tucked up her skirt, and helped her mother clear the garden for cabbages, carrots, spinach, beans, and radishes. Hesper had already weeded the herb garden; scents of rosemary and sage teased Emma's nose as she worked.

"You should walk into town," Hesper protested as the sun, going its way, began to shift the patterns of tree shadows around them into the garden. "Breathe the sea air, see some younger faces."

"Right now I'm doing this," Emma answered, attacking a prodigious burdock root with satisfaction. "I'm seeing you."

Later, when they had downed tools, washed off the dirt, and perched themselves on a sunlit log for cups of mint tea and a bowl of wild strawberries, Emma asked her mother, "Why did you leave Aislinn House if you were only going to sit in the tree house thinking about it? There, you could just open a door and see more pieces of the mystery."

Hesper shook her head. Her thick, springy hair had collected an assortment of petals, twigs, a couple of insects trying to find their way out, sprigs of herbs she had tucked behind her ear for later. One of the insects, a tiny red beetle, flew away at the movement; Emma reached out and brushed the spider off.

"I never saw like you did. I caught glimpses of a great many people doing incomprehensible things. Some of them made me uneasy. The knights fully armed. That great pack of crows flying rings around the tower. Once when I opened the stillroom pantry, I thought they would come streaming through the doorway after me. I couldn't say for certain that anyone even saw me. Except the crows. Maybe it's a rare thing in her world that your friend Ysabo sees you as clearly as you see her. I left Aislinn House because I wanted more time of my own to find out about it. And because—" She smiled, tilting her face into the light. "I like being outdoors. I guessed that people would come seeking my remedies no matter where I kept myself. And out here, I can go barefoot."

Emma stayed for supper, which was great fat dried mushrooms plumped up with water and fried in butter, a salad of dandelion and violet leaves, and the curly tips of ferns, fish from the market her mother had smoked, and ale—another payment. Emma, a bit sore from her exertions and pleasantly relaxed from the ale, heard the bell on her way through the woods. The light faded around her. The trees thinned, opened to reveal the unkempt hedges and overrun gardens of Aislinn House, all but lost in wildness.

She went in the way she had left, through the boot room. She took the back stairs to her room to rebraid her hair and change her shoes before she went down to the kitchen for gossip and to see if anyone noticed she had gone.

Mrs. Blakeley found her in the hallway between the stairs and the kitchen. "Emma!" she exclaimed. "Where have you been? We looked everywhere for you."

"Why?" Emma asked quickly, searching the housekeeper's face. Her normal pallor was blotchy with color; her eyes, usually weary and preoccupied, looked wide and a bit stunned. There was no sign of tears; Lady Eglantyne must still be alive. "I took my half-day. I went to see my mother."

"Oh, if only the gentlemen had come earlier; you could have taken them with you."

"What gentlemen?"

"You might have told us, Emma. Well. At least they came in time for the letter."

"What letter?"

"It's down in the kitchen. Mr. Fitch was reading it to Mrs. Haw. She kept something warm for you. Oh, Emma." She pressed her fingers against the ancient black fabric over her bosom. "We have so much to do."

"She's coming?" Emma breathed, her skin prickling oddly.

"Miss Miranda Beryl, and her maids, household staff, friends, carriages, horses, stablers—I don't remember who all. Fortunately, we were able to warn Mr. Cauley. Come down, read the letter yourself. You'll see what we need to think about."

She hurried Emma downstairs. Fitch was writing a list, while Mrs. Haw, involved in a seemingly endless comment about life that was interspersed with items to be purchased, broke off mid-mutton at the sight of Emma.

"Oh, there you are," she said tremulously. "We thought you'd run off and left us to ourselves with all this."

Emma pulled out a chair, sat down. "All what?" she asked Fitch. He pushed the letter across the table, looking more alert than he'd been in years at the prospect of company. Even the tufts of hair above his ears seemed glossier.

"Lady Eglantyne's heir will be here in two days," he told her. "We must prepare the house."

"Two days!" She stared at him incredulously, then ran her eyes quickly over the letter, which was mauve, lightly scented, and in clear, quite elegant handwriting. She stared again at the butler, and whispered in horror, "Oh, Mr. Fitch."

"Now, don't panic. Once the lady is here, we'll have plenty of staff to help us."

"Help themselves to our jobs, more likely," Mrs. Haw muttered.

"An undercook, three kitchen maids, two housemaids, stablers—"

"What about the stable roof? It's all but fallen in. And the bedrooms haven't been dusted for decades. And where will we put everyone?"

"We can only do what we can, Emma," Fitch said firmly. "The lady will have to understand that. And since Judd Cauley from the inn was here when the letter came, we were able to show him Miss Beryl's request that he ready rooms at the inn for friends and staff we might not be able to accommodate."

"I see," Emma said. Her voice still shook, but it was regaining strength. She rubbed her face with chilly fingers, trying to grasp an elusive thread of thought. "Judd Cauley." She found it finally. "Why was Mr. Cauley here at all?"

"He and his friend came to see you," Mrs. Blakeley answered.

"Me!"

"Well, your mother, actually. But they stopped here to ask you for directions. We couldn't find you."

"I was there, helping her with her garden," Emma said dazedly. She looked at Mrs. Blakeley. "His friend?"

"Mr. Ridley Dow." To Emma's astonishment, the housekeeper came within memory of a smile. "Quite a handsome, nicely spoken young man he is, too. From Landringham, and staying at the inn as well."

"But what did they want with my mother?"

"Who knows? An herb, an ointment, something for the horses—They were quite disappointed that we couldn't find you. Mr. Dow was all for wandering about in the woods on the chance they might run across the tree house. But then we showed Mr. Cauley the letter, and he said he had to get back and put his own house in order."

"The harbor inn is much closer to Aislinn House than his inn," Emma said practically.

"Judd Cauley pointed that out, too," Fitch said, "to his credit. The staff might be moved there later. But according to her letter, Miss Beryl preferred the inn on the cliff with the magnificent view for her friends. One of them must have known about it, I would guess. Mr. Cauley seemed a bit panicky himself when he left."

"He at least has a working stable. What has he to panic about?" Mrs. Blakeley demanded.

"His cook," Mrs. Haw said pithily, rapping a stirring spoon against the stew pot on the stove. "One night of her, and they'll all be moving to the harbor. Are you hungry, Emma?"

"I ate with my mother, thank you, Mrs. Haw."

"Nettles and bark, no doubt."

"Close," Emma agreed. She was silent, still wondering what a Mr. Ridley Dow from the great city of Landringham, in which presumably one could find everything in the world, would want with a wood witch in Sealey Head who lived in a tree. "They didn't give any reason at all for wanting to see my mother? If it was urgent, she could go to them."

Fitch shook his head slightly. "Not urgent, no." But he seemed slightly puzzled. "Mrs. Blakeley offered to open up the old stillroom for Mr. Dow, let him look for what he needed there. He wasn't interested. He did ask an odd question. But maybe it only seemed odd because he's a visitor and we're used to it."

"Used to what?" Emma asked.

"The bell. He asked if we heard it more clearly in the house than outside. I don't know why he thought we might." He scratched a feathery brow. "I had to admit I scarcely hear it anywhere, anymore."

"I never do," Mrs. Blakeley agreed. "It's just another noise the world makes. Doesn't mean anything." She reached out, patted Emma's shoulder, and Emma, rendered transfixed in her chair, blinked oddly gritty eyes and felt herself turn human again. "We must be up and doing before the birds, tomorrow. Best get your rest."

Nine

J udd gathered the staff of the Inn at Sealey Head in the taproom. Everything, he noted, looked suddenly dusty, shabby, worn. Chair legs were chipped, tabletops dry and splintery, the great fireplace stones stained; even the windows, letting in the bright afternoon light whereby he could see these flaws, were dim with smoke and ancient grease. Four faces, including his father's, were gazing at him expectantly.

"Right," he said briskly, resigning all to destiny. "In two days we'll be having more guests than we'll know what to do with. Miss Miranda Beryl, the heir to Aislinn House, is coming from Landringham with an entourage of staff and friends." He paused while Mrs. Quinn sat down abruptly with a squeak. His father punched his chair arm with a fist, grinning hugely. "We're to put up those who can't be accommodated at

Aislinn House. Every room must be spotless, the kitchen and bar need replenishing, the stables need cleaning and repairs. You're fine workers; I don't need to tell you what you must do." He paused again, drew breath. "Mrs. Quinn. Since you won't be able to cook and clean for such a large group at the same time, I'm appointing you head housekeeper. I'll hire someone else to take over your duties in the kitchen. As of today." Inspiration struck; he abandoned himself to it recklessly. "Now."

"Mr. Cauley," Mrs. Quinn protested. "I'm in the middle of cooking your suppers."

Judd hesitated. Behind Mrs. Quinn, he saw the single fierce shake of his father's head. "You'll have to put up with my cooking for a change, Mrs. Quinn. I need you too much for other things."

"But you don't know how. I've had years of experience. Where will you find a replacement for years of experience in two days, Mr. Cauley?"

"I'm sure I'll never be able to replace you, Mrs. Quinn. I can only do my best. I hope you'll look upon my efforts kindly, and be patient."

"But—"

"What, for instance, can be done with this room, Mrs. Quinn? Lily? What would you suggest that might make our guests inclined to linger here and not move immediately over to the harbor inn, which is more convenient by far to Aislinn House?"

Even his father looked around at that, straining to see some room for improvement. Lily and Mrs. Quinn, challenged by the threat, their eyes narrowed in eerily similar expressions, studied the room silently.

"Everything needs a good scrub," Lily pronounced firmly. "Including and especially the windows. Maybe some curtains to soften the stones?"

"A good dusting," Mrs. Quinn suggested. "If bottles there must be, those bottles should shine. And the tankards. A carpet by the hearth. And a few chairs around it." She was on her feet abruptly. "And these tables—all scattered every which way. They need some kind of pattern. There's a great deal of charm in a good pattern. I'll show you. Help me, Mr. Quinn."

Judd helped his father up and out of their way. In the hall, he found Ridley Dow. Still in his coat and on his way out again, he had paused to listen.

"You were brilliant," he murmured to Judd.

"Was I?" Judd asked him, suddenly dubious. "Can you cook?"

"I don't know. I've never tried. Ah—you have no one else in mind?"

Judd shook his head. "Not an inkling."

"I don't care," Dugold sighed contentedly. "I'd as soon eat a boiled boot than another bite of Mrs. Quinn's cooking."

"Let's hope I can do better than boot leather. I don't blame you," he added to Ridley, "for fleeing the confusion. I'm sorry for it. We shouldn't be driving our only paying guest out on the rumor of others. Though I suppose you might know some of Miss Beryl's friends?"

Ridley hesitated. "I might have met one or two," he said slowly and without his usual easy smile. "I doubt they would remember me." He paused again; Judd heard the screech of table legs across the floor. "One especially, I would prefer to avoid. But more than likely he would be staying at Aislinn House."

"I'm sorry," Judd said abruptly. "You're the last guest I would want to make uncomfortable. I could put Mrs. Quinn back in the kitchen; she'll get rid of everyone in no time."

Ridley's smile rose to the surface again. "Please—anything but that. And I'm not driven out by the noise. I'm going to ride back to the wood, see if I can find the tree house. If at all possible, I would like to explore Aislinn House before Miss Beryl gets there. I think the herbalist might be the perfect guide."

"For what?" Judd asked incredulously. "What can the bell possibly have to do with that faded old house? Or Emma's mother?"

"I won't know unless I find out," Ridley answered imperturbably. Something crashed in the taproom; there was a confused gabble of voices. Ridley nodded speechlessly, dropped his hat on his head, and went one way quickly; Judd grasped his father's arm and bore him the other.

He left Dugold in his rocker, raptly contemplating their good fortune, and descended into the kitchen to see what he had inherited from Mrs. Quinn. He found beef boiling merrily in a pot above the dying fire, and, in the oven, burning bread. He pulled the bread out in a cloud of smoke and thought briefly of tossing it onto the fire, for the loaves seemed to have the density and texture of nicely seasoned wood. He poked at the beef with a fork. The prongs bounced off the meat. He pulled the pot off the hook, set it on the floor, and contemplated, with some bitterness, what might have appeared on his plate in the guise of supper.

He put his hand in his pocket, counted what came out of it. He went back upstairs to the taproom, where the three Quinns were busy transforming the room into total chaos.

"I'll be back," he told them tersely.

Halfway down the cliff road into town, he met Gwyneth Blair and her sister Pandora, walking up the road toward the inn.

He stopped, wordless, entranced by that long golden hair streaming back from Gwyneth's face, then suddenly scattering every which way as the wind changed its mind and turned. She was laughing; so was her younger sister, and Judd felt his own mouth tugged into a smile.

"What?" he demanded. "Did I forget to take my apron off?"

"We were coming to have tea with you!" Pandora exclaimed. "And here you are."

"And lucky you are," he told them. "The inn is in shambles, and I've taken Mrs. Quinn out of the kitchen to put everything back together again. There's no one left to boil water for you."

"Oh," Gwyneth said, her brows crooking above her lenses. "Is this to do with Miss Beryl? We've been hearing rumors."

"Already?"

"Dr. Grantham told my father that he'd received a note from her. Is she staying with you?"

"No, only some of her party. Which inspired me to ban Mrs. Quinn from the kitchen. So now I must find another cook. Do you know of any cooks at loose ends, roaming about Sealey Head begging for a position?"

"Let me give it some thought... Are you absolutely adamant that you'll give us no tea?"

"You'll thank me," he assured her. Then he paused, struck by a likely possibility; he added slowly, "Mr. Dow might find it well within his capabilities to boil water, but he has fled the scene as well. I'm very sorry. I'm on my way to find something to replace the disaster in the kitchen that was to be our supper. Since I got rid of the cook, I seem to be responsible for feeding people."

"Ah, well," she said composedly. "Another time, then. Though—" She hesitated, an odd expression in her eyes as she gazed over his shoulder at the inn on the bluff. "I did want a word with Mr. Dow."

"Ah."

"Has he mentioned magic to you?"

"Once or twice. He gave me a book to read. It's quite entertaining, a sort of romance about some sorcerer who came to Sealey Head long ago."

"Really?" A little color fanned across her cheekbones; he recognized, in her eyes, the cupidity of another whose reason was lost to books. "May I read it when you're finished?"

"It may be a while, if I actually have to stop reading and behave like an innkeeper."

"Perhaps your guests won't stay long," she said fervently, then laughed at herself as he smiled. "I'm sorry. I can imagine a little of what all this means to the inn. First the wealthy Mr. Dow and now Miranda Beryl's entourage. But what am I thinking, keeping you standing here when you must go hunting up a cook? I'd ask at the bakery, if I were you. And I'll ask Aunt Phoebe. She might know someone who knows someone. Pandora!" she called abruptly to her sister, who was bent over and digging perilously at something down the side of the cliff. "Be careful! The wind will push you right over."

Pandora straightened finally. "I've found a perfect fossil!"

"Good for you! Come over here before you become one at

the bottom of the cliff." She looked at Judd, seemed to read the thought in his eyes, to hear the words lined up in his impulsively opened mouth. "I promised to take her to the top of Sealey Head," she said apologetically. "Otherwise, we would walk with you back into town. She wants to see if she can see the ghostly ship going under as the bell rings."

"That's a couple of hours from now, and a walk back in the twilight," he reminded her gravely.

"I know. I doubt we'll stay out that long today. Do you still?"

"Do I—"

"Still look for the ghost ship?"

"Of course. Always, if I'm watching the sunset."

"Mr. Dow seems to think the bell has nothing to do with a ship," she said puzzledly. "I wanted to ask him what he truly thinks. But we always seem surrounded by Sproules, when we meet, so it's hard to talk coherently about ghosts."

"I noticed."

She threw him a sudden, mischievous smile. "That's partly why I promised Pandora this excursion. And if we go back down too soon, they'll most likely be there still in the parlor with Aunt Phoebe."

"Ah," he said, enlightened and relieved, at least on that score. He added, reluctant to bring the wealthy and charming Mr. Dow into the conversation again, but it seemed only fair to tell her, "Ridley Dow seems to think the bell has something to do with Aislinn House."

"Really?" she said, astonished. "How could it? The house never had a bell tower, did it? And there's no local lore suggesting a connection."

"That's where he is now, trying to find Hesper Wood and

all her local lore. He thinks she must know something about the bell."

"Why on earth?"

"I have no idea, beyond that she is obsessed with the history of the inhabitants of Sealey Head."

"Tenuous," she remarked after a moment.

"Perhaps. But sometimes strangers see something more clearly than those who have been looking at it all their lives."

"Well. I'm working on my own theory about the bell. It does involve Aislinn House, but many other aspects of Sealey Head as well."

"You're writing this?"

She nodded, flushing again. "The twins like it."

"I'll trade you Ridley's book for a glimpse of it," he said promptly.

She laughed. "That's unfair! How can I say no? But you'll have to wait; I'm still working my theory out."

"Maybe by then, there will be someone in the kitchen to make you tea. I hope you'll come again," he added. "I can promise you access to any number of odd books. And I'd love to read one of your tales."

She studied him silently a moment, then gave a little nod. Her gray eyes, he saw, were the exact shade of the clouds gathering at the edge of the world, preparing to grapple the sun into the sea. "I remember we used to like the same books when we were young," she said. "I'd like you to read what I'm writing." She turned, shading her eyes. "Pan—Oh."

Her sister was with them suddenly, a whirlwind of lavender skirts and dark, wild hair. She held out her hand, showed them the spiral shell caught in crumbling layers of stone. "Mr. Trent has a book of drawings of fossils. I'm going to see if this matches any of them. I'm sorry you didn't have tea for us," she told Judd. "I liked your Mr. Dow."

"We'll come again," Gwyneth promised.

Smiling, Judd watched them pushing uphill against the wind, skirts billowing and twisting around their ankles, until he remembered, with a start and a sudden turn, the ruins of overcooked supper and the triumphant Mrs. Quinn who awaited him if he returned empty-handed from his quest.

Ten

They were not your ordinary merchant sailors, Gwyneth wrote the following morning in her tiny room under the eaves. *Not hairy and hardworking, dressed in blue gabardine trousers and mostly barefoot. Nor were they in any kind of uniform. Nor, Mr. Blair hastened to assure himself through the end of his telescope, were they pirates, unless the wild marauders of the deep seas wore breeches and coats of silk all the hues of mother-of-pearl, and boots so brightly polished they reflected sunlight like metal. Like the ship, they carried no arms, no pistols or swords. At least, he amended grimly, none were visible. And, oddly enough, no hats. As the ship had turned from the channel into the harbor, he had noticed something even stranger. The vessel slowed as sail was taken in, but Mr. Blair could see no one at all—no bustling sailors, bellowing in answer to orders below, clambering among the rigging on the masts, loosening, taking in, taking up—no one tending to the sails at all. It seemed as though they cupped their windward hollows to a wish, like giant ears, luffed in answer, and rolled themselves up.*

The ship glided to the center of the harbor, lowered an anchor, and sat there admiring its reflection. It seemed, with its colors and lovely grace in the limpid, blue-gray water, like some rare bird come to light upon the waters of Sealey Head.

Nothing happened.

Mr. Blair waited.

Nothing happened.

He heard steps pounding up the stairs to his office on the second floor of the warehouse along the docks. He kept the telescope trained on the ship, waiting for the splash of a longboat, a raised flag, even a blast on a hunting horn from that odd crew: any kind of a courtesy signal greeting Sealey Head and assuring the populace of friendly intentions.

Nothing.

The door opened; his son Jarret, lithe and dark-haired, stood panting, staring over Mr. Blair's shoulder out the grimy mullioned window. "Did you see what—"

"Yes."

"Who in the world—"

"I have no idea."

They were not the only ones watching the ship. Sir Magnus Sproule, riding despondently back to his house after viewing his desiccated fields, and pleading vociferously with the cloudless sky, had reined in his horse along the cliff. He sat there staring in disbelief at the elegant vessel. "Lost," he muttered finally, but made no move to ride away. On the other cusp of the town, on Sealey Head itself, the innkeeper, Anscom Cauley, crouched on his roof and hammering down patches over the leaks, had been transfixed as well by the unexpected

*sight. He felt his face trying to do something it had nearly forgot-
ten how: to smile. "Guests," he breathed. And in Aislinn House,
becalmed and morose in its penniless state, Lord Aislinn's daughter,
Eloise, gazed down the hillside at the gleaming ship. Her small,
mushroom brown eyes took on a gleam unaccounted for by the gloomy
shadows. "Wealth," she saw, and "men," perhaps even "marriage-
able men." At that point in her tedious life, she would have wedded
the Pirate King himself just to get away from Aislinn House and her
dissolute father.*

And as they watched, they were watched.

"Gwyneth!" Aunt Phoebe called from the bottom of the
attic stairs. "Are you coming?"

Gwyneth jumped, having forgotten, for the moment,
which world she inhabited: her aunt's voice boomed incon-
gruously across the yardarm of the mysterious ship.

"Coming!" she answered, wondering where, and then
remembered: she had promised to accompany Phoebe for
various errands along Water Street. She left her page to dry,
wiped her pen nib, and capped the ink, all while getting to
her feet and dodging, out of habit, the sharply sloping roof.

She opened the door, peered down; her aunt had already
bustled away, calling to the twins. Gwyneth, still feeling the
tidal pull of her story, closed the door firmly and regretfully
upon it, and went down to join Phoebe.

The young maid Ivy was with her, looking flurried, her
arms full of Dulcie. "I can't find them, ma'am."

Phoebe put her fingers delicately to her eyes while her
voice gathered power enough to be heard behind couches in
the parlor, potted palms in the library, and whatever books
the twins might have vanished into.

"Pandora! Crispin! I need you to watch Dulcie while we

are gone! Those two. They melt into the air at any hint of responsibility. You'll have to find them, Ivy."

The girl's eyes grew wide. "Yes, ma'am. But ma'am, the cook wants me to run to the butcher for a pork roast she forgot—"

How does one forget a pork roast? Gwyneth wondered, then thought, for some reason, of Judd. Cook, she remembered. Cook.

"Ivy, do you know anyone looking for a position as cook? Mr. Cauley at the inn is desperate."

The maid gave a faint giggle and slid her hand over her mouth. "Sorry, miss. It's just we've been wondering what he was going to do about Mrs. Quinn."

"If you hear or think of anyone, will you tell me? And ask the cook."

"Yes, miss."

"Meanwhile," Aunt Phoebe demanded fulminately of the chandelier, "what are we to do about the twins?"

Mr. Blair threw open the library door. "I cannot hear myself think," he said testily, then bellowed like a bull, "Twins! I've heard less noise from an army taking over a government and dethroning a king."

"I'm sorry, Toland," Aunt Phoebe said a trifle crisply. "They're apparently in hiding; we're all going out and—"

"Yes. I heard." He held out his arms. "Give Dulcie to me. I'll find the twins. Stop grinning, you little bundle of trouble. I'll put you in the cage with the parrot. Pandora!"

"Yes, Father?" she said, gliding with dignity down the stairs behind him. "What is everyone shouting about? I've only been in my room, trying to finish a sentence in my diary."

"It must have been an excruciatingly long sentence," Aunt Phoebe said acridly. "We're going out. Watch the child."

"Of course, Aunt Phoebe," Pandora said mildly, receiving the bundle and setting her on her feet. "Come, child. We'll go and teach the parrot some new words."

Phoebe opened her mouth, closed it, watching their slow amble down the hall toward the parlor. She closed her eyes. "Toland."

"Yes, Phoebe."

"The parrot is stuffed."

"Fortunately, don't you think, knowing the twins?"

He disappeared back into the library. Aunt Phoebe gripped Gwyneth's arm.

"I need air," she said. "Now."

On the street, her hold loosened a little; the brisk wind from the sea, the busy, glittering water behind the shops along the harbor, the smiles and greetings of townspeople growing more and more familiar to her, eased the severity of her expression, replaced it with one that made Gwyneth suddenly wary. Her aunt shifted closer to her, patted her arm a couple of times, mentioned idly that they must remember to go to the confectioner's for tea cakes, since the Sproules would surely stop by that afternoon.

"Especially since they missed you yesterday," she said.

Gwyneth, who was absently searching the harbor for the ship in her story, blinked at the suddenly meaningful note in her aunt's voice.

"Yes," she answered. "Pandora and I went for a walk."

"Raven especially expressed his disappointment that you weren't home. Couldn't you have taken your walk earlier in the day?"

"I was working earlier."

"Writing."

"Yes."

"You are a well-to-do merchant's daughter being courted—very seriously, I must say—by the squire's son and heir. Don't tell me you haven't noticed."

"I was trying not to," Gwyneth sighed. "Aunt Phoebe, I know he's nice enough, and very sweet to Dulcie. But—"

"Obviously longing for a family of his own," Phoebe said briskly. "Outside of niceness and sweetness, what objections could you possibly have? His family is wealthy and eminently respectable; you could not find a better match in these parts, except at Aislinn House, and there is no one eligible for you there. Not that the family would even consider a merchant's daughter. That the Sproules would is to their credit, and obviously only because of the strong feelings the young man has for you."

"Aunt Phoebe, they are descended from farmers! Now, they're farmers with a title."

"Well, at any rate, you don't have one," Phoebe said a trifle nebulously, "and he does. Or will. Well. Besides that, I mean. Do you have objections to his suit?"

"Yes, I have objections," Gwyneth said roundly; her aunt's fingers, tightening again on her arm, checked her impulse to stride. "We don't have a thing in common to talk about; he has no chin; he is better at charming you and Dulcie than me; I suspect that at heart he believes that marriage is the proper cure for a woman who writes. And he thinks a great deal too highly of himself. He loves himself far more than I could ever love him."

Phoebe was silent. They passed the stationer's shop. Gwyneth cast a wistful glance into the window, saw Mr. Trent placing the latest fashionable novel to advantage on the windowsill.

Will I? she wondered wistfully. Will my name? Will complete strangers read mine? What, she thought more coherently, is Aunt Phoebe thinking?

Her aunt told her abruptly. "Are you in love with someone else?"

Gwyneth froze half a step; her aunt's fingers finally slid away. "No," she answered fiercely. "Of course not. That has nothing whatsoever to do with my feelings about Raven Sproule. Must we talk about this? He might as easily fall in love with somebody else next week."

"He might," Phoebe agreed. "That's why I think you should encourage him a little more. Be home when he comes to call. Talk to him. You gave most of your attention last time to Mr. Cauley and Mr. Dow. That was good of you to be solicitous of Mr. Cauley, who has been going through difficult times. But you don't seem to notice his feelings toward you, and it isn't fair of you to encourage him."

Gwyneth stared at her aunt, felt the warmth, despite the wind, in her face. "What feelings?"

"Mr. Dow, of course, is another question." She paused again, revealing to her fascinated niece what kind of question. "Wealthy, well-mannered, very sympathetic, very handsome. I don't blame you if you have discovered feelings for him."

"Mr. Dow," Gwyneth echoed faintly.

"But we don't really know anything at all about him. It's wiser not to risk your future on the unknown, the charming stranger whose own heart might already be taken, and lose both him and the comfortable life you might have had with the more familiar."

Gwyneth stepped wordlessly around a pile of crab traps a fisher was unloading at the end of a dock. "You don't think Mr. Dow could love me?" she asked finally. Her aunt, she realized, had just handed her the plot of the previous latest fashionable novel. She might as well use it to cloud the issue, since Phoebe didn't want to hear anything Gwyneth had to say, anyway.

Her arm was taken again, gently. "I would think far less of Mr. Dow if he couldn't. I see no reason why he shouldn't. But he may have very good reasons: family obligations, or an engagement of his own in Landringham, for example. He frequents quite a different world from Sealey Head and has a life there of which we know nothing. Besides, you wouldn't dream, I hope, of living so far from your family."

"I lived most of three years there," Gwyneth reminded her, "and here I am, back again. I missed the wildness here. The sense of living on the edge of the world, the borders of the unknown."

"Your father would be very glad to hear that. He would miss you if you went to live anywhere else. And Raven Sproule would give you the best of all reasons to stay here in Sealey Head. Far be it from me to tell you what to do," she added, as Gwyneth opened her mouth. "I am only trying to give you a sense of direction you seem to lack. Just think about what I've said. And—Oh! Here's the chandler's; we're running low on candles. And then to the grocer's for tea. I'm glad we were able to talk, Gwyneth. Sometimes our lives are so full of people we can't hear what anyone is saying."

"Indeed," Gwyneth breathed dazedly, and followed her

aunt into the shop, where they found Judd Cauley placing a very large order for the inn.

"I hope, Mr. Cauley, you will spare a few for us," Aunt Phoebe said affably.

He looked even more harried than usual, Gwyneth saw as he turned to greet them. But, meeting his eyes, she found the pleased smile in them, and then felt her own. As simple as that, she thought, then wondered what that meant.

"Are you ready for your onslaught of company?" she asked.

"I'm dreading it," he confessed. "The inn is in complete confusion; I still don't have a cook, and we seem to have driven away our sole lodger with our noise and disorder and my cooking. I haven't seen Mr. Dow since yesterday."

"If he reappears, please send him to us for his tea," Aunt Phoebe said with bewildering inconsistency.

"Thank you, Miss Blair; I'm sure he'll appreciate that."

"We'll send word immediately if we find a cook for you," Gwyneth promised.

"Just send the cook," he pleaded. "I can make do as long as we have to feed only ourselves and rumor. But the truth of the matter will appear under our inn sign tomorrow, and if I must send them all into town to eat, I doubt they'll be with us long."

"There's my cousin," Ross Carbery, the chandler, said abruptly. "You might talk to her. She cooks nicely, and since her husband was laid up with a fever and is too weak yet to go out in his boat, she's had to take in mending and laundry."

"Of course I know Hazel," Judd said gratefully. "I'd be happy to give her a try."

"She's just a door or two down on Mackerel Street. I don't

know how she'd feel about cooking for a crowd. But she's got a cool head and busy hands; she might just do."

"Good. I'll go there immediately. Thank you, Ross." He nodded farewell, backing toward the door; his eyes returned to Gwyneth. "Next time you ask me for tea, I might just have it for you, Miss Blair."

"I'll hold you to your challenge, Mr. Cauley."

"Whatever did he mean?" Aunt Phoebe asked with mystification of the closing door.

"Pandora and I got tired walking up Sealey Head yesterday," Gwyneth explained, and found herself smiling at the memory. "We begged Mr. Cauley for tea, but he wouldn't give it to us."

Phoebe pulled the door open; the cowbell rattled alarmingly. She pronounced judgment tartly as they stepped into the street.

"How very peculiar of you both."

GWYNETH wrote in the scant hour she had free between errands and tea:

After a night and a morning of waiting for some sign of intention from the silent ship in Sealey Head harbor, the townspeople discussed the matter and decided to send a boat out to visit the ship. Mr. Blair would go, of course; he had traveled farther than anyone, and might recognize at least the origins of the mystery. Sir Magnus Sproule, who needed to take his mind out of his dying fields, and who was handy with a sword if the occasion warranted, volunteered. Mr. Cauley and Lord Aislinn, along with several other merchants, would be among the party onshore to welcome the visitors. Another party would be hidden away in Mr. Blair's warehouse, watching for any signs of violence. These were hardy fishermen and field-workers, whose weapons of choice were the gaff, the shovel, and the poacher's pistol. Lord Aislinn carried an ornate pistol as well, but since it hadn't been fired in a century, he was persuaded to leave it unloaded. Another pair of fishermen rowed the boat across the harbor, where Mr. Blair hailed the still figures watching them from the deck of the ship.

They replied quite readily; their words were oddly accented but understandable. A rope ladder was run down over the side. Mr. Blair and Sir Magnus, strong men impelled by curiosity, hauled themselves up without incident, and stood on the shining deck, blinking in wonder.

Those who surrounded them were all tall, lean, and astonishingly elegant for the rigors of a life at sea. They wore their hair long, unbound, and unencumbered by anything resembling a hat. A dark-haired man spoke first. He wore a pale blue silk coat and breeches, and what looked like a spray of pearls set in gold pinned at his throat. He was quite handsome. They all were, Mr. Blair saw with amazement; they might have been the members of the same sprawling family.

"Welcome," he said in a pleasant, easy voice, his words colored by the music of an unknown language, "to the Chimera.*"*

Eleven

J udd trudged back to the inn after a pleasant but futile
interview with the chandler's cousin Hazel. She was aware
of his problem with Mrs. Quinn, she had said. As was the
entire town, he thought glumly. But the young woman looked
quite apprehensive at the thought of cooking for such a punc-
tilious crowd. And who could blame her? Besides, she had
confided shyly. What with one thing or another, while she
took care of her ailing husband and made ends meet, she
hadn't really noticed her own condition. Until now. And
he wouldn't want a cook who turned green in the mornings
and got queasy looking at an egg dribbling out of its shell
and lolloping into the frying pan, now, would he?

No amount of money would tempt her.

Just as well, he thought as he left her. There wouldn't

be much once the guests had been driven away because he couldn't feed them. Even Ridley had found another place to eat, and Judd could hardly blame him for that.

Odd, though, that he'd stayed around for Mrs. Quinn's lumpy porridge and rubbery fish, only to vanish at the prospect of Judd's cooking. He, at least, could follow his mother's recipes. Judd scratched his brow bemusedly, wondering. More likely it had been the tumult he'd fled. Mr. Quinn and Judd pounding on the stable roof, while Mrs. Quinn and Lily shoved things around in every room, chattering nonstop as they cleaned everything in sight. What was it Ridley had gone off to do? Something about looking around Aislinn House for the bell? It sounded a great deal more peaceful than trying to study at the inn. At least until someone noticed the stranger flitting about the house.

Judd made a few more stops, at the butcher's and the grocer's to place orders, at the tailor's to have himself measured for a new coat. Mrs. Quinn had practically demanded he do that, and his father, sight of Judd's present coat unseen, had backed her. That tedious chore done, he spent a moment at the stationer's shop, inquiring of Osric Trent if he had seen anything of Mr. Dow.

"No, I haven't," the bookseller said. "Not since you were here with him last. When you see him, tell him I found a couple of books on local history that might interest him."

"I will," Judd said, wondering if Ridley had finally fallen over a cliff.

At the inn, he took a quick look at the Quinns' handiwork before he started supper. The taproom was amazingly burnished; tabletops, bottles, copper taps, even the windows gleamed. There were a few startling touches: mugs of wildflowers on every table, some exceedingly lacy curtains framing pristine views of the sea and the flowing green slope of the headlands that had been nearly invisible, what with layers of soot and salt air, for years. Decades. In fact, Judd realized, since before he was born. He felt the fierce tidal flow of worry in his heart begin to turn. The floors, both oak plank and flagstone, looked freshly scrubbed; he marveled at them as he walked down the hallway to see his father. The candles had arrived before him; the glowing brass sconces along the walls each held a fresh wax taper. With, for some reason, a ribbon tied around it. He blinked, and refrained from glancing into the sitting room, guessing that, in their zeal, Mrs. Quinn and Lily had swagged and beribboned the entire room.

Dugold, listening to the sea in his rocker at the window, recognized his son's step. "Well?" he asked a trifle fretfully. He must be getting hungry, Judd thought. "Did you find us a cook?"

"I asked around. Nobody yet." He dropped his hands on his father's shoulders. "You'll have to bear with me tonight."

"That's easy to do," Dugold said, turning in the chair as though he might see Judd's face if he looked hard enough. "With you in the kitchen, I can at least recognize what I'm eating. But they'll be here tomorrow! What then?"

Judd shrugged. "I'll keep looking. And cooking."

"You're good," Dugold said glumly, "but you're not good enough. Not for rich folk out of Landringham."

"I know. But not much else I can do, is there? I'll feed them until they leave, and then we'll only be back where we were before, except a lot tidier. Don't worry. I let the towns-people know what we need. As if they didn't already know," he added ruefully.

"Everyone in town knows about Mrs. Quinn's cooking except Mrs. Quinn, is that it?"

Judd nodded, then remembered and spoke. "That's it."

"Funny about that."

"One day it will be," Judd promised, and gave Dugold's shoulders a final pat. "I'd best get cooking."

"Where's that Ridley Dow?" his father asked. "I remembered a thing or two I wanted to tell him about Sealey Head."

"I'll let him know when I see him."

In the kitchen he chopped leeks and potatoes to fry together, and put the loaves he had left in their pans to rise into the oven. Then he stood leafing through his mother's cookbook, trying to work his way through her stained, hurried writing for what to do with the slab of mutton on the table that wouldn't take all night.

Someone rang the bell outside the door.

He froze. Can't be them, he thought desperately. Can't be. Not today. Not in time for mutton.

He listened, heard Mr. Quinn's footsteps in the hallway, then the front door opening. Breath stopped, he listened for a gabble of voices, a wave of footsteps clicking and clomping, spilling across the floorboards.

He heard only Mr. Quinn's again, coming toward the kitchen stairs and then down. "A Mr. Pilchard, sir." He seemed extraordinarily excited by the stranger, his thick mustache working with emotion. "Says he cooks."

"Oh," Judd said soundlessly. He slammed the book shut and recovered his voice. "Send him down, Mr. Quinn, at once, and tell him to hurry."

Mr. Pilchard, too bulky to hurry, looked more like a

frogfish, with his plump, lumpy face, than the sleek fish whose name he shared. He descended with concentration, breathing noisily, a rather shabbily dressed man somewhere between youth and age, with most of his fair, thinning hair still on his head, and one ash-colored eye disconcertingly larger than the other. He weighed anchor at the bottom of the stairs and nodded amiably at Judd.

"Hieronymous Pilchard," he said. "I hear you're looking for a cook, Mr. Cauley."

"Where?" Judd asked curiously.

"Where? Ah—where did I hear. I've been staying at the tavern in town; that's where I heard. Some were laying bets on whether you'd find a cook or not before the gentry came to town."

"Did you bet?" Judd asked dryly.

"I?" Mr. Pilchard smiled slightly. "Oh, I should have, I suppose. Didn't think of it. I just wanted a job. I've been a ship's cook for twenty years, cooking for as many as a hundred on the *Mother Carey*, and for as few as six on the *Merry Eel.* I washed ashore up the coast at Petrel, and made my way down, looking. It came to me, a few weeks ago, that if I ever wanted to marry and settle, now was the time. I'd somehow forgotten to get around to it before. Sealey Head is a pretty town, and friendly. I took to it right away and hoped I'd find a way to stay. Will you give me a try, Mr. Cauley?"

"Mr. Pilchard," Judd answered fervently, "if you can persuade my father with that piece of mutton, nothing would make me happier." He untied his apron, tossed it to Hieronymous Pilchard. "We will be five for supper—six, if our only lodger shows up. Tomorrow we may well be twenty-five. There's bread in the oven, potatoes and leeks on the table, and anything else you can find in the pantry. Have at it, Mr. Pilchard."

"Thank you, Mr. Cauley. I'm grateful."

"Not," Judd breathed to the air at the top of the stairs, "more than I am."

An hour or two later, he ate supper with his father, since Mrs. Quinn, designated housekeeper, refused to let anyone but guests sully the taproom, and Ridley didn't appear. Just the smells of the food set in front of him made Dugold sigh with pleasure.

"Just like your mother's."

Sharing a little table in front of the darkened window, the two made their way quickly, methodically, and with reverent silence through a soup of leeks and cream, peppered mutton chops as tender as they could be gotten, fried among chopped onions and potatoes, accompanied by warm, crusty, crumbly bread that didn't fight back between the teeth.

Dugold dropped his fork after the last bite, sat back in his chair, and stared at his son so intently that Judd wondered if the cooking had cured his sight. But no: he had to grope a little for his beer.

"That was incredible," he said after a gulp. "That was—what's that word Ridley uses? Magical." Judd, still chewing, could only nod. "Keep him," Dugold ordered. "Give him whatever it takes. I haven't tasted the like of that since your mother died. What was his name again? Halibut?"

"Pilchard."

"Whatever you do, keep an eye on him. Don't let anyone else make off with him."

Judd smiled. "What would you do with yourself if you didn't find something to worry about?"

"I'm looking after you, boy. I'm still your father."

"Right you are. But just for tonight, revel in your well-cooked mutton and pretend we've solved the last of our problems."

He took the dirty plates to the kitchen, found Mr. Quinn there, drawn inexorably down below stairs to bask in the company of the paragon who had cooked his supper. Hieronymous Pilchard, his arms in the suds, cocked a bushy brow over his oversized eye at Judd.

"Well?" he said. "Does he approve?"

"Mr. Pilchard, you have no idea. If you leave, he'll probably go with you." He put his dishes down, surveyed the kitchen. It was unexpectedly tidy, so soon after Mr. Pilchard's culinary labors.

"At sea, you get into the habit of cleaning up as you go along," the cook explained, reading his thoughts. "There's not much working space on a boat."

"Still, I should get someone in to help you," Judd said. "You may need it, when there's a crowd."

"Lily," Mr. Quinn suggested.

"No. She'll be busy enough as it is. Maybe one or two of the baker's dozen; they all must know their way around a kitchen. Where did you put Mr. Pilchard's things?"

"What things?"

"They're back at the tavern," Mr. Pilchard said. "I came up here just on the off-chance . . . I'll go down for them when I've finished here."

"Mr. Quinn will show you a room when you're ready."

"An entire room," Mr. Pilchard marveled. "I've barely gotten used to half a mattress."

"The best," Mr. Quinn promised, "of the servants' quarters. Too bad Mr. Dow missed that supper tonight."

"Mr. Dow?"

"Ridley Dow, our only lodger," Judd explained. "Until tomorrow. Well. I think he is, at any rate." Mr. Pilchard, groping under the suds for the sponge, cocked his brow again. "Still lodging with us, that is."

"Still hasn't been sighted?" Mr. Quinn asked. "Must have been all our hammering. Couldn't hear himself think."

"I hope that's all it is," Judd said slowly, wondering suddenly if he should add their lodger to the list of his worries. But, he reminded himself, Ridley was an intelligent and resourceful man on a quest for some beast called Magic; he couldn't be expected to behave like ordinary people. He felt eyes on him, looked up to find Mr. Pilchard studying him, hands moving rhythmically underwater, his mismatched eyes as unreadable as oysters. As Judd met them, the cook looked down at the water, pulled a plate out of it, and dipped it into a pot of cold water to rinse it.

"I'll keep his supper on the coals for a while, in case he comes in later," he offered, and Judd nodded.

"You might keep an eye out for him in the tavern when you go back for your baggage," Mr. Quinn suggested. "Tell him it's safe to return."

"What would I be looking for?"

"A dark-haired young man wearing fine clothes and a pair of spectacles. Most likely with a book in his hands," Judd said.

"Spectacles," Mr. Pilchard murmured. "Book. I shall certainly do that, Mr. Cauley."

Mr. Quinn left to find Mrs. Quinn to dust and air a room for the cook. Judd lingered to discuss his terms of engagement, which, owing to Mr. Pilchard's years at sea and his ignorance, at the moment, of his own worth, were arrived at easily and with mutual satisfaction. That done, Mr. Pilchard walked down Sealey Head by moonlight to fetch his things, and Judd went to read his father to sleep with the improbable adventures of one Nemos Moore, who had apparently more magical powers than he knew what to do with, and, more astonishingly, had once made his way to the rugged and isolated coastal town of Sealey Head to use them.

Twelve

Emma was pulling great swaths of muslin off card tables and gun racks and the billiards table in the game room when she heard the creaky boot room door open. She froze, muslin swirling around her like ghosts. Nobody but she ever used that door now. Had Miss Beryl's staff descended already upon the house, to explore, compare, criticize, and complain? She heard a comment in a deep, unfamiliar voice, as another door opened across the hallway: the stillroom.

She heard her mother's voice in answer.

Surprised, she dropped the dustsheets on the floor and waded across them.

She found Hesper in the stillroom with a stranger, a dark-eyed, bespectacled young man. He dressed as though he might have been part of Miranda Beryl's rich and indolent entourage, with those pale, golden butterflies all over his black waist-coat, and the satin piping on his cuffs. But he wore a vivid, attentive expression upon his face as he listened to Hesper, which, Emma suspected, was unnatural among the delicately brought-up city folk, especially when they were spoken to by wood witches with naked shins and twigs in their hair. He had, Emma realized, a fair sprinkling of bracken in his own long hair. His fine clothing was rumpled and stained. His eyes, like her mother's, seemed heavy, red-rimmed with sleeplessness. They both looked, to put it plain as a pot, as though they had spent the night together under a bush.

Emma's brows flew up in wonder. Her mother saw her then; a smile sprang into her eyes.

"There you are, Emma! We were just talking about where we might find you." She put her bare, brown arm around Emma's shoulders. "This is Ridley Dow." Emma nodded briefly, speechless. "We've spent a good part of yesterday and last night going through my papers and talking about this house. We were going go find our way in here at night through the boot room, and wake you before Miss Beryl got here, but I think we fell asleep on our way here."

Mr. Dow nodded, rolling one shoulder around a crick. "I remember losing an argument with a tree root."

"You were going to sneak around Aislinn House in the middle of the night?" Emma said faintly.

"Well, everyone but you is half-deaf; nobody would have noticed."

"But why?"

"Mr. Dow thinks he might be able to help Ysabo," Hesper said. "We need you to open doors."

Emma edged sideways toward the solid worktable, leaned

against it, wondering how many different ways a body could possibly be surprised in a minute. She found her voice again finally. "Nobody," she said, gazing wide-eyed at Mr. Dow. "Nobody but us has ever known her name before. Ever in my life."

"Your mother has told me everything about her," the mysterious Mr. Dow explained. "Everything you have told her. I've been putting bits and pieces of the story together for years. You see, I think one of my ancestors was responsible for the spell on Aislinn House."

"Spell." The unlikely word took shape and meaning in Emma's head, became suddenly comprehensible. "Spell. Is that what it is?"

"I think so," Mr. Dow said, watching her intently from behind his lenses.

"I don't—I never thought about such things before. But it does—When you said it, it felt right. It could explain so many strange things." She heard Mr. Dow gather breath, loose it in a slow, deep, satisfied sigh. She studied him, brows rising again, fretting together. "But what could you do? You don't know that place. It's eerie—full of great, noisy, armed knights, flocks of crows that look at you like they'd swarm over you and pick your bones if they didn't like the expression on your face. What could you do for Ysabo?"

"I don't know. I can't know until I've seen. Your mother told me you open doors to that secret world, you talk to Ysabo across thresholds. Would you open one for me?"

Emma opened her mouth; nothing came out.

"Mr. Dow just wants a glimpse of Ysabo's world," Hesper told her quickly. "He might see a great deal, like you, or very little but the odd detail, which is all I ever see. He won't interfere. And she needn't see him at all. He could stand behind the door and peer through the crack along the hinges. Couldn't you?"

Mr. Dow looked at her, his spectacles reflecting light, hiding his expression. He said quickly, "Yes, of course."

Hesper nodded encouragingly at Emma, who said dazedly, "But I never know what door I'll find her behind. Any door, it could be, anywhere in this house, from cellar to attic."

"Then I'll follow while you work," Ridley Dow said. "Very discreetly, of course; no one will know I'm here. You can try the doors of whatever room you're in. I promise I won't get in your way, and I'll be very patient while you're busy."

"And I can help you work," Hesper offered.

"I could use help," Emma admitted. "And the house is very quiet, now. There's only Mr. Fitch, who mostly stays down in his pantry, and Mrs. Blakeley, who hates climbing stairs. Sophie never leaves Lady Eglantyne's bedroom, and Mrs. Haw never leaves the kitchen except to shop."

"So there we are, then," Mr. Dow said briskly. "Where shall we start? What were you doing when we came in?"

"Pulling the dustsheets off the billiards table."

"And which way is that?"

"Wait," Hesper interrupted. "You're both missing what's under our noses."

"And that would be?" Mr. Dow asked with alacrity.

"The stillroom pantry door. Right over there. It's where Emma first saw Ysabo."

They all looked at it: Mr. Dow hopeful, Hesper expectant, Emma with sudden weariness as she remembered everything in the pantry lying under a decade-old coat of dust that would need to be dealt with, along with a hundred other things that needed . . . She moved toward the closed door with a shrug; it had to be looked into, and it was a place to start.

She gave Mr. Dow a moment to position himself at the hinges, then opened the door.

And there was the princess, framed by stones as always at that time of the morning, standing in an arched walkway near the top of the house, with the restless sough of sounds splashing up from the great chasm of the hall behind her. She smiled instantly at Emma. But her speckled eyes seemed wary, oddly secretive.

"I'm exploring," she told Emma very softly. "I'm trying to understand things."

"Oh, be careful," Emma begged.

"I am, I am." Her wild, curly red hair hung loosely down her back; on her pale, plain face the mark of the knight's fingers had faded to a startling shade of greengage plum. "I can't talk now; I must be very quiet."

"I know; I can't, either. The house will be full of guests by evening. The heir is coming."

"Ah—did your lady die?"

"Not yet. But she's no better."

Ysabo nodded gravely. Then her eyes shifted. She stared in utter astonishment at what was going on at Emma's elbow, which was Ridley Dow, touching Emma's arm gently, and saying, as he eased past her to step across the threshold, "Princess Ysabo, I am Ridley Dow. I believe you might have crossed paths with an ancestor of mine, Nemos Moore."

"Emma!" Mrs. Blakeley called just outside the stillroom door, and Emma's bones leaped in her skin like a deer at a pistol shot. Her fingers slid off the door. Mr. Dow reached

129

out, closed it deftly behind him as the housekeeper entered the stillroom.

"Oh, there you are, Emma. And Hesper, too! I do hope you've come to give us a hand; I'm sure Emma's told you what's happening."

"Yes," Hesper said, blinking rapidly at the afterimage of the vanished Mr. Dow. "Yes, I'd be happy to, Mrs. Blakeley. I could give this room a good tidying, for instance."

"That would be extremely helpful. Emma, the servants' stairway needs sweeping badly, if we're to have strangers running up and down them."

"Yes, Mrs.—"

"And the windows in the breakfast room are appalling, Mr. Fitch discovered when he went to gather up the silver pieces to polish. You'll need to examine the linen in the drawers for moths."

"Stairway," Emma repeated mindlessly. "Windows, linens—"

"And—oh, I know there is so much we depend upon you for, but please remember Lady Eglantyne's lunch tray. Though why we bother when she won't eat—" Mrs. Blakeley finished worriedly.

"I can take that up," Hesper offered quickly. "I'd like a look at her, to see if anything comes to mind to help her."

"Yes, Hesper, please do. I just don't know, all this turmoil, and the poor woman trying to die peacefully."

"I'm sure you're doing your best, Mrs. Blakeley."

"Well, we are, and I'm glad to see you back, Hesper."

Emma waited until the housekeeper turned finally, and the last of her black hem fluttered through the door. Then she flung herself at the pantry door, her mother close behind her. She wrenched it open.

Nothing but shelf after shelf of dusty bottles and jars, dried herbs and cobwebs hanging overhead, a couple of bluebottles banging away at the small, high, grimy windows.

She and Hesper stared at one another wordlessly. Then Hesper said sharply, "I'll finish the game room and clean the stillroom. You go and open every door you see."

She did, all through the house, pitting herself as desperately and randomly as any bluebottle searching for its freedom, at all the doors in the house.

Not one opened to Ysabo's world.

THE carriages rattled down the cobbled, weedy drive in the early afternoon. Emma, sitting on the breakfast-room carpet, awash in a pile of tablecloths and napkins upon which the moths had feasted without remorse, heard the sound with horror. Here they all were, with Miss Miranda Beryl, and nothing would ever be the same again. She scrambled out of the linen pile, threw everything into a laundry basket, and shoved it behind the first door she passed: the cupboard under the stairs, which gave her a good look at brass polish and cleaning cloths, and nothing at all of either Ysabo or Mr. Dow.

She pulled her apron straight, hitched up a stocking, and ran to the open front door to join the rest of the staff of Aislinn House on the steps to welcome the heir. Mr. Fitch, in his black and looking stately, had a cloth stained with silver polish hanging out of his back pocket. Mrs. Blakeley gestured sharply to Emma, who hurried into the gap between the housekeeper and Mrs. Haw, whose annoyance at being pulled out of the kitchen was rapidly melting into terror.

Even Hesper had been given an apron and pulled into the receiving line. The ruffled apron hem dangled oddly between her torn skirt and her bare feet in their clogs.

Seven carriages, a dozen men on horseback, filed down the drive, came to a halt at the front steps. Emma watched numbly as steps were placed, carriage doors opened, ladies placed a satin slipper, a gilded shoe upon the first step and came out in streams and clouds of color, their hats completely veiled in swaths of flowing net and lace. They stood on the drive, faces hidden within their private clouds, turning this way and that to examine the ancient, tired house, the over-grown lawns and tangled gardens, the stables no one had remembered to open, the dry fountain and the fish pool so murky that even the frogs had abandoned it.

Mrs. Haw gave a weary sigh, flung up her hands, and low-ered her bulk heavily onto the steps. "Might as well just walk straight into the wood," she muttered. Mr. Fitch hissed at her; Mrs. Blakeley gave a small, despairing moan. Even Hesper shifted, backed up a step, as though she wanted to yield the house to its fate and go take off the ridiculous apron.

Then the head carriage trembled on its axle; a streak of cobalt blue filled the doorway. A white kid boot with a heel like a spindle positioned itself upon the wooden steps amid the flurry of white lace underskirt and dark blue. A head, star-tlingly bare in that company, ducked under the lintel, tilted upward to survey the motley assembled on the porch. They stared at her; she gazed back at them. She had ivory hair with shades of gold in it, done up in a bouquet of curls on top of her head with a violet tucked into each curl. She looked like something out of a fairy tale, Emma thought: skin as white as snow, lips as red as blood. Great eyes the color of her name, green as sea on a turbulent day, but no expression in them at all; no telling what she was thinking.

She unfolded a tall, slender body and descended grace-fully to the ground. Nobody around her moved. They simply watched her silently, as though waiting for a sign that they would stay or go.

She walked up the steps, stopped in front of Mr. Fitch.

"I'm Miranda Beryl," she said, as though he hadn't guessed. Her voice was deep, cool, and crisp. "I wish to see my great-aunt."

"Yes, miss," he said quickly, and turned his head. "Emma. Take Miss Beryl upstairs."

"Yes, Mr. Fitch," Emma said, her own voice so high and tight in her head she sounded like the hinges on the boot room door.

Miranda Beryl said nothing more, gave no instructions to the world suspended outside Aislinn House. She followed Emma inside, barely glancing at the house, the broad rooms opened for the first time in years, and respectably tidy, except, Emma noted, for the dust cloth dangling over the marble head of somebody in the drawing room. But no time left to deal with it now. They went up the grand staircase, polished and dusted until the old rosewood gleamed; the painted faces of Miranda Beryl's family along the walls seemed to watch her with interest as she passed.

Emma opened Lady Eglantyne's door. Sophie, startled out of a nap in her chair beside the bed, rose, blinking with won-der at the astonishing woman in blue. She curtsied suddenly in confusion, as though to the fairy queen. Miss Beryl flicked a glance at her, then ignored her. She went to the bedside, stood looking down at her great-aunt a moment. She laid her long fingers on the bird-bone wrist, and Lady Eglantyne's eyes fluttered open.

Her sunken, cloudy eyes gazed back at her grandniece. Did she see her? Emma wondered. Or only a dream?

She breathed something, a half word, the beginning of a comment, the beginning of a name. Her eyelids fell again, closed.

"H'm," was all Miranda Beryl said before she turned and walked out of the room. She went downstairs again, the amazed Emma following, and out the front door. To all the silent figures turning to her, including Mrs. Haw still sitting on the steps, she announced,

"She's alive. We're staying."

Thirteen

All sound ceased in the great house when Ridley Dow closed the door behind him. It was as though the ocean itself had stopped dead in the middle of its thunder. So Ysabo felt, as the strange abrupt silence buffeted her ears. The young man, still looking at her, opened his mouth to speak again. Then he simply dissolved into nothing, and the world started speaking around her again.

It sounded familiar enough: no vast rumblings of astonishment and rage, no raucous rattle and clamor of crows pouring like black wind among the stones. The house had ridded itself of the stranger that easily. It had swallowed him. It had blinked him out of sight. No need for disturbance, except in Ysabo, whose trembling would stop eventually, whose terror would recede. Who would compose herself, for the sake of her days, and continue on her way.

Which she did, when she could finally bring herself to move, to step through the place where the man had vanished. Her eyes still burned dryly; her heart still pounded at the memory. He had looked at her; he had given her his name and hers. And for that, he had ceased to exist.

It might have been Emma, she realized dazedly. Stepping so easily, in curiosity, across the threshold, the first time she had seen Ysabo's world. But they had always been wary, both of them, of the random, capricious threshold across which they met. So it had not been Emma, blinked out of existence in front of Ysabo.

It had been a stranger who knew her name.

Who had he said? Crossing paths . . . an ancestor . . . Something urgent had brought him to that door. But what?

She drew breath, loosed it wearily. Another question without an answer.

She had no more courage for exploring, for wondering, for asking. The incident had stopped her heart; she wanted no more surprises. She went upstairs to where it was safe, to Maeve's chambers, where her mother and her grandmother spent their mornings. It was not yet noon; she didn't have to be elsewhere. Maeve and Aveline gazed at her absently as she entered, their eyes full of some interrupted discussion. Ysabo sank into her chair near the windows, took up the needlework she had left on the small table beside her.

"Where have you been?" Aveline asked. It was more a greeting, an acknowledgment of Ysabo's presence than a question demanding an answer. She went on without waiting for her daughter to cobble a half-truth. "We've been planning your wedding."

"Oh." She straightened in her chair, remembering it herself then, and tried to assume an interest. "I don't know what happens. What must I do?"

"Just say yes to anything you are asked," Maeve said. She glanced dubiously at Ysabo. "You will, won't you? You won't argue, you won't ask why—"

"No," Ysabo answered softly. "I promise. They frighten me, the knights."

"Well, that won't last. And, of course, he may begin to love you. That has been known to happen. Usually, they forget who you are within the year. I mean," Maeve amended, at Aveline's indignant stare, "you become as necessary as all women here: you have your place, you are seen, you become part of the ritual of their lives. It is not an encumbrance as long as you ask nothing unreasonable of him."

"May I ask his name?"

Maeve and Aveline consulted one another silently.

"Nieve?" Aveline guessed.

"I thought it was Zondros."

"You don't know?" Aveline said a little fretfully to Ysabo. "It seems the kind of thing one should, at such a time."

"He only said it once. And then he asked the question. I was so surprised that his name flew out of my head."

"Well," Aveline said, pushing a needle trailing black thread into her frame, "somebody should know. I'll ask among the ladies. Now. As for your wedding. You will be married in the great hall with all the knights and lords and ladies attending. You'll wear my wedding dress. Rose-colored satin with webs of pearls all over it. The ceremony is ancient and simple. You pledge yourselves to one another, drink from the same cup, and kiss. You'll marry in midmorning, after you feed the crows, who, of course, will be watching, too. That way the rituals will not be disrupted. That evening there will be a sumptuous wedding feast. You will wear the dress to that, and you and your knight will sit in places of honor at the table. Then, for that night and until you conceive, you will sleep together in the marriage chamber. After that, you will both be free to return to your own chambers; your husband will come to you or not, as you both decide."

"I don't go to him?" Ysabo said faintly.

"It's as you decide," Aveline repeated. "But your chambers are more private than the knight's. You see?" She smiled at her daughter. "Nothing difficult, nothing confusing, nothing to fear. And sooner than you can imagine, you'll have a child of your own to love." She paused; her perfunctory smile grew deeper, more genuine. "For us all to love. Can you do all that? Without causing trouble?"

Ysabo sank deeper into her chair, tried to vanish into the tapestry. She gave the only possible answer. "Yes, Aveline."

She worked her needle silently a while, two faces appearing, one after another, in her head: one with black brows and a bold, proudly planed face, the other with dark eyes behind flashing spectacles. One had seen her when he looked at her; the other never saw her. She heard Maeve's and Aveline's voices again as they reminisced about their own weddings, then wandered off into more distant, improbable times.

"Do you remember," Aveline said, "those long, long summer days, just before the leaves began to turn? I ran barefoot across the meadow grass while you dallied in the pavilion among the courtiers with Queen Hydria and the wizard Blagdon, watching knights ride in all their colors through the distant wood..."

They were tales, Ysabo had decided long ago. Stories Maeve and Aveline put themselves into in order to pass the time, worlds full of trees, seasons, sky, castles, worlds where hearts were pierced by a glance or a sword, where magic wove like bindweed through past and present, where people fought and loved and died without regard to ritual. Places they could visit whenever they wanted, for they had found the only door out of Aislinn House: the door into tales and dreams.

"And one turned aside from his company," Maeve murmured, "rode across the meadow to me."

"Did you know him before I did?" Aveline asked.

"Who?"

"Nemos. Before I was born."

"I always knew him. Always, all my life..."

Ysabo threaded a needle with the color of foam and began to fill in the wing of a swan gliding across a pool full of flowers like cups of light. She had only seen such a pool in someone else's tapestry. I borrow worlds, too, she thought. I pretend I have been in them.

"When we rode with him down that long road in the rain? Do you remember? Dark it was, so dark, even at noon that day. Do you?"

"Yes."

"Where were we going?"

"We rode in Queen Hydria's entourage, home from visiting some enchanted place that Blagdon wanted her to see, to honor."

"Old ruins. I remember now."

"They were, yes. They were ancient stones, trees so twisted and tangled by age they crawled along the ground as white as old bones. But the place was still alive. I could feel it, the memories it held. The compelling magic of it."

The sun had shifted its light beyond the stone frame of the window, too high overhead to be seen. Ysabo put her needlework down and rose quietly, to change into her white gown for the midday ritual. Aveline gave her an approving smile. She put her own work aside, but lingered for one more memory, one more sweetmeat. Ysabo, crossing to the door, heard it.

"When we walked into the wood in the soft spring rain? Just the three of us? I was very small. All the white violets at the stream's edge seemed like lovely, astonishing bits of treasure. And everything around us a mist of new green. Nemos picked a violet, put it in your hair. But it refused to stay, kept falling down again, and disappearing in the weeds..."

Ysabo's hand, closing on the door latch, jerked away from it as though it had pricked her. Aveline glanced around at the rattle. A servant came forward swiftly to open the door, bowed Ysabo through. She kept her shoulders back, her pace even, until she turned a corner.

Then she slumped against the wall, blinking, her eyes gritty, swollen with memory.

Nemos, the stranger had said as he came into her world. Nemos Moore.

And then Ridley Dow was gone. Aislinn House had closed over him like water, and he had drowned in nothing.

Again she found the strength to move: nothing else to do. She followed the ritual path of her day as mindlessly as the sun, holding the goblets with Aveline and Maeve in the great hall for the knights, watching the doors close behind them. Opening this window, lighting that candle, locking the door at this end of the house, unlocking the door at that. Lighting the lantern, carrying it into the dark, leaving it on the boat to cast its frail light across the black water.

Someone spoke then, and she nearly reeled into the water with shock.

"Princess Ysabo."

Ridley Dow was sitting on a ledge of stone, an outgrowth along the cavern wall. She could barely see his face, but she recognized the flash of his lenses.

"I thought—" Her voice had gone somewhere; she could only whisper. "I thought you were dead."

"No." He rose, came closer to her, but only as close as the edge of shadow around the light. He spoke very softly. "I'm sorry I startled you. I made myself disappear. I take after my ancestor in that I can learn to do such things. I thought it would be safer for both of us. I've been following you."

"You should not—" Her voice, gaining strength, shook with urgency. "You should not be here, Ridley Dow. This house is no place for you."

"I know."

"If anyone sees you—If even the crows see you—You are not part of the ritual. The knights don't understand anything that is not ritual. They punish it."

"I understand." He touched his spectacles with a forefinger, studying her. "I'll be very careful."

"But what is it you want?" she asked him desperately. "Why have you come at all? There is nothing for you here but trouble."

"I know," he said. "Exactly what I've come to find. How much trouble my ancestor caused through the centuries he's been alive. How much I can cause him."

She stared at him, wordless again. He shifted shape in front of her eyes, then, from the reckless innocent as unarmed as a maiden come to tweak the eyelid of the ancient sleeping monster, to a man with hidden powers who might possibly understand more about her life than she did.

"Nemos," she whispered. "Maeve and Aveline talk about him. They make up tales with him in them. They ride with him to impossible places, to meadows and ancient ruins, to the court of a Queen Hydria, who seems to hold her court here in Aislinn House as well, because everyone says her name at supper. But no one ever sees her there. So how could Maeve and Aveline know her? How could they know Nemos Moore? They've been in Aislinn House all their lives."

"And Nemos Moore," Ridley said grimly, "has been in and out of this house at will. I don't understand everything he did here, but he is very powerful and seems capable of any mischief, including riding into someone else's tale." He was silent a little, as though contemplating his wicked relation in the dark water. Then he seemed to see the water again. "I don't suppose," he added, "you know if there is any meaning whatsoever to this boat. The lantern."

"Don't ask." The words came out with unexpected fierceness. "That is all I understand. All anyone has ever told me."

"I see," he breathed.

"I must go. The ritual doesn't like to wait." She turned her back to him, told him as she moved away, "If you follow me, don't let me know."

When she looked back before she left the underground chamber, he was nowhere to be seen.

He appeared again sometime later, when she unlocked the door to the east tower and went up the winding stairs to the top to turn the page in the book on its stand in the empty room. He was there suddenly, at her elbow, peering at the empty page.

"How very strange . . . Is it simply cruelty, or some extreme subtlety of magic?"

"Ridley!" she exclaimed, her hands closing tightly onto the edges of the stand.

"Sorry," he said penitently. "It's a book. I have no common sense around them." He reached out, to her horror, riffled through the blank pages. "I'll have to study it more closely later."

She stared at him again, this creature from some world beyond her comprehension. He bore her scrutiny with composure. No knight would ever have allowed her to study him like this, she thought. Their eyes would grow angry, warning her, as though her gaze had challenged them.

"Who are you?" she asked with wonder, and he smiled.

No knight would ever have smiled at a question from her.

"Ridley Dow," he said. "I like to read, to lead a scholarly and eccentric life, to learn peculiar things. Why, for instance, a bell no one has ever seen has rung the sun down at Sealey Head every day for centuries."

She drew back from him a little, puzzled. "The bell."

"Do you ring it?" he asked, watching her steadily, the smile gone now.

"No."

"Who does?"

"I don't know. Maeve, maybe. One of the other ladies. It's someone's ritual; I don't know whose."

"What do you do when it rings? Where are you at that moment?"

"In my chambers waiting to be called for supper."

He blinked. "It's a dinner bell?"

"It's the bell that rings when the sun disappears."

He looked a little bewildered. "But you go to eat, then."

"I continue my ritual," she explained. "I go down to the great hall where the knights are gathered after their return. I light some candles but not others, place this chair here, fill this cup but not that. When I have finished everything, I sit where I am escorted by one or another of the knights. They usually speak only to one another unless it's part of their ritual. For instance when the knight asked me to marry him." She shook her head slightly, her eyes widening, stunned and bright with pain at the memory. "I didn't know him. They change constantly, it seems. But it didn't matter, since they barely see us. Any more than you would see a candle, which always changes and always looks the same until it dies and you replace it with another just like it. He spoke to me. Asked me that question. And I asked why? Why should I? I was just another candle in his eyes." Her hand slid to her cheek. "So he hit me."

"He—"

"It was ritual, Aveline told me later. It was ritual and I had stopped everything to ask why. He had no other answer. And then, two nights ago, he escorted me to the chair beside him, and told me we would marry when the moon is full."

Ridley opened his mouth, found no words, either, for a moment. "What will you do?" he asked finally.

"Marry him. Have his child. That much is ritual. But not even he can tell me not to wonder, not to look for answers. He won't ever care what I'm thinking, only that I continue the ritual. What I do outside of the ritual he will never ask."

She heard his breath, softly loosed, as he gazed at her. "Emma's mother told me something about this. But hearing it from you makes it so much more complex."

"Why?" she asked curiously. "It is what it is, no matter how you hear it."

"Yes." He hesitated again. "But then I didn't know you. Before I met you, you were just a princess. Just another candle. Now you are Ysabo, braver, I would bet my small but comfortable fortune, than any knight in that great hall. And," he added, gazing at her, "you have the most amazing face."

She smiled. "I know. Aveline says I'm a goblin."

"If goblin you are, with that great mass of curly hair, those eyes speckled like birds' eggs, that smile that illumines your entire face, then goblins must be of such beauty that only the rarest of beings can recognize it."

She felt that smile in her again, even as she shook the words away, like a bird flicking rain from its wings. "The knights never, ever, ever, say such things."

"Then they are—well. They are spellbound. Unfortunately, not by you."

"Spellbound," she repeated, a word she had never spoken before. Then she started, stepping away from the book. "I must go. You are spellbinding me, making me forget the ritual."

He nodded, taking her place at the stand; she left him in silent contemplation of the empty book.

She thought about him as she cleaned the crows' tower,

145

picked up feathers and scrubbed the stones. As usual, the crows gathered around her while she worked, watched her, croaking softly, their coarse, thick feathers rustling. Their crow noises mingled with the sough of trees, other birds, the distant sounds from the sea. She didn't notice at first when they grew silent, stopped picking at their feathers and commenting to one another. She looked up finally, saw them ringed on the wall around her, as still as though they had been turned to stone.

Spellbound.

Abruptly they all fluttered up into the air, still silent as smoke, in a great spiral, turning and turning until the highest flier broke their pattern and made a straight line for the sea.

The rest followed.

Ysabo sat back on her heels, wet from the scrub water, and watched them with wonder. She heard the breathing beside her finally and started. Ridley was crouched beside her, watching as well.

"Not part of the ritual?" he guessed.

She shook her head. "They've never done that before. They have always stayed with me until I'm finished." She put her hand to her mouth suddenly, wet cloth dangling from her fingers. "I wonder," she whispered, "if they saw you."

He blinked. "Not ordinary crows, then."

"I've never known any but those. I don't know what's ordinary," she answered, watching again as they streamed over the wood toward the craggy headland. "They seem to know things. The way they look at me. They seem to understand things. And I've seen what they do to other birds. They are ruthless."

"Ah."

"Perhaps you shouldn't follow me."

"Not today," he agreed, following their flight to the sea. "I'll find some other ritual to watch. And I want, above all, to find that bell." His eyes loosed the birds, looked at her again, smiling. "So. If you don't see me for a while, don't worry. I'll be very careful."

She nodded, unable to summon an answering smile. "I'll know," she warned him, "if you're not."

But supper that night was uninterrupted by any break in the ritual, any challenge to the knights, anything at all out of the ordinary, not even so much as an unexpected word, an interested glance from the knight who had escorted her to the chair beside him, and whose name, by the end of the evening, she still did not know.

Fourteen

Gwyneth rode up the weedy road through the wood to Aislinn House with Raven and Daria, half-listening as they argued about propriety. The rest of her mind was on the elegant ship she had left anchored among the fishing boats in Sealey Head harbor. Exactly who were those fascinating strangers in their rich garb who could lower a sail by lifting an eyebrow? She knew what she wanted them to do. But how to explain who they were, where they came from, and what had lured them to the shabby little sea town that was growing poorer and more desperate by the day?

"Well, of course we won't call it a ball," Daria said. "Not under the circumstances. However, Miss Beryl must be used to a constant round of amusements—parties, dinners, dances, concerts, riding, picnicking—in Landringham society. She might be grateful for any entertainment here. And the sooner the better, as Mother says. Anything could happen at any moment, and then they must all be plunged into mourning clothes."

"Still, a small, intimate supper might be more suitable first," Raven mused. "Just our closest family—"

"And Gwyneth."

"Of course Gwyneth." He turned his head to bestow his most intimate smile upon her. "I scarcely remember anymore that she is not part of the family, we are all together so often."

"Perhaps you should make a greater effort to remember that she is not, as yet," Daria said so pointedly that Gwyneth brought her thoughts away from her handsome, dangerous adventurers with something akin to panic.

"I think you could call it a supper," she said quickly, "and still invite a few neighbors as well."

"And have a little music," Daria added.

Raven rolled his eyes and sighed expansively. "Then we might as well invite half of Sealey Head, and have dancing, and call it a ball."

"What do you think, Gwyneth?" Daria appealed. "We can have music and dancing in a tasteful way that wouldn't be disrespectful to Miss Beryl's sentiments, couldn't we? It would be perfectly proper, wouldn't it? Your aunt seemed to think so yesterday, at tea."

"Aunt Phoebe thinks everything you do is proper."

"An amiable woman," Raven said, looking gratified. "How fortunate we were to have her come and live with you after—" He paused, cleared his throat. "After your misfortune. She seems extraordinarily fond of you and very

149

concerned about your future happiness. So she gave me to understand yesterday."

"Did she?" Gwyneth said, dismayed. He gave her another meaningful smile.

"Very much so. In fact—Well." He checked himself again. "This is hardly the time—and we are in the midst of deciding what to do about Miss Beryl. It's difficult to know what might be proper according to Landringham standards: society is so much more complex there."

"They can't be that different from us," Daria objected. "Anyway, we set the standards in Sealey Head. And it's not as though we would be dancing in Aislinn House itself, with poor Lady Eglantyne upstairs in her bed. A ball might be exactly what's needed to alleviate the dreariness of the occasion. And soon. If she dies before our party, we certainly can't have it after the funeral. I know!" She bounced a little, excitedly, in her saddle. "Let's go and ask Ridley Dow. He'd know what's proper in the city."

"Surely not this minute," Raven protested. "He's the opposite direction."

"Oh, why couldn't he have come to tea at the Blairs' last night! What more interesting or important could he have been doing instead?" She turned to Gwyneth. "What can he do with himself all day in Sealey Head?"

"He reads a good deal, I think."

"He must rest his eyes sometimes."

"The inn might be full of people he knows from Landringham," Raven suggested. "Perhaps he was unable to detach himself."

"Let's go there and find out," Daria said firmly. "After we've paid our call on Miss Beryl."

"Then we wait to consult with Mr. Dow before we invite Miss Beryl to Sproule Manor?"

"No, there's no time to wait," Daria said, contradicting herself. "Besides, what if he's not there to ask?"

Raven exhaled noisily again, turning his eyes toward the sky, where a squirrel on a branch above his head testily chided the interlopers. "Then what do you want to do? Invite her to a small dinner party, a full-blown ball—Which?"

"Why don't you ask Miss Beryl?" Gwyneth suggested, inspired. Both Sproules gazed at her wordlessly. "Just ask her if she would feel comfortable at such a gathering, and with or without music."

The Sproules' eyes left her face; they consulted one another, still silent, and came to an accord, apparently, for Raven said appreciatively to Gwyneth, "Very nice, very proper. How neatly you found our way out of that tangle. Worthy of your Aunt Phoebe."

"Music," Daria said, moving along to the next item of discussion. "Something more refined than country dancing? We can't have people red-faced and stomping on the floorboards at such a delicate time."

"Where," Raven asked, "do you propose to find anything refined around here?"

"Well, I don't know. Surely somebody knows somebody. We'll ask Mr. Trent." She was abruptly still again, her hand reaching across to grip Gwyneth's, reins and all, at the sight of the half dozen carriages in front of the stables. "So many people," she sighed contentedly. "It will be a grand party."

Barely had they dismounted when stablers came to take their horses. Old Fitch opened the door for them. The changes in the house were immediately apparent as they crossed the threshold. Swathed ghosts looming in the rooms had become furniture again. Curtains were pulled back; windows opened; the house smelled of trees and wildflowers instead of polish and ancient soot. Even more unexpected was the faint, continuous tension in the air of people moving, breathing, rustling, doors swinging open, closing again on half-heard words. The house felt full, Gwyneth thought, vibrant with so many invisible people, and she wondered in sudden horror if they had come too early, at midmorning, interrupting, with their country ways, the leisurely habits of those who thought the sun rose at noon.

Fitch showed them into an aired and polished drawing room and went to inform Miss Beryl of their presence.

Miranda Beryl came to greet them almost immediately; no sign, at least from her, that she didn't know when morning began. Her rather chilly beauty seemed a bit frayed, Gwyneth thought, after the initial, startling glimpse of it. The pale skin around her sea-green eyes was shadowy; she looked, as she crossed the threshold, as though she were trying to summon a smile and swallow a yawn at the same time.

"Good morning," she said in her deep, sweet voice. "I am Miranda Beryl. How kind of you to take the trouble to come and call on me. Fitch, please tell Emma to bring us tea."

A tall, thin man had accompanied her into the room. He had fair, lank hair as straight as straw, and remarkably bright eyes, vivid as mother-of-pearl, in a lightly lined, expressionless face. He cleared his throat very softly; Miss Beryl added indifferently, "Oh. And this is Mr. Moren, who was kind enough to ride up from the inn this morning to inquire after my great-aunt."

Daria made a little mewing sound, her lashes fluttering

like wings. "Oh, so have we. I do hope she is better this morning. At least no worse. Miss Beryl, I am Daria Sproule, and this is my brother, Raven. We are pleased to meet you, Mr. Moren. Our father, Sir Weldon Sproule, owns most of the local farmland. We've ridden over from Sproule Manor to welcome you to Sealey Head."

Raven seemed to be having trouble finding his voice. He cleared his throat a couple of times. Gwyneth, fascinated, watched the blood well into his face, color it an even strawberry from chin to brow. Gazing into those emerald eyes, he looked as though he had been walloped with the business end of an oar.

"Good—good morning," he managed at last.

"Yes, isn't it?" Mr. Moren murmured in his thin, dry voice, while his eyes lingered with sudden interest upon the afflicted young man.

"And you are?" Miss Beryl inquired of Gwyneth.

"Oh, sorry," Daria said hastily. "May I present our good, dear friend Miss Gwyneth Blair. Her father, Toland Blair, owns all the big ships in the harbor."

"How do you do?" Gwyneth asked faintly under the cool, disconcerting gaze.

"I confess I am a little tired," Miss Beryl answered with unexpected candor. "I had no idea there was so much of Rurex outside of Landringham. And so many people one doesn't know who choose to live in it."

"Miss Beryl inhabits such a rarefied constellation in Landringham, one might as well expect the sun to notice his neighbors," Mr. Moren remarked with rather perfunctory attention to his pronouns, Gwyneth thought. The brilliant eyes were on her face, suddenly, as though she had commented aloud, and she felt herself flush.

"Also," Miss Beryl continued, "I was awake early this morning, expecting a visit from Dr. Grantham, who came to see my great-aunt."

"Any improvement?" Raven asked heartily, making an effort that deepened the hue of his face to burgundy.

"No. No change. Ah, here is Emma with the tea." The maid backed through the door, half-hidden behind an elaborate silver tea service. "Emma, I am learning quickly, is the one upon whom we all depend, especially my staff, who have not yet found their way around this great old house."

"You've never been here before?" Gwyneth asked.

"I think once. Very long ago, when I was a child. But it may have been another house," she added vaguely, and reached for the teapot. "Please sit down. Thank you, Emma. How do you take your tea, Miss Sproule?"

"Oh, please call me Daria. Sugar, no lemon. I want us all to become great friends, especially if you decide to take up residence in Sealey Head." The flow of tea into her cup dried up briefly at the idea, but Daria didn't notice. "I was hoping," she confided, "we were all hoping that you and your friends might come for supper at Sproule Manor some evening soon. To meet a few more of your neighbors. We were wondering. If you felt it appropriate. We know how deeply concerned you must be about Lady Eglantyne. There could be music, if you would like."

Miss Beryl, standing with the teapot in her hand, watching Daria until she ran down, put the pot on the tray finally. "So kind," she answered, handing Daria her cup and leaving her baffled. "Miss Blair?"

"Lemon, please."

"And you, Mr. Sproule?"

"In a cup is how I take it," Raven said, chuckling at his own pleasantry. His pale blue eyes, fixed upon Miranda Beryl's face, seemed unusually close together, Gwyneth saw; perhaps the avidity of his gaze had caused them to cross slightly. "I do hope you will accept our invitation, Miss Beryl. With or without music."

"How kind," Miss Beryl said again, blinking. "But I can't think how. Not with poor Lady Eglantyne. How could I leave her now that I'm finally here?"

"My dear Miss Beryl, would she notice?" Mr. Moren asked, pouring his own tea. "Lady Eglantyne, I would guess from what I saw this morning, is quite comfortably inhabiting her own world."

Miss Beryl gazed at him across the tea table. "I am trying, Mr. Moren, to live above myself. It's confusing, when one is used to one's more familiar habits. Surely it would be considered unfeeling among the folk of Sealey Head?"

"We invited you, Miss Beryl," Raven began heartily, and ran up against Mr. Moren's tensile voice.

"It's not only your aunt you must think of," he reminded her. "Your friends might enjoy some idle entertainment."

"It's true we have all been tiptoeing around the place," she said doubtfully.

"Besides, when have you ever turned down a party?"

A dimple appeared unexpectedly in Miss Beryl's cheek. "As you can so well testify, Mr. Moren."

"And why not? When I take such pleasure in watching you enjoy your life?"

"You take too much pleasure in my frivolous life," she answered idly, hiding her expression behind a tilted teacup. She put it down, and asked the drawing room in general, "Oh, why not?" Muslin over the open windows puffed in answer. "I must meet my neighbors sometime."

"Good!" Raven exclaimed, his cup rattling into the saucer. "We'll make a long evening of it, then. Music, a little dancing, a late supper. I warn you: half of Sealey Head will be there to meet you. And we can even surprise you with an acquaintance of yours from Landringham."

"From Landringham?" she echoed. "Someone I might know in Sealey Head?"

"Mr. Ridley Dow," Daria explained, laughing at her perplexity, and Gwyneth saw Miranda Beryl's face turn oddly mask-like, still dimpled with the tilt of a smile, while all expression faded from her eyes.

"The scholar in Sealey Head?" Mr. Moren wondered. "I thought he had left Rurex to travel abroad. He must have had a book under his nose and gotten lost." He added with a faint chuckle, "No doubt, when he finally looked up from his reading, he thought he had reached a different country."

"Sealey Head is very much a part of Rurex," Daria protested warmly. "And anyway, Mr. Dow is far too intelligent to mistake where he is in the world."

"Mr. Ridley Dow?" Mr. Moren queried her lightly with a raised eyebrow. "Who can spend a good hour trying to separate you from your ear with the subject of damselflies?"

"He has never mentioned damselflies," Daria said staunchly, "and he found his way on purpose to Sealey Head."

"Did he now? Ah, well, then, a different Mr. Dow."

"No, no; he has mentioned being in Miss Beryl's company in Landringham. Didn't he, Raven? In fact, he is staying at the inn on the cliff with the rest of your party. I'm surprised you have not met him there, Mr. Moren. And, Miss Beryl, I am sure he will be delighted to see you."

Gwyneth watched their eyes meet over the tea table: Mr. Moren's blandly questioning, Miss Beryl's fading toward boredom on the subject.

"Perhaps a certain type of fossil in the cliffs drew him," she suggested, and rose abruptly, smiling charmingly upon them without quite seeing them. "We shall all anticipate your party, I'm sure. Let us know which evening you want us. We have no plans."

Her visitors left half a teacup later, scattering pleasantries across the threshold.

"A fascinating, admirable woman!" Raven exclaimed, as they waited for their horses.

"So beautiful," Daria murmured, clasping Gwyneth's arm. "Oh, I can hardly wait for the party. Can you, Gwyneth? Though I am not sure that I quite liked her friend, Mr. Moren, did you, Gwyneth?" She watched her brother pawing the gravel like a steed, his eyes on a flock of warblers flitting overhead, and whispered, without waiting for Gwyneth's opinion that, indeed, she found Mr. Moren unsettling, yet somehow intriguing, "Raven seems a bit smitten. But don't pay any attention to it. Men get this way. I've read about it. It's like a rash. They wake one morning, and it's gone. Now," she said aloud, as Miss Beryl's stablers brought their horses up, "let us go over to the inn and find Mr. Dow, who is spending entirely too much time without us."

They continued their journey back downhill and around the harbor, where Gwyneth's thoughts strayed to her mysterious ship, anchored, surely, just in that brilliant splash of light rippling across the bay. Not pirates, she determined, nor faery, nor from any earthly realm. But what then? And from where?

Beyond the town, they rode abreast up the headland, Raven in the middle, where he veered randomly between discussing the details of the party with Daria and extolling the remarkable qualities of Lady Eglantyne's heir.

"Such grace and composure in her time of trouble. Not only must she tend to her great-aunt, but she must keep her friends amused as well. We must help her in that as best we can." He cast a solemn look at each of the young women beside him. "I expect you will be able to come up with suitable ideas to entertain her. I can think of nothing better than a brisk ride every morning. Perhaps along the waves. The sea air would do her good."

The sea air was busy tying Gwyneth's hair in knots and trying to push them all out of their saddles. Daria clamped her hat, a straw confection wreathed in pale green tulle, on her head with one arm; its broad brim flapped, tried to fly. Down the cliff, the waves boomed like cannon fire against the rocks and broke with frothy glee. A pair of seals dived effortlessly in and out of the tide. Gwyneth watched them, envying their grace, their composure in the wild waters.

Seals, she thought. Selkies. Sea people.

Princes of the sea.

Come to Sealey Head for . . .

"Sealey Head," she said aloud, involuntarily. She felt the Sproules' eyes on her, and turned to meet them, smiling. "Sorry. I was lost in my story."

"The pirate story?" Daria asked eagerly.

"No. Not pirates," she said firmly. "Better than pirates."

"What an extraordinary thing to be thinking about after visiting Aislinn House," Raven remarked. Gwyneth, glancing at him, wondered why his uplifted profile seemed more parroty than usual. Exaltedly beaky.

"One must think of something," she said, amused. "Presumably Miss Beryl is thinking enough about death and its awesome responsibilities for us all."

"Yes, but pirates?"

"It's the way my mind works. I doubt that any chiding or lecturing will change it, since I feel most comfortable this way."

Raven found nothing to say to that, which he said with significant silence the last quarter mile to the inn. Daria chattered for all of them. Gwyneth's thoughts rode ahead to the inn, where the innkeeper would come out smiling to welcome them to his suddenly bustling establishment. Or not smiling, she remembered abruptly, if he had not found a decent cook for the crowd.

And crowd there seemed to be, judging from horses saddled in the yard, awaiting riders, from the carriage being readied, from neatly, soberly dressed underlings venturing out to the cliff edge to marvel at the sea. Were they all leaving so soon? she wondered with concern. Had the worst occurred already: Mrs. Quinn had cooked them breakfast?

But the innkeeper, helping Mr. Quinn with the carriage, smiled with pleased surprise upon them as they rode into his yard.

"Welcome," he called. Raven, surrounded by horses, dismounted quickly, and, with one of his unexpected and charming gestures, went to help with the very handsome matched set of four grays being harnessed to the carriage. Judd relinquished the task to him and came to greet the ladies.

"You found a cook," Gwyneth guessed immediately, and he laughed.

"An exceptional one came to my door in the nick of time. He spent the last twenty years at sea, cooking for any number of people; he was completely undaunted by the impending throng from Landringham and cooked an amazing supper for them that brought praise even from Mrs. Quinn. But what brings you here on such a boisterous day?"

"What, indeed!" Daria exclaimed, dismounting with a sigh. "I thought the wind would blow us out among the gulls. We have come to recapture Mr. Dow's attention; he has been neglecting us all, and we miss him."

"Oh." Judd's smile vanished. "You haven't seen him, either, then."

"He's not here?" Daria said incredulously. "After we rode all this way?"

"You don't know where he is?" Gwyneth asked, surprised. "When did you last see him?"

"Several days ago," Judd said slowly. "He said he was going to ride into the woods to look for Hesper."

"Hesper?"

"Why Hesper?" Daria demanded fretfully. "What could he want with the wood witch?"

Judd shook his head. "Something about that bell and Aislinn House. That's all he said." He glanced down the cliff toward the shadowy trees on the hill behind the harbor. "I haven't seen him since."

"Is he staying somewhere else?" Gwyneth suggested, though it hardly seemed likely. "He wouldn't do that without telling you."

"All his things are still here. All his books. He hasn't

even been back for a change of clothes, so far as I know. And you know how he likes to dress. Mr. Trent hasn't seen him, either."

"Aunt Phoebe asked after him; he hasn't come to tea again."

"He seems to have vanished... What trouble could he possibly have gotten into between here and Aislinn House?"

Gwyneth looked back at him silently, equally mystified. Daria, her eyes flickering between their faces, filled her lungs abruptly and bellowed across the yard in a voice not even her brother recognized, "Raven! Stop dawdling among the horses and come here! We are riding back to Aislinn House."

She had mounted and turned her horse onto the road before her bewildered brother extricated himself from the carriage harness. Gwyneth sighed, moved reluctantly to her horse.

"I'm sorry," she said to Judd. "We are never able to talk."

"No," he agreed somberly. "Let me know if you find him?" She nodded; he added quickly, "Let me know if you don't."

"Yes," she said, and followed the impulsive Daria. Midway down the headland, Raven, raising a formidable army of arguments, including rudeness, inconvenience, and the prospect of disturbing Lady Eglantyne, finally persuaded his sister not to gallop back to Aislinn House and announce her intention to search for the missing Mr. Dow in the closets or under the beds.

"Miss Beryl would surely have mentioned it if he were staying there," he said at least half a dozen times. "She seemed quite surprised that he might be in Sealey Head at all. He probably left town suddenly on business, and of course he will be back. He would have told us otherwise."

Gwyneth stopped with relief in front of her house, let them return to Sproule Manor without her.

Daria, leaning from her saddle, whispered fiercely, "Keep looking for him; so shall I. Let me know if you hear anything at all."

"I will. I promise."

Gwyneth watched them ride sedately down the street, Raven leading the horse she had ridden, and no doubt thinking of Miranda Beryl, his sister riding silently beside him, her thoughts no doubt in a turmoil over Mr. Ridley Dow.

Sproules in love, she thought with wonder, and went upstairs quickly, before Aunt Phoebe noticed she was back, to continue her story.

She wrote:

You could recognize them for what they weren't by looking deeply into their eyes. Unfortunately neither of the humans standing on the deck of the Chimera *was in the habit of looking deeply into anyone's eyes; they hadn't looked so at their wives in years. But had Sir Magnus Sproule or Mr. Blair done so, they would have seen the restless wilderness within, the vast expanse of an unknown kingdom the strangers viewed daily; it left its imprint on their pupils, in their very thoughts. They saw to the depths of what mortals, with their little lines and hooks and nets, barely penetrated.*

Princes of the sea, they were, lords of the watery realm beneath the waves. And following the same impulse the sea has had toward land since tides began, they longed to conquer it, to claim and to possess it, beginning with the rugged rocky shore and crag of stone that was Sealey Head. That humans already claimed and possessed it was a fact to which they were entirely indifferent. The wave, after all, does not consider the lives it feeds, the dead it washes away, when it overwhelms a village of barnacles on a rock. Its sole concern is its own power.

So, too, with the visitors on their pretty ship. It was not armed because they had all the power they needed within themselves to take Sealey Head.

All they needed was permission.

"Gwyneth!"

Gwyneth sighed and put down her pen.

Fifteen

Miranda Beryl's entourage of friends and their servants lodged at the inn showed no signs, after several days, of leaving for more convenient quarters. Indeed, they had already given a predictable shape to their days. Just after noon, never before, they began to appear in the taproom, one by one, like a gaudy and ruffled flock of birds homing in on their favorite watering hole. Mr. Pilchard ran errands early to be back in time to cook for them. He sent up their breakfasts as the orders came down: hot, crisp rolls, butter and strawberry jam, baked eggs flavored with herbs and cheese, sausages, a hash of finely chopped onion, smoked salmon, and potato, hot slabs of clove-scented ham, plenty of tea and coffee and ale. All of this was delivered to the taproom by two of Colin Baker's boys, who were used to kitchen chores, dodging choppers and elbows, and remembering the sudden, urgent whims of the guests.

When the guests finished breakfast, they wandered outside, where their servants, for whom Mr. Pilchard had cooked much earlier, had horses saddled, carriages ready and waiting. By noon, the guests had rattled away to Aislinn House. The inn was quiet all afternoon. Mrs. Quinn and Lily tidied the rooms. Mr. Pilchard cleaned the kitchen and began to prepare for the next meal. Judd walked into town, placed orders for the evening meal at the fish market, the butcher, the grocer, as Mr. Pilchard suggested. He kept an eye open for Ridley Dow, whom he did not see, and for Gwyneth, whom he did once or twice, at a distance and accompanied by a Sproule.

Finished with his errands, he made a brief appearance at the stationer's. He would poke his head in the door, catch Mr. Trent's eye. Mr. Trent would shake his head, then raise a brow. Judd would shake his own head. They would both shrug. Judd would return to the inn.

The guests would wander back in the evenings sometime between sundown and midnight. Those who came back earlier usually began earnest and quite ruthless card games in the taproom. Mr. Pilchard made them sandwiches or entire suppers, whatever they requested. Judd stayed in the taproom, serving them, relaying orders to Mr. Pilchard, who seemed tireless and constantly inventive. By midnight the guests retired with their cards, bottles of brandy, and late-night repasts to their rooms. Judd and a yawning Mr. Quinn cleaned the taproom. Judd checked the kitchen before he went to bed, found it empty, the cook in bed, he assumed, and the spotless pots ready for the morning. As always, he read himself to sleep.

In the late afternoon, before the guests began appearing and duty called Judd back to the taproom, he visited his father.

Dugold took an innkeeper's interest in the daily business. After Judd described the most exotic of the outfits their guests wore that day—a cloak lined with lemon satin, a pair of gold shoe buckles shaped like spaniels—he would produce whatever vexations had plagued him during the day. Dugold always had some advice to share, whether or not Judd had already solved the problem with the leaky pipe, the broken beer tap handle, or Mrs. Quinn wanting to tie bows on all the doorknobs.

Then Judd would fetch a mug of beer for his father, and, in that idle hour before sundown, continue reading *The Secret Education of Nemos Moore*. Dugold, after offering the opinion that magic he couldn't see wasn't of much use to him, usually napped through much of the book. But he woke up when Nemos Moore found his way to Sealey Head.

"Must have gotten lost," he muttered. "All that magical power he says he has, and he winds up in a town full of dead fish."

"No, no; he was following the sound of the bell."

"The bell." His father's eyes sought his, came close. "Our bell? The one in the water?"

"Yes."

"What for?"

Judd skimmed the page silently. "A source of great power, he calls it. An ancient, labyrinthine mystery."

"Which was—what?"

"Like a maze. A puzzle. Not," he added, scratching his head, "the simple echo of a bell on a foundering ship."

"A mystery in Sealey Head?" his father asked incredulously. "Where does he think he is?"

"I don't know," Judd said, flipping the page avidly. "Let's find out. Ah—New chapter. 'In Which He—'" His voice stopped; he sat still, staring at the page.

"You've gone off without me," Dugold commented. "I may not care for the book, but I like the sound of your voice."

"'In Which He Finds His Way to Aislinn House.'" He raised his eyes, stared at his father. "That's what it says."

"So?"

"So. That's why—that's why Ridley Dow went there."

"To Aislinn House."

"Looking for the bell . . ."

Dugold closed his eyes, screwed them up tightly, and shook his head as though to get rid of extraneous notions, empty words, paradoxes. He opened his eyes again, reached for his beer. "You lost me, boy. Where is that Ridley, anyway?"

"I don't know," Judd breathed, turning pages again. "Let's see if we can find him."

But the adroit and knowledgeable Mr. Moore grew strangely vague once he had entered Aislinn House. Odd details—a flock of crows, a broom closet—drew his notice. The bell was scarcely mentioned. A beautiful woman named Hydria, with a long and mysterious past, took up most of the pages. She sounded, Judd thought, like someone out of a very old ballad, the queen of a rich and magical realm accessible easily to anyone with a little imagination. Dugold began to snore in the middle of the descriptions. Judd read on, searching in vain between the lines for Ridley Dow, until the sound of his own bell, and the thump of boots on the floorboards, drew him back to the taproom and his thirsty guests.

They were growing bored, he understood from their comments as they drank his ale and brandy. Bored with the imposed quiet, the desultory afternoons in Aislinn House, where they waited for Lady Eglantyne to die, bored with the quaint fishing town, the little tedious boats coming and going, the rides along the beach or in the wood where one never met anyone, not anyone one knew, or cared to, at any rate. Their noisy card games began earlier and earlier; they gambled and drank through the evening, joined by others staying at Aislinn House who were tired of the sedate evenings there. The taproom, full of brightly dressed people calling for food and drink as they shuffled their cards, certainly had a prosperous air about it. Judd, who missed his own long evenings with his father and his books and the sound of the sea, found himself perversely wishing, even as gold clinked into the till, that they would all go away.

One afternoon, when they had begun to drift in especially early for their games, the doorbell jangled yet again, and Mr. Quinn came to join him behind the taproom bar.

"You have visitors," he told Judd. "I showed them into the sitting room. I'll take over here."

Judd, cheering up at the thought of Gwyneth, was only mildly disappointed to find a Sproule with her instead of her sister Pandora. At least there was only one of them.

Gwyneth was gazing with astonishment at the bedecked little room, the only place in the inn that the guests avoided.

"It looks like a ball gown," she said to Judd. "All lace and bows. Even the mantelpiece is swagged with silk."

"I didn't do it," Judd assured her.

"Oh, come, Mr. Cauley. You're among friends. You can confess."

Daria picked up a conch shell trailing a pink ribbon from one of its spikes. "I think it's sweet. Shells are quite naked, fresh out of the sea, aren't they." A shout, followed by a wave of laughter, rolled out of the taproom. "Gracious, Mr. Cauley, whatever is going on in there?"

"Miss Beryl's guests are playing cards."

"Really?" Gwyneth looked out the sitting room door, and encountered the closed taproom door, with its narrow window of crackled glass. "Can we peek in?"

"Whatever for?" Daria demanded.

"Are they playing with dice? Are they betting?"

Judd smiled at her. "A dozen men on their way to being drunk are busy trading their considerable wealth back and forth over a handful of painted paper cards." He crossed the hall, opened the door a little, and she applied her eye to the scene.

She stepped back finally, looking oddly contented. "I thought as much. But I wasn't certain."

"My dear Miss Blair, what kind of tale are you writing?"

"The kind that tells you what it is as it goes along. Thank you, Mr. Cauley, that was extremely helpful."

"Would you like to go in and try a hand?"

"Don't tempt me. I don't want the experience, only the details." She hesitated, her smile fading a little. "No Mr. Dow in there."

"No."

"How very odd."

"Yes."

She lowered her voice almost to a whisper. "Daria talked almost of nothing else as we rode up here. I think she's in love."

"I am sorry," Judd said sincerely, as they went back into the sitting room, where the beribboned Daria, upon the sofa with bows pinned all over it, seemed to be merging with her background. "I do wish very much that I had some inkling of where Mr. Dow has gone. But I haven't heard a word." At least, he thought but did not say, nobody has found the body washed ashore.

"Oh," Daria sighed, melting a little more into the sofa as she slumped. "I was so hoping...Well." She straightened determinedly and opened the reticule she carried. She took out an envelope, handed it to him. "We rode up here to invite you to a party at Sproule Manor in honor of Miranda Beryl. Music, dancing, supper. Please come. All of Miss Beryl's guests and half of Sealey Head will be there. And," she added wistfully, "I very much hope Mr. Dow as well."

Judd looked at Gwyneth. "Will you be there?"

"Of course."

"Then so will I."

"Of course she's coming," Daria said a trifle moodily. "She's practically family. My brother wrote her down first on his invitation list. Well, first after Miranda Beryl, of course."

"And who was first on your list?" Gwyneth teased. Daria blushed a little and got to her feet restively.

"Tea?" Judd offered, but nothing, he saw, would have kept Miss Sproule except the prospect of Mr. Dow.

"Thank you. We have other invitations to deliver, and we promised Gwyneth's aunt...My brother should be there, by then. He rode to Aislinn House to give the invitation to Miss Beryl. I hope," she added to Gwyneth, her eyes widening, "she does not keep him. He seems a bit distracted these days, with the party."

"Indeed," Gwyneth murmured.

"Oh, my dear," Daria said quickly, her hand closing solicitously upon Gwyneth's elbow. "You mustn't take it seriously."

Gwyneth drew breath, held it for a moment; Judd watched her, brows crooked, wondering. She loosed it finally. "Yes," she said decidedly. "I think I must."

"But it's not as if—"

"Your brother seems infatuated with Miss Beryl, and I for one could not be happier."

Daria blinked at her. "But—he—she couldn't—"

"How do we really know what another's heart will do? Until they do it? I think it's a lovely idea."

"But—Well, of course it is, but—"

"And as you say, he does regard me as part of the family. A dear sister. I'm quite content with that. Mr. Cauley, we will see you soon, then, at Sproule Manor."

"But, Gwyneth," Daria protested, following her out the door. She glanced pleadingly at Judd as she passed him. "If you hear anything at all of Mr. Dow—"

"I'll send word, I promise. Thank you for the invitation. I look forward to it."

She nodded glumly, cast an appalled glance at the taproom door as laughter exploded out of it, then a more grateful one at the innkeeper as he escorted her out the front door.

The sun set, but if the bell rang, Judd didn't hear it over the ringing of the inn bell, as more and more of Miranda Beryl's guests left the dreary silence of Aislinn House for the boisterous, convivial company in the taproom. Judd left Mr. Quinn behind the bar and helped Mr. Pilchard, who was alone in the kitchen by then. He took orders from the guests, for whom drinking and cards were a hungry business, conveyed them to the cook, and brought the dishes up from the kitchen. Finally, around midnight, he began snuffing out candles. Miranda Beryl's guests rattled away in their carriages. His own finished their hands, gave final orders to Mr. Quinn and Mr. Pilchard, and took their cards and trays upstairs. Judd helped Mr. Quinn clean the taproom, then stuck his head back down the kitchen stairs. All was dark and quiet there.

On impulse, he said to Mr. Quinn, who had locked the taproom and was checking the doors, "I'm going for a breath of air. Don't lock me out."

He hadn't seen the waves under his nose for days, it seemed. Months. The breath of air was more a blast of wind, misty with spindrift, for the tide was frothing up the side of the cliff, trying to shake the inn into the sea. A little coracle moon drifted serenely among the briskly scudding cloud. Dimly, within the wind, Judd could hear the laughter of the gamers, or the memory of it, anyway, for most of the windows were dark. A couple, his own among them—Mrs. Quinn must have kindly lit his lamp—cast little pools of light into the dark.

Within one of them, he saw someone standing.

He started, then stepped eagerly forward, calling softly, "Ridley?"

"No," Mr. Pilchard said, his bulky figure turning. "Only your cook, Mr. Cauley. I came out to hear the tide. Haven't stopped listening for it yet."

Judd joined him at the cliff's edge. "I know," he sighed. "I've missed it, too. It's been years since we've had such a full house. I forgot how much work it is."

Mr. Pilchard chuckled. "You're doing well." He held some-thing, Judd saw; a bowl that smelled vaguely like supper.

"Thanks to you. I could have gone back to my books if Mrs. Quinn were still in the kitchen."

"Ah, it's almost too easy, cooking in all that room, on a floor that doesn't throw you off your feet and toss all the plate out of your cupboards."

They watched a top-heavy wave welter drunkenly up to the cliff, lose its balance, and career into it, sending spray up over the top. Judd wiped his face and nodded at the bowl in the cook's hands.

"Your supper? At long last?"

The cook glanced down at it. "No. Only scraps. I got into the habit of feeding them to the birds. Hungry buggers, always. Any news of your Mr. Ridley?"

"Mr. Dow. No."

"Ah. Where was he off to when you last saw him?"

"Aislinn House, he said. He took his horse. Maybe he was called back to Landringham and didn't have time to send us word."

"Aislinn House. That's the great house up the hill where all the extra gamers are coming from. Maybe he's still there."

Judd turned, saw the faint gleam in the distance, among trees tossed in the wind like kelp, of windows still alight in the house. "Maybe," he said slowly. "He did disappear around the time Miss Beryl arrived. I believe he knows her."

"There you are, then."

"Maybe..." Judd said again, doubtfully. "But I think he wanted to go there before she came."

"Well. Then she came, and he changed his mind. Such happens."

"It does, indeed, Mr. Pilchard. No mystery, then?"

"From where I can see, no mystery at all. But then, I'm no expert at these things, Mr. Cauley," he added apologetically. "Not as though I know what I'm talking about, when I'm not talking about food. But I'd say if that's all it is, no use worrying or going looking for him. He'll wander back when he's ready."

"You're probably right. Well. I think I'll go upstairs and read his books. Coming in?"

"Not just yet," Mr. Pilchard said. "I'm still waiting for the birds. Blustery night. Takes them a while to catch the scent. I've left the kitchen door unlocked; I'll go in that way."

"Good night."

He left Hieronymous Pilchard to feed the gulls and retired to his bed with the arcane mystery of the life of Nemos Moore.

Sixteen

E mma stood beside the kitchen stove with Mrs. Haw,
watching the egg poaching in its pan for Lady Eglantyne's breakfast. Everything else was on the silver tray: the
teapot and cup, the sugared strawberries, the buttered toast
triangles kept warm under napkins, the morsel of porridge
in its pretty bowl, the pink rose in the bud vase. At the other
end of the long table from the tray, three stern, silent girls
chopped great piles of vegetables for Mrs. Haw to work into
wonders and marvels for the evening meals of close to a couple dozen guests.

"They're good workers," Mrs. Haw murmured to Emma,
her voice muted by the brisk thump of blades on the boards.
"But they keep themselves to themselves. They're civil
enough, yet they make a body feel even our cucumbers aren't

what they're used to, let alone our scallions and rosemary. And as far as our cabbages go—well, poor cousins they are indeed to the queen of the crop, the Landringham cabbage. Mr. Fitch stays in his pantry when they're here; I hardly see anyone to talk to."

The bright yolk grew filmy, like a dreaming eye. Mrs. Haw spooned the egg from the water, slid it into a bowl, and covered it. She added the dish to the tray; Emma picked it up.

"Let me know how she's doing," Mrs. Haw pleaded. "Nobody tells me anything anymore."

"I will," Emma promised, knowing that the tray itself would tell Mrs. Haw as much as anyone that Lady E was still alive and chewing. Though how or why, Emma had no idea. What kept that delicate, aged, weary body alive in such a house? she wondered as she trudged upstairs. Nobody came to see her but her grandniece, once every morning, just to check if she was still alive. Everyone sat around in the afternoons, beautifully dressed and bored, waiting languidly for her to die.

Why bother? Why didn't they all just go back to Landringham, where they could party from one end of the night to the other? Aislinn House was hardly a prize to be taken when one old lady finally drew her last. It was a moldering, dusty pile in an obscure fishing town. Probably the best Miranda Beryl could do with it would be to sell it outright to the Sproules, who would consider it another giddy step toward the lofty respectability to which they aspired. ·

Except, she remembered, for the secrets within its walls.

She balanced the tray carefully, opened the door to Lady Eglantyne's chamber, holding her breath and hoping against hope for a glimpse into that rich, powerful, extremely peculiar world. She only saw, as usual, Lady Eglantyne sitting up precariously, her head bobbling in her cap, her eyes watching Emma as though she were part of a dream and only remotely familiar: she might as well have been a flowerpot or a pillow crossing the room. Miranda Beryl sat in a chair beside the bed facing her great-aunt; Sophie sat anxiously at the window, her own breakfast tray, which one of the aloof creatures in the kitchen had brought up earlier, a clutter of crusts and yolk stains on the window seat.

At least Sophie recognized Emma, gave her a smile, looking grateful for the sight of a friendly face.

"Thank you, Emma," Miss Beryl said, rising as Emma laid the tray on the bed next to Lady Eglantyne. She left the feeding of her great-aunt to Sophie, who took her place at the bedside with relief. Usually, Miss Beryl waited in the room until Dr. Grantham came. That morning, she turned and followed Emma out.

"I am to go riding with Raven Sproule," she said so abruptly that Emma glanced behind her to see who else was in the hallway. It was empty. Behind the closed doors of the bedrooms, very little seemed to be stirring. She turned back, found herself the focus of the intent green eyes. "After Dr. Grantham comes, of course. Mr. Sproule wants to take me to Sealey Head so that I can see the famous view that my guests there are enjoying; we will ride down to the beach from there."

"Yes, miss," Emma ventured, wondering.

"You were born here, weren't you? You know everyone in Sealey Head."

"Yes, miss."

177

"So you would recognize a stranger come to town."

Emma nodded. "Everybody would, miss. Especially the way they dress."

"But perhaps this one might not be so gaudy."

"Mr. Ridley Dow, miss?"

The eyes gazing at her withheld expression, but Emma felt a heartbeat's worth of pause in the air, a blink that was suppressed. "You know him?"

"He was the stranger who came to town first."

"Ah. No. Not Mr. Dow. Someone not so noticeable. That I might not recognize as not belonging here, but you would."

Emma thought. "Oh," she remembered suddenly. "You mean like Judd Cauley's new cook."

"Judd Cauley?"

"The innkeeper on Sealey Head, where your other friends stay. He was desperate for a cook. His other one, Mrs. Quinn, would have driven all the guests away, she was that bad. The entire town was watching to see what he could do about it. Everyone likes Judd Cauley; he's just had some bad luck, until Mr. Dow came. That was the first of his changing luck. And then Mr. Pilchard came a few days ago, just in time for your guests."

This time she did blink. "Pilchard?"

"I think that's the right fish. Mrs. Haw told me about him, after she went to town to give her orders and pick up gossip."

"H'm," Miss Beryl said. Her gaze left Emma, refocused on something nebulous just beyond her. "It hardly seems likely," she added after a moment. Neither comment seemed to require a reply. "Anyone else?"

"No one that springs to mind, miss." She hesitated, asked before she lost courage, "Is Mr. Dow one of your party?"

The green eyes came back to her, wide and chilly. "Ridley Dow? I believe we occasionally meet. But no. Why, Emma?"

Because he's lost in a mysterious world behind a door within this house, Emma thought, in case he's a friend of yours. But nothing in Miranda Beryl's expression suggested anything of the sort. Her own eyes dropped; her voice dwindled. "If there's nothing else, miss, I'll take Sophie's tray down."

Dr. Grantham was in the room when Emma returned later for Lady Eglantyne's tray. Slipping unobtrusively to the bedside, she counted the number of bites taken: missing points on two toast triangles, the highest on the tiny mound of strawberries gone, a bleed of yellow into the egg white. Lady Eglantyne was sleeping now, her breath so light the coverlet scarcely moved. Emma picked up the tray, heard Dr. Grantham speak softly, echoing her own thoughts.

"I have no idea why she clings . . . Were you ever very close? Is she staying alive for you?"

Miranda Beryl, gazing inscrutably down at Lady Eglantyne, looked as though she might emanate mist like an ice block at the question. She didn't bother answering it, only said, "There's nothing else you can try?"

"Against time? No. I haven't a cure for that in my bag. She seems in no pain; that is the best we can hope for. Of course, if you wish, you could ask one of your Landringham physicians to visit her. I've done all that I can."

"I'm sure they would tell me exactly that," Miranda Beryl murmured. "So it seems we must wait."

Emma eased out the door. There was little more life in the silent rooms around her; as yet no one had even sent a servant down for coffee. They would snore until noon, then all demand to be fed at once, like nestlings. She went down the hallway toward the stairs, then, on impulse, passed them. She turned a corner and then another, beyond the bedchambers, where a little peaked alcove held nothing but a dormer window and a linen closet.

She put the tray on the window seat and opened the door.

She had so little expectation of seeing anything but folded sheets and towels that she jumped at the sight of Ysabo. She stared, tongue-tied with relief. The princess, carrying the scrap bowl as usual at that time of the morning, had started as well, looking apprehensive, as though anything might have come at her out of the abruptly opening door.

Then she smiled tremulously and put her finger to the smile at the same time.

"I'm glad to see you," she whispered.

"I've been trying so hard to find you! Is Mr. Dow—"

"He's somewhere. He comes and goes; I never know—" She glanced behind her, then tried to speak even more softly than a whisper. "He shouldn't have come, but he refuses to go. So far no one else has seen him."

"What is he doing there? What is he looking for?"

"Mostly, the bell. And other things. Why we are all caught up in this strange life. Emma, I always thought it was odd, but no one else did, and now that someone has told me yes it is a spell, it is enchantment—now I'm terrified twice. Of it coming to an end. Or of it never ending." She tried to smile again; her skin, always pale, seemed bluish, more whey than milk. "And above all, I am afraid for Ridley Dow. I wish he would go away. Then I think of him gone, no one to answer my questions, ever, and that is even more frightening."

"Let him stay, then," Emma said, more firmly than she

felt. "Let him find his answers. This strange house has ruled your life long enough."

"But it's so dangerous for him," the princess breathed.

"And for you?"

"So far, no. He is very careful around me. I think no one would notice him at other times; they'd think he belonged somewhere else in the house, or to some other part of the ritual."

"Where is he now?"

Ysabo shook her head. "I don't know. I haven't seen him yet today. He said he wanted to study all the pieces of the ritual. That's a lot of lives."

"How can he?"

"He vanishes. He becomes invisible and watches. He's magical, Emma. That's how he recognizes magic."

"I hope he's magical enough," Emma sighed, "for a house full of it. I'm so glad I found you again. I was terrified when he closed that door behind him. I thought the roof would fall in, or Aislinn House would disappear or something."

"I know. So did I." She glanced worriedly up at the lofty stones, then added, "I had better go. Maeve and my mother are waiting for me to try the wedding dress on. Aveline is taller than I; the sleeves and hem must be shortened." She paused, her thin red brows peaked; she asked suddenly, "Do you know when the moon will be full? We never pay it much attention. It's outside of our lives."

Emma tried to remember; she hadn't been paying attention lately, either. A thin, cold, tilted smile in the sky outside her own bedroom window emerged from behind a cloud in her memories. She said, "I think—"

What she thought was overwhelmed by a great tangle

of sounds—thick wood clouting stone, a man shouting, the fierce yammer of crows growing louder and closer. She clapped her hands over her mouth. The princess had pulled the scrap bowl against her, hugging it hard, her white face turned toward the clamor. In the hall below, the familiar, echoing din from the great hall ceased.

The silence was abrupt, eerie, and it didn't last long. In the next moment came the roar of men's voices, swelling in fury to meet the harsh cawing of the crows.

A figure ran through the open door at the top of the tower and down the steps, pursued by a black cloud of birds. They were swooping, slashing with beaks and claws at the nebulous figure, who seemed oddly faceless and mostly formed of a long black cloak. Ysabo gasped. Emma, guessing what it must be, pushed a scream back into her throat. The knights' shouting spilled ahead of them; boots pounded on stone steps; swords scraped the walls as they clamored up to deal with whatever had set the crows going.

"Mr. Dow," Emma wailed, then dropped her hands, hissed as loudly as she dared across the threshold, "This way! Come through the door!"

The empty hood turned away from the birds toward the princess and the housemaid standing there, one on each side of the world. The first knight appeared at the top of the inner stairs, baring his teeth and an unsheathed blade. He shouted at the sight of the drifting cloak attacked by crows. It shook its empty sleeves at the two young women as though, Emma thought, it were shooing away geese.

Someone cried behind Emma, startling all of them, "Ridley!"

The name seemed to shape him, pull him out of nowhere.

His face appeared, bloody and astonished; crows seized his visible arms, his hair, stabbing at him. Then a light flashed out of him and the crows leaped away from him, screeching. He vanished again. The cloak collapsed on the floor, instantly smothered in a furious rain of crows. Ysabo swayed back against the walkway wall, still clutching the scrap bowl, and closed her eyes. Emma stood frozen, watching the flowing tides of men and birds converge in front of the princess.

Then the door was wrenched out of Emma's grip; it slammed with a bang, and someone careened into her, pushing her over on top of Miranda Beryl's feet.

Miss Beryl joined her on the carpet a second later, kneeling beside the prone figure between them. He was facedown, his coat and shirt tattered and flecked red.

"Help me get him up, Emma," Miss Beryl said. Her deep voice sounded crisp, unshaken. But one of her curls, which Emma had thought must be glazed into place by the frost in her maid's eyes, sprang loose suddenly, went trailing down her back. "Is there an empty room?"

Emma's eyes widened. "In this house?"

"Attic, servants' quarters, anywhere—A closet?" Her green eyes, unblinking on Emma's face, tried to compel the impossible out of her. Impossibly, they succeeded.

"Lady Eglantyne's dressing room. Nobody uses it now. Sophie naps in her room after breakfast and Dr. Grantham's morning visit; she won't see us go in."

"Yes."

Somehow they wrestled Mr. Dow to his feet, not without further damage to Miss Beryl's hair and the front of her lacy morning dress. Emma, wearing black, fared better. Ridley helped them toward the end, his eyes opening, his legs finding some balance.

"Is that truly you, fair Miranda?" he asked in wonder as they stumbled down the mercifully empty hallway. "How wonderful. And the faithful, lovely Emma. Just in time to rescue me. Ysabo was right about those crows."

"Ridley, be quiet," Miss Beryl commanded.

"Yes, my own," he whispered. Emma closed her eyes tightly in disbelief, opened them again.

"If anyone looks out and sees us," Miranda said softly, "you were wandering in the woods reading a book and fell into a bramble bush. You found your way upstairs after being delivered to the doorstep by—oh—"

"Dr. Grantham," Emma suggested.

"Good. No. Why didn't he stay—?"

"Because the doctor was in a hurry, and he found Mr. Dow stumbling around in the yard. You said we'd take care of him."

"Good."

But no one opened a chamber door, came out to wonder at the procession. "Emma," Miss Beryl said, her voice very low.

"Yes, miss."

"I know you keep your secrets."

"So do you," Emma commented with amazement. "How much of the other Aislinn House do you know?"

"What Ridley has told me." She waited, balancing Ridley between her shoulder and the doorjamb while Emma opened Lady Eglantyne's chamber door.

She was relieved at the absence of crows, as well as of Sophie. The faint breathing, the muted light and soft summery air, made the room seem safe, as far away as possible from the strange, violent, incomprehensible world within the walls around them. She looked into the dressing room, an airy chamber nearly as large as the bedchamber, full of dusty wardrobes and chests, a daybed, and a stand with a jug and basin, both harboring forgotten puddles.

Ridley collapsed with a sigh on the daybed. Miss Beryl sent Emma for water, linens, blankets. Emma, returning with blankets and a full water jug, saw her peeling away Mr. Dow's torn clothes with breathtaking efficiency. On her way back from the linen closet, with her arms full of sheets and towels, she was startled by a voice in the quiet hallway.

"Emma, is it now?" Mr. Moren drew up beside her, idly spinning a monocle on its ribbon. "I have been looking for Miss Beryl. Is she still abed?"

"No, sir," Emma said, before she thought, then stood groping for something plausible, while Mr. Moren flipped the monocle into his fingers and fitted it into his eye. It made one bright eye seem larger than the other, she saw, and twice as difficult to think.

"Ah, you've seen her, then. Where is she?"

"I think with Lady Eglantyne, sir."

"I think not." He raised a brow, dropped the glass circle from his eye socket, and spun it again. "I just looked in. She is not there."

Emma blinked. She had closed the dressing room door, she remembered, lest Lady Eglantyne open her eyes and spy a half-naked man on her daybed. "Well, then," she heard herself gabble, "perhaps she's dressing. I heard her mention a ride on the beach this morning with Raven Sproule."

He let the monocle fall, looking mildly amused at the idea

of the squire's son. "There's a thought. Perhaps I'll ride out and join them. You needn't mention it. I'll surprise her."

"Yes, sir," Emma said woodenly, her mouth as dry as day-old ashes. She didn't move until he had turned down the stairway, and she heard his footsteps on the floorboards below. She returned to the dressing room to find Mr. Dow neatly bandaged, and beginning to breathe quietly. Miss Beryl helped her unfold sheets and a blanket, settle them over him. Emma glanced around the room, saw the streaked towels, the bloody water in the basin.

"I'll clean these up, miss, as soon as I can. There's a potion in the stillroom my mother made up for soothing pain. Shall I get that for him?"

Miss Beryl nodded. "That would be good." She blinked at the dried stains on her dress, then brushed at them, her long fingers trembling slightly. But her voice was still cool. "I must hurry and change to go riding with Mr. Sproule."

"Now?" Emma said incredulously.

"He'll be here soon. I must still be seen as the rich Miss Beryl, idling away my time while my great-aunt fades."

"Whatever will your maid think about your dress?"

"Who knows? We lead unsavory lives."

For some reason that made Emma remember the monocle, the enlarged, peering, glittering eye. "Oh. Mr. Moren stopped me in the hallway, looking for you."

Miss Beryl's face took on its mask-like calm, as though she had turned herself into porcelain. "What did you tell him?"

"That I thought you were dressing to go riding with Mr. Sproule. So he went away, to surprise you on the beach."

The porcelain blinked; Emma heard it breathe. "Emma, you are astonishing. I am so grateful." She paused, her eyes no longer chilly, remote, but wide and shadowed with what they had seen. "I walk always, always on thin ice," she said softly. "Emma, the best you could do for all of us now is to find that stranger whom I would not recognize as such in Sealey Head. You know him as Mr. Moren, in one of his guises." Emma opened her mouth, closed it wordlessly. "He has been among my friends—" Miss Beryl checked, waved the word away with her hand. "My following—my disguise, I suppose you could call it. He has been close enough to watch me all of my life. And now that I'm here in Aislinn House, about to become its heir, he wants me even closer still. He wants what I cannot, would never give him. But, oddly enough, he is rarely with me now. He disappears; no one sees him outside of Aislinn House, and only then early in the morning, when I visit my great-aunt, or late at night. He told you that he would meet me on the beach. But he won't be there."

"He said—he asked me not to tell you."

"So. You'll think he is there, and I would never expect him to be there. But where will he really be? I think he disguises himself during the day from those of us who recognize him."

"But why?" Emma's voice barely cleared her throat. "Why would he hide himself? What does he want? Who is he?"

"The man who controls the secrets of Aislinn House." The implacable voice shook finally. "He is Ridley Dow's uncle far, far too many times great. He is Nemos Moore."

Seventeen

That evening Gwyneth read to the twins:

So charming were the unexpected visitors to Sealey Head that in no time at all both Mr. Blair and Sir Magnus Sproule were possessed of the same idea: they—at least the highest-ranking among the strangers—should come ashore and be given a sumptuous dinner. Exactly where the necessary succulent viands were to be found in the desperate and impoverished town, neither of them knew. Somebody probably had a pig left. Or a sheep. Surely Lord Aislinn hadn't drunk up his entire wine cellar. There must be cabbages around somewhere. And leeks. And—

But, alas, the handsome man they assumed was captain, since he did most of the speaking, told them apologetically. For various reasons, neither captain nor crew could leave the ship. The reasons were vague: things were hinted at, allusions were made to the nature of the cargo, to a distinguished unnamed presence, to the contract with the ship's owner, a formality surely, but they had given their word of honor not to leave the ship until it was safely in port. You understand, being men of the world.

Indeed the two men did. They glanced down at the boards beneath their feet and understood that either a woman of unearthly beauty, or the heir to a great realm, or a hold crammed with gold and jewels lay just beyond eyesight.

But, the captain continued, there was no reason why he should not extend his own invitation to the dignitaries of Sealey Head. They should come to supper on the ship the very next night, and they would be given such a repast as they would remember for the rest of their lives. And they should, of course, bring their wives.

Mr. Blair and Sir Magnus Sproule agreed with alacrity. Such was the miserable fare in town the past months—thin fish soups, ancient bread and cheese, withered vegetables, hard, sour fruits— that they were already dreaming, as they clambered down the side into their boat, of rich creamy sauces and hot, bloody, peppered meat.

They hastened to shore, spread a general, appeasing word of their visitors' peaceful intentions. And then they conferred in private with Mr. Cauley and Lord Aislinn.

The four of them were pretty much the extent of the dignitaries in town, besides the owner of the stationer's shop, a most intelligent man who might even discern where the strangers came from. But he grew dizzy and was prone to fainting just putting one foot into a rocking rowboat; there would be no persuading him. The four of them it would be. Wives had been mentioned, it was reluctantly remembered. Wives should be brought, lest the omission be considered rude or suspicious. Lord Aislinn's wife, having come to the conclusion that anything must be an improvement over life with her selfish, profligate, untrustworthy, misery-making libertine of a hus-band, had departed this vale some years earlier. He would bring his daughter, Eloise, he decided immediately, his eye brightening at the thought of a wealthy, charming husband who might be away at sea most of the time, leaving his possessions under the care of his father-in-law.

That determined, they hastened home with the news, causing four pairs of eyes to gleam with anticipation for the first time in months. And of the four, the eyes of Lord Aislinn's daughter shone the brightest.

Gwyneth stopped. The twins, Pandora on the sofa, Crispin prone on the carpet with his chin on his hands, looked at her expectantly.

"Go on," Crispin urged. "Tell what they ate at the feast."

"She doesn't find a husband, does she?" Pandora asked uncertainly. "Gwyneth, does this have a happy ending?"

"I don't know. Which way would make it happy? That she does find a husband, or she doesn't?"

"Well, she can't marry one of them, can she? They're wicked!"

"So," Toland Blair murmured over a palm frond, "I'm beginning to think, is my eldest daughter. What have you in mind for those poor unfortunates?"

Gwyneth considered her plot and reddened slightly. "Nothing good, I'm afraid."

"I think it's a marvelous story," Crispin said staunchly, sitting up. "Only I wish you didn't write it in fits and starts. You should just finish it."

"Well, I would if my writing life didn't go in fits and starts."

"Do you know what's going to happen?" Pandora demanded.

"Yes. I think I finally have all of the pieces."

"Speaking of invitations," Mr. Blair said, rummaging around his desk. "Your aunt Phoebe and I have both been invited to the Sproules'—ah—what did they call it? 'Evening affair, with supper and dancing, to meet Miss Beryl,'" he read from the card. "Phoebe is very pleased. Though it's quite soon: they give us only two days to choose our dancing slippers."

"I believe they were concerned about Lady Eglantine," Gwyneth answered as vaguely as possible. Her father slewed an ironical eye at her.

"Ah."

"May we go?" the twins demanded together. Crispin's voice, sliding perilously into the upper registers, sounded so much like his sister's that he blushed scarlet; his mouth clamped shut.

"Of course not."

"But I am so rivetingly curious about Miranda Beryl," Pandora exclaimed. "Please, Papa!"

"You weren't invited," he said pitilessly. "We'll tell you all about it. And hope that it doesn't end in the kind of disaster your sister's story portends." He contemplated Gwyneth in silence a moment, smoothing his mustache. "It can't have been your extremely conscientious governess. Or that bland educational establishment in Landringham. I can't imagine what it was that gave your mind such an aberrant turn."

"Luck, I suppose," Gwyneth said cheerfully, and went to put her papers away.

At tea the next afternoon, Aunt Phoebe could talk of nothing else—of shoes and silks and Gwyneth's hair and the generosity of the Sproules—until the twins moaned in torment, and Gwyneth felt like joining them. Fortunately, Daria arrived with news that wrested everyone's attention from the party.

"Mr. Dow is back at the inn!" she exclaimed almost as she entered. Her stricken eyes, very round and for once unblinking, kept them from instant, general rejoicing; held in abeyance, they all waited for the bad news. "He has had an accident! But—" She held up her hand, cutting short the immediate agitation. "He will be fine, I heard. He will attend our party."

She waited; so did everyone else, trying to anticipate the next emotional hurdle.

Finally, Aunt Phoebe said, rather bewilderedly, "That's wonderful news—I mean about—Gracious, child, what kind of an accident?"

"I'm not really—Nobody quite—" She turned to Gwyneth; her face was bright now, with relief and delight. "I am so happy!" she breathed, clutching Gwyneth's hands, which Gwyneth had fortunately just emptied of her last bite of cherry tart. "I can't wait to see him."

"I can't, either," Pandora sighed. "Why didn't he come tonight? He must miss us."

"I'm sure he does," Daria said quickly. "He is resting this evening. That's what Judd Cauley told me, when I saw him at the stationer's shop. Mr. Trent was delighted with the news, of course."

"As we are, as well," Aunt Phoebe said, pouring Daria tea. She glanced at the door, missing something else.

Under the table, Dulcie asked through a mouthful of crumbs, "Tantie, where's the bird?"

"Raven!" Aunt Phoebe exclaimed. "Yes. Where is your brother this evening? We miss him as well."

Crispin opened his mouth, closed it again under Gwyneth's narrow-eyed stare. Daria took a precipitous gulp of hot tea, which rendered her speechless a moment.

"He—ah—rode over to Aislinn House. To ask after Lady Eglantyne, of course, make sure her condition has not worsened."

"Of course," Aunt Phoebe said smoothly. "Very proper."

"Yes."

They both gave little, darting glances at Gwyneth, who, unable to work up a sufficiently mortified expression, reached for a cherry tart instead and handed it to Dulcie.

"Oh, don't encourage her!" Aunt Phoebe cried, instantly diverted. "Dulcie, come out from under that table before you turn into an uncivilized hooligan."

"Are there civilized hooligans?" Pandora asked sweetly.

"Yes," Gwyneth said. "Both of you twins. Go away, as I know you're longing to do, and let us talk."

"Raven promised he would stop here on his way home," Daria told Gwyneth earnestly and unconvincingly. "Oh, Gwyneth, all Miss Beryl's guests are coming, and most of those from Sealey Head whom we invited. Sproule Manor will scarcely hold such a crush! We will be forced to dance on the cliff."

"Did you find some musicians of delicacy and refinement?"

"No," Daria said complacently, choosing the plumpest macaroon. "But they're young and energetic, and they'll play the moon down. Now, tell me what you will wear."

Gwyneth wore thin pale green muslin over a shift of white

silk so embroidered and beribboned it reminded her of the sitting room in Judd's inn. Her father brought out the carriage for the half-mile journey to Sproule Manor. The moon, while far from full, was at least congenial, smiling upon them as they rattled up the coast road. Half of Sealey Head seemed to be walking along it, everyone dressed in their best, waving cheerfully at the intermittent carriages. Gwyneth heard the vigorous, spirited fiddling even over the tide before they reached the manor.

Every window blazed; lamplight splashed upon the cliff, revealing the dancers that Daria had envisioned. Along one side of the grassy knoll, great fires blazed; a pig, a couple of lambs, a side of beef turned nakedly on their spits above the flames. The smells of brine, smoke, and meat mingled enticingly in the wind. Gwyneth wondered what Miranda Beryl's elegant guests would think of that eyeful of country ways.

Inside, the house smelled of a hundred beeswax candles in chandeliers, candelabras, sconces, and sticks. Fires raged in the hearths at either end of the hall, for the doors were wide open to the wind, cooling the crowd within. Boots pounded among dancing slippers on the oak floors; the city folk, glasses of wine or punch in their hands, watched from the sidelines. Their gowns, Gwyneth noted with envy, were of simple, subtle lines, whose fabrics dazzled the eye with hues over which light shifted like water, changing teal to blue, and rose to crimson, and glinting through lovely, nameless colors along the way.

Rooms on both sides of the hall were open to reveal groaning boards within, already surrounded by unabashed townspeople, who knew that the Sproules, above all, liked their guests to make the most of their bounty, and who seldom got such a feast as this anywhere else.

Aunt Phoebe and Toland Blair were hailed by Dr. Grantham almost immediately. Gwyneth listened to news, or lack of it, about Lady Eglantyne, then wandered off for a glimpse of the guest of honor. She found Daria first, who pulled her across the floor at the edge of the dancers, then into the crowd.

"Look at her!"

Miss Beryl wore purple, the wine-dark shade visible just under the surface of the sea where the great kelp fronds grew closest to the light. Against it, her skin turned a flawless cream; her pale hair, wrapped around miniature purple irises the color of her gown, looked like a garden after a snowfall.

She extended an arm languidly; Raven, flushing with pleasure, took her empty glass and worked his way toward the bottles and jugs and punch bowls on a table just outside the door.

"Oh," Daria groaned. "I do wish she would go back home. She is spoiling everything."

"Never mind," Gwyneth said.

"But I do mind. I mind for you! And for myself—I so want you as a sister. If he proposes to her tonight, I will smack him with a beer jug."

Gwyneth laughed. "You will always have me for a sister. We don't need Raven for that."

Daria glowered a moment longer at the lovely Miss Beryl, then sighed, her face easing.

"Well, she would never have him, anyway. Look at all those admirers around her. Mr. Moren has scarcely left her

side all evening. She'd hate Sealey Head. And Raven, esti-
mable as he is, lacks a certain—oh—dashing quality most
pleasing to women with nothing better to do than fall in and
out of love."

"Indeed."

"Eminently worthy, though," Daria assured her, "on a
practical, daily basis." She grew abruptly silent; Gwyneth felt
fingers, tense and chilly, close around her wrist. "Is that—
Just coming in—"

"Yes," Gwyneth said, taller and able to see over more
heads. She smiled at the sight of the fair head beside the dark.
"I believe it is Mr. Dow. With Mr. Cauley."

Daria tugged her so quickly into the crush again that she
left a trail of splashed punch and apologies before she entirely
caught her balance.

Ridley Dow saw them as they squeezed through a final
tangle of elbows and backs, into the quieter realms along
the wall. He looked pale, Gwyneth thought, and shadowy
beneath his lenses. He didn't move to meet them; he hovered
near the protection of the stones but greeted them warmly as
they reached him.

"Miss Blair, how are you? Miss Sproule, what a delightful
gathering. How kind of you to think of it."

"Mr. Dow, how are you? Where have you been?" Daria
asked precipitously. "We heard you had an accident!"

"A minor one. I'm much better now."

"But you look far too pale, even in this light, doesn't he,
Gwyneth? What happened? Nobody will tell us."

Ridley Dow shrugged slightly, then seemed to wish he
hadn't. "It was foolish enough. A sort of hunting mishap."

"Did you fall off your horse?"

"In a manner of speaking."

"Where have you been? Poor Judd Cauley thought you had abandoned him. I do hope you are well enough to dance, Mr. Dow. But where were you? And why didn't you tell poor Mr. Cauley where you had gone?"

"Where," Gwyneth said, diverting Daria's solicitous intensity from the patient Mr. Dow, "is Mr. Cauley? I thought you came in together."

"He went to fetch some ale for us," Mr. Dow answered. "There's quite a mob around the bottles."

"Ever the innkeeper," Daria said fondly. "But, Mr. Dow, you haven't told us where—"

"You ladies both look lovely tonight," he interrupted. "You look like spring itself, Miss Blair. And Miss Sproule, how well that purple brings out the green in your eyes."

"Yes," Daria answered a trifle moodily. "Thank you."

"To answer your question: I had some business to take care of, and I simply forgot to tell Judd Cauley where I was going. I didn't expect to be away quite so long."

"You didn't tell anyone," Daria chided him. She leaned against the wall beside him, looking mollified. "Everyone wondered. You forget that you have friends in Sealey Head who feel your absence."

He blinked at that, looking a little nonplussed. A streak of winy purple across the room caught Gwyneth's eye. She took pity on him, though every bit as curious as Daria about his mysterious adventure, and said quickly, "I'm sure Miss Beryl was pleased to see you again."

Daria rolled an indignant eye at her; something unfathomable surfaced in Mr. Dow's face.

He said only, lightly, "It's often hard to tell exactly what

197

pleases Miss Beryl. But I must remember to claim a scrap of her attention and pay my respects before I leave."

Daria straightened abruptly, as if the wall had poked her. "Mr. Dow, you can't leave before the moon sets! You must drink and eat and dance, at least with me. You will feel so much better for it, I assure you. Dancing always does me good; the more the better. I'll prove it to you."

"Miss Sproule, I'm quite persuaded already that you are right. But—"

"Ah, here you are, Mr. Cauley," Gwyneth interrupted contentedly, as he came up with two foaming mugs in his hands. He looked as happy to see her, and as polished, in his new coat and shining boots, as she had ever seen him.

"Miss Blair. And Miss Sproule," he added, sighting her at Ridley Dow's elbow. "Thank you again for inviting me," he added to her, while his eyes returned to Gwyneth's face. "I'm already having a wonderful evening."

"Mr. Dow is already thinking of leaving," Daria complained. "Tell him he can't possibly, Mr. Cauley."

"Of course he can't," Judd said, handing him a mug. "He must at least keep you company while I fetch you some refreshment. What would you like?"

"Punch, please," requested the placated Daria.

"And you, Miss Blair?"

She came to a sudden decision. "I'll come with you. Keep you company while you fight through the press."

He smiled. "How kind of you, Miss Blair. What a brilliant idea."

They strolled outside, took a place somewhere beyond the crowd around the bottles, waiting while it dispersed a little.

Judd, studying Gwyneth in silence, alarmed her into touching the pins in her hair.

"Is it falling down?"

"No," he said, surprised. "Sorry. I've never seen you with your hair up like that. It's usually tossed about like an osprey's nest by the time you reach the inn."

"You have a memorable turn of phrase, Mr. Cauley. Do you like the bird's nest better?"

He didn't answer. She looked into his eyes, saw moonlight reflected in them. She swallowed suddenly, hearing the air between them speak, the night itself, the running tide.

"Miss Blair," Judd said finally, huskily.

"Please call me Gwyneth." Her voice sounded strange, oddly breathless. "You used to. When we were children."

"Gwyneth."

She felt the sound of it run through her. "Yes. That's better. What did you ask me?"

He put his ale mug down in a patch of wild iris. "To come for a walk with me along the cliff to look at the waves."

"Yes," she answered softly. "That's what I thought I heard."

They came back sometime later, windblown and damp and hungry. Judd courageously plunged into the throng around one of the banquet tables, where great platters of roast meat had been added to the fare. Gwyneth found a couple of empty chairs around the dancers. Raven seemed to be making a speech of some kind, possibly introducing Miss Beryl, for she stood near him, not talking, but not really listening, either; she seemed to be searching the crowd for someone.

"Lovely addition to—" Gwyneth heard Raven declaim. "Welcome—Our support in this difficult—Sure you all—"

Someone took pity on him and began clapping, for everyone was chattering; even the musicians had begun to retune their instruments. The applause spread enthusiastically through the hall, cheers and caps tossed in appreciation of the feast that they could all get back to now that the ceremony was over. Raven looked gratified. Miss Beryl smiled her charming, perfunctory smile, turned her back just as Raven stepped toward her; she was drawn away from him into the dancers by Mr. Moren. Another of her friends clapped Raven on the shoulder, said something, and shrugged. He smiled again, reluctantly.

Judd came finally, laden with plates, forks, napkins.

"How clever of you to find us chairs, Miss Blair!"

"Wasn't it? And how brave of you, Mr. Cauley, to battle the mob to forage for us."

"That," Judd said, "is to make you admire me so much that you might even dance with me."

He sounded hesitant, waited for her answer before he even took a bite. Gwyneth waited to swallow hers.

"You mean," she said shrewdly, "in front of my father and my aunt, the Sproules and the better part of Sealey Head?"

"Yes," he said without smiling. "It would mean that much to me."

"A declaration," she guessed abruptly, with unladylike precision.

"Of serious intent. Yes."

She held his eyes, seriously moved. "Judd. I can't answer for my aunt, or the Sproules, or most of Sealey Head. But my father will most wholeheartedly think the better of me for choosing to dance with you."

He flushed. "Really?"

"Yes. So eat your supper in peace."

She herself was pleasantly surprised, a little later, by the sight of her aunt Phoebe and Mr. Trent taking a turn on the floor. The bookseller smiled from sideburn to bushy sideburn; Phoebe, her bun slipping down her neck, laughed unexpectedly at something he said. Gwyneth glanced around, wondering if her father had been tempted by anyone. But no: there he was beside the fire, discussing the affairs of Sealey Head, no doubt, with the ruddy and brawny Sir Weldon Sproule and other local businessmen.

There was a scrape and a flounce beside her as Daria pulled an empty chair up next to her and sat down.

"Mr. Dow left," she announced dolefully. "He was unfit for dancing, he told me, and not much better for company. He disappeared into the crowd to pay his respects to Miss Beryl, then he left without saying good night to me. Exactly what kind of an accident did he have, Mr. Cauley? Did somebody shoot him or something?"

"I'm not certain of the details," Judd answered. "But he seems a bit feverish, I think. That's probably why he forgot."

"But I know the very remedy for that!" she exclaimed. "It's a concoction of my grandmother's. I'll ride to the inn tomorrow, bring some to him."

"I'm sure he would be——" Judd began, and gave up, dropping his fork without finishing the thought. "Have you eaten, Miss Sproule? May I get you a plate?"

"That would be so kind of you, Mr. Cauley," she said glumly. "My feet got so tired from holding the wall up with Mr. Dow." She waited while Judd, exchanging a wry glance with Gwyneth, put his plate down and took himself out of earshot. Then she said softly to Gwyneth, "You shouldn't encourage him, you know. He has such feelings for you, poor man."

"There you are, Daria!" boomed a voice that made them both start. Lady Amaryllis Sproule, resplendent in blue taffeta with a beehive of lace the color of old ivory over it, put her hands to her ample waist and tapped her slipper at her daughter. "Why on earth are you sitting when there are hosts of young men to dance with? Everyone has been asking where you are." She extended a hand the size of an ox hoof and hauled Daria to her feet.

"Mother, Mr. Cauley is fetching my supper!"

"Supper! Who needs supper on such a night, with all this music and these eager lads? Go on, girl, get out there."

"But I can't leave Gwyneth—"

"From what I see, Gwyneth is doing just fine as she is." She flashed a pair of deep dimples at Gwyneth and hurried away to boom cordially at a neighbor.

"Whatever did she mean by that?" Daria asked Gwyneth puzzledly. "I haven't seen you dance at all." Gwyneth shrugged wordlessly; Daria heaved a sigh. "How I wish Mr. Dow had not left. Oh, well. I suppose I must cajole somebody into dancing with me."

She adjusted the expression on her face and went off to flirt. Gwyneth, left alone, studied her plate hungrily, chose a forkful of cold potatoes dressed in dill and oil and vinegar, and looked up, inelegantly chewing, to find Miss Beryl's shimmering skirt swirling in front of her. She and Mr. Moren were attempting one of the local dances, more gracefully, Gwyneth thought, than many of those born to it, yet not, apparently, without mishap.

"Oh, Mr. Moren, was that your foot?"

"I believe it was. No matter, my dear. Another dance, and I think we'll have it."

"Fortunately," Miss Beryl commented, looking down at her feet, "we have only two; what would we do with a third to keep track of? I promised the next dance to Raven Sproule. Since he is feeding us those great roast creatures, I think it only polite to oblige him."

"Let him wait," Mr. Moren suggested without pity.

"No. I think they take such things seriously here. They aren't accustomed to our casual rudeness."

"You are letting me wait."

Miss Beryl was silent; Gwyneth swallowed her bite quickly and sat suspended, willing herself invisible.

"You know I take forever to make decisions," Miranda Beryl said finally, lightly. "And I always forget immediately what it was I had made up my mind to do. Don't let's talk about it. Words get in the way of my feet."

"I won't take no for an answer," Mr. Moren warned her, a smile on his sallow, clever face. His eye fell on Gwyneth; he nodded to her amiably, the smile deepening in his eyes as though he had heard her listening. Miss Beryl stepped on his foot again, and his expression changed abruptly.

"I am so sorry—"

"Are you?"

"That must have been my third foot, clumsier than the others." The music spun a merry flourish and stopped; Miss Beryl drew back. "Rest a little, here with Miss Blair, while I practice with Raven Sproule."

Mr. Moren sat rather heavily down next to Gwyneth, to her discomfort. "Miss Blair, I hope you don't mind if I keep you company until your friends return."

"Nothing could please me more," she said, and he looked at her with interest.

"How strange words are, don't you think? They can mean their exact opposite so easily. Don't you find that fascinating?"

"Yes, I do," she answered with considerably more feeling, and he nodded. "These country dances can be a bit rough," she added. "I hope you aren't badly injured."

"To say that I am would be to imply blame," he answered smoothly, "and that would be ungallant. Let us say that the injury done is not to my foot, but to my pride, which is worth far less. I think both will heal nicely before the evening ends. Was that Mr. Dow on the edges of the gathering earlier? I noticed you talking. About newts or mushrooms, no doubt?"

"He is rather bookish," she agreed.

"We haven't seen him lately. Off wandering the coastal thickets? The cliffs of Sealey Head? He, at least, was wise enough not to try to dance."

"He has not been well, I believe."

"Ah. That must be why he didn't brave the crush to pay court to the guest of honor."

"Didn't he?" she said, surprised. "Someone said he had. I must have misunderstood."

"Miss Beryl remarked upon it," he said carelessly. "She likes her courtiers to be attentive even though she tires of us easily."

"Mr. Dow had an accident recently," Gwyneth said carefully. "Perhaps he simply was not feeling strong enough to get through such an energetic mob."

"No doubt." He strained with a sudden energy of his own against his chair, causing the wood to protest. "No doubt. A delicate soul, I've often thought. Unassuming and rather more interested in trifles than in life. Even I can be wrong occasionally. Now," he added, as the music swooped to an exuberant finish, "I believe I'm cured. And there is your friend Mr. Cauley, making his way toward you. I must find Miss Beryl and persuade her that I am completely uninjured and ready to try again."

He left, rather precipitously, to Gwyneth's relief. She turned in her chair to look for Judd, and her aunt dropped down immediately beside her.

"Gracious," Phoebe breathed, patting her rosy face with a bit of lace handkerchief. "I haven't danced like this since I was your age." She peered at Gwyneth's plate. "Is that poached salmon?"

"Yes. Would you like a bite?"

Phoebe leaned back, fanned her face. "Mr. Trent is bringing me a plate. Why aren't you dancing? All these handsome men from Landringham—you must have met a few of them while you were there."

"Not a one," Gwyneth said, biting into braised celery. "They're far too grand for me. I prefer the bookish types."

"Like Mr. Dow, you mean." She patted her niece's shoulder. "I saw you talking to him. He left quite early, didn't he?"

"Not feeling well, I think."

"Yes, I heard . . . Ah, here's Mr. Cauley. He'll do for a dance with you instead, won't you, Mr. Cauley?"

Judd put Daria's plate promptly on a chair, stepped in front of Gwyneth. "Whatever you say, Miss Blair." He held out his arm. "Gwyneth?"

"Nothing would make me happier, Judd," she answered, and left her aunt staring at them, surrounded by a little island of abandoned chairs and plates.

Later, riding home in the carriage with the moon in her window slipping gently into the waves, Gwyneth felt a sudden qualm about the fates she had devised for her characters, as she considered her own contentment. But this was life, she thought remorselessly. That was story. Each had its own demands, and she had made her choices.

No choice but to follow the story into their watery graves.

Eighteen

The inn was unusually quiet the entire morning after the Sproules' party. Hardly surprising, Judd thought, since guests had wandered back in at all hours: midnight, the wee hours, the darkest hour, the crack of dawn. Rising shortly after sunrise himself, wakened by a ray of light in his eyes and the smile on his face, he had felt his heart floating lightly as a bird upon a wave. Everyone else, it seemed, had just gotten to sleep. He dressed quietly, wondering if he and the fishers already putting to sea were the only ones up in the entire town.

But no. As he creaked a floorboard in front of Ridley Dow's door on his way to the kitchen, he heard the doorknob turn. He felt an eye on his back, turned to see it watching him.

He said softly, "Ridley?"

The door opened a bit farther. "I had to be sure it was you," Ridley whispered. He was fully dressed in the clothes he had worn to the party. They looked slept in. So did his hair. "Do you have my book?"

"Which?" Judd said, studying him. "Ridley, are you ill?"

"No, not at all. I just need my book."

"I have a dozen of your books in my room. Which in particular?"

Ridley put his finger to his lips, lowered his voice to the thinnest of whispers. *"The Secret Education—"*

"Of Nemos—"

"Sh!"

"Moore?" Judd whispered back. "Yes. Do you want it now?"

Ridley's shoulders slumped in what looked like relief; he leaned against the doorframe. "Yes. Please. If you would be so good."

"It's in my room. I've been reading it to my father. Would you like some coffee? Breakfast?"

"I can hardly think of anything at this moment except that book."

"All right," Judd breathed. "I'll get it for you."

He found Ridley in the same position, wedged between the doorpost and the door, when he returned. His eyes were closed. His face, beneath its dark shadow, seemed very pale, except for the smudges of fatigue under his eyes and the fiery streak along each cheekbone.

He murmured without opening his eyes, "Thank you, Judd," took the book, and closed the door.

Judd, fully awake now, and with memories of Gwyneth beginning to recede under the weight of day, went down to the kitchen to brew himself some coffee.

Mr. Pilchard, hearing a disturbance in his kingdom, wandered in yawning as Judd sat drinking it.

"Good morning, Mr. Cauley." He glanced up as though he could see the prone bodies through the floorboards. "Didn't expect you up so early."

"Me, neither," Judd said. "I didn't mean to wake you. I doubt that anyone will need you for hours. Oh, except for Mr. Dow."

"Ah. Back, is he?"

"He appeared yesterday afternoon, somewhat worse for the wear. And still is," Judd added slowly, remembering the strange details Ridley had dropped, fantastic, complex, and exasperatingly vague. He found Mr. Pilchard's disconcerting eyes upon him, the one seeming to loom large with speculation, and remembered Ridley's plea for absolute secrecy about what he had been doing. He changed the subject. "I think Mr. Dow could use some breakfast. Something simple and hot."

"Feeling poorly, is he?" Mr. Pilchard turned to pull a pan off a shelf. "I know some herbs that are good for fever, indigestion, such as that. I'll add a few to his eggs. A bit of warm bread and butter with them, a pot of hot tea?"

"That should help," Judd said. "Thank you, Mr. Pilchard."

He took the tray upstairs, found Ridley slumped over the open book on his desk. Other books lay scattered on the floor, on his bed, as though he had been searching for something. Judd put the tray down gently, glanced at one of the open books. It seemed to be an anecdotal history of Sealey Head, one of Mr. Trent's, probably, and contained, within a paragraph, a brief reference to the bell on the sinking ship.

Judd looked at Ridley, who was struggling upright, reaching for the teapot. "What happened to you in Aislinn House?" he asked. "Exactly?"

Ridley shook his head, pouring tea. "The less I tell you, the better. But this much I can tell you: it is under a spell and has been for some time. I don't know if Nemos Moore is responsible for the spell or only for meddling with it. But he is very much aware of it. And I know he is here in Sealey Head."

"Here?" Judd said, startled. "In my inn?"

"No. He's not one of your guests. I checked as they came in. I don't know where he keeps himself. He's been on the edges of Miranda Beryl's widespread circle of acquaintances for many years. He came to Sealey Head with her, I know that much. She will, after all, inherit Aislinn House, and everything in it, which is considerably more than meets the eye."

"How much more?"

"You would not believe..." He peered at his omelet, picked up a fork, prodded it, finally took a bite. "It's quite good," he said, surprised. "Mr.—What was it? Perch?"

"Mr. Pilchard. Cooked at sea for twenty years, came ashore finally to look for a wife. Is your relative a danger to you? Is that what happened to you?"

"I'm not sure exactly what happened, except that I ran afoul of the spell itself. There is some quite ancient magic within Aislinn House, as well as my ancestor's meddling. As soon as I'm stronger, I'll go back, take a more circumspect look at it." He took another bite of eggs, as Judd gazed worriedly at him.

"Why?" he demanded finally. "Why must you challenge whatever evil there is in that house? Can't you find someone else to do it? Why must you risk your life? What's in it for you?"

"Knowledge." He buttered a piece of bread, avoiding Judd's eyes for some reason. "After all, I am a student of the ancient arts. How else can I learn except by studying them?"

Judd left him flipping pages while he ate and went downstairs to check on the state of the taproom. He glimpsed a fluttering on the stairs ahead of him: a couple of disheveled heads, homespun skirts above bare feet skittering down. Souvenirs, he realized sourly, of last night's party. They moved too quickly out the door for him to recognize them.

He found Mrs. Quinn and Lily busy in the taproom, readying it for whatever guests ventured in when they finally opened their eyes. He backed out silently and walked down the hallway to the room overlooking the cliff to see his father.

Dugold was awake. Judd helped him dress, chatting absently about the Sproules' party, until Dugold interrupted him, his filmy eyes trying to find his son's face.

"Your voice sounds like a neap tide on a fine spring morning. Washing in slow and calm and barely waking the barnacles. Something you want to tell me?"

Judd felt himself flush. Yes! he thought. I want to tell you Gwyneth, I want to shout Gwyneth, I want to toast Gwyneth between two mugs that sing Gwyneth when they clink, I want... "No," he said, and Dugold, hearing the smile in his voice, grinned back.

"It's about time."

211

The guests staggered out of bed at midday; the baker's children careened through the hallways with trays as the cook directed them. Judd, noticing one of the boys tapping at Ridley Dow's door, was surprised but relieved that the scholar was still alive and requesting further nourishment. The outer doorbell jangled, announcing company. He hastened downstairs to greet them himself, knowing that Mr. Quinn was busy in the stable. It was not Gwyneth, as he had unreasonably hoped. It was a couple of visitors from Aislinn House, looking bleary and a trifle ragged around the edges but ready to start yet another merciless card game in the taproom with anyone who might be up.

They came and went, the butterflies of Miss Beryl's entourage, keeping both Judd and Mr. Quinn busy. He didn't see Ridley or his father all afternoon. Answering the bell in the late afternoon, he found the languid Miss Beryl herself at his doorstep, on horseback, with a mounted Sproule on either side of her.

He stared. He had seen her the evening before, but from a distance. That close, just above his head, she was even more incomprehensibly beautiful. Except, he thought, pulling himself out of his undignified stupor, for the thoroughly bored expression on her exquisite face.

"Afternoon, Judd," Raven said affably. "Miss Beryl expressed a desire to visit the inn where so many of her friends find themselves in the afternoon."

"Miss Beryl," Judd said. "Please, come in. And Miss Sproule. How delightful to see you again so soon."

"Thank you," Miss Beryl said, dismounting with such graceful efficiency that the hovering Raven was left with nothing to do but hand his sister down.

212

Daria looked far from bored. Anxious, apprehensive, and determined, Judd thought, and felt a twinge of pity for Mr. Dow. However, if he had any of his ancestor's gifts, he might be able to magic himself invisible to her myopic intentions.

"I brought my grandmother's conserve of roses for Mr. Dow," she told Judd immediately upon landing. "Excellent for distresses in the throat and lungs. I do hope he is here," she added fretfully. "Tell me he is, Mr. Cauley."

"I saw him in his room this morning," Judd said, ushering them in. "I can say only that much with certainty." He opened the door to the sitting room, the sight of which caused even the jaded Miss Beryl to hesitate for a quarter of a second before she entered. Mrs. Quinn had attacked again; there were raspberry-colored doilies underneath everything, even the table legs. "Please sit down. I'll order tea for you and see if Mr. Dow is in."

He resisted a desire to check the yard again, see if Gwyneth had somehow appeared, pulled inexorably into the wake of Sproules. One of the baker's children crossed his path; he sent the boy to the kitchen to request tea in the sitting room immediately for Miss Beryl and friends. Then he went upstairs to tap on Ridley's door.

He got no answer but what sounded like a book crashing to the floor. He opened the door, puzzled. Ridley was on his bed with a book over his face; a *History of Sealey Head with Anecdotes and Recipes* lay askew on the floor. Ridley still hadn't changed his clothes from the previous evening. A tray with a half-eaten bowl of chowder and some drying bread sat on his desk. More books had been added since morning to the general clutter, randomly strewn like driftwood on a beach.

Judd said softly, "Ridley?"

A hand rose after a moment, pushed at the book on Ridley's face until an eye became visible, partially open and not entirely aware. Then Ridley grunted a question, shoved the book away, and sat up.

His face had the sort of greenish pallor of someone lurching endlessly from wave to wave in a boat without a rudder. It disappeared for a moment behind Ridley's hands.

"You look terrible," Judd said. Ridley murmured something incomprehensible. Judd added, "I am sorry to have to tell you that the Sproules and Miss Miranda Beryl request your company in the sitting room."

Ridley's hands parted; he looked incredulously at Judd. "She came here?"

He nodded. "With her grandmother's cure for a chest cold."

"Her grandmother's—Oh."

"Do you want me to extend your apologies?"

"No." Ridley stood up after a moment. He swayed, but managed to stay on his feet. "Just tell them I'll be a moment."

"All right," Judd answered dubiously. "Don't fall down the stairs."

He checked on his father along the way, apologizing for missing their afternoon reading and promising to send some cheese and ale to keep him company. A thump on the stairs cut short his visit; he found Ridley, in clean clothes at least, clinging to the newel post.

He said apologetically to Judd, "If you could just help me to the sitting room."

"I am at a loss," Judd told him, as they limped down the

hall, "to fully appreciate the attractions of Miss Sproule, but love, they say, only the lover understands. Do you want me to send for Dr. Grantham?"

"No," Ridley murmured, as Judd opened the sitting room door. "I have a better idea."

His appearance brought cries of sympathy and distress from Daria Sproule, and a wide-eyed glance of astonishment from Miss Beryl, who looked as though he had dropped a jam tart on her kidskin boot.

"Mr. Dow, you are quite unwell," she told him accurately.

"Oh, poor Mr. Dow, this will help you," Daria cried, pushing the rosy concoction in its glass jar into his hands. "A tea of wintergreen leaves and juniper berries will cure most ailments; my aunt Florida swears by it. I'll bring you some tomorrow."

"Daria, Miss Beryl," Raven said hastily, "I think we must leave Mr. Dow to rest, especially since we have no idea of the nature of the illness."

"Wisely spoken, Mr. Sproule," Ridley said. "The ladies should indeed stay away from me. I do have a favor to ask of Miss Beryl if you will be so good."

"What?" Miss Sproule and Miss Beryl demanded together.

"Would you be so kind as to ask Lady Eglantyne's housemaid Emma to ask her mother to pay a visit to me? I think she will find a remedy as quickly as Dr. Grantham, who has far better things to do."

"What a peculiar request," Miss Beryl remarked to the air. "Well, I suppose I might remember if I do it immediately upon returning."

"I would be so grateful."

Ebon Baker entered, staggering under a tea tray laden with delicacies; Judd caught it as it slid toward a table.

"Tea?"

"I'm afraid I must decline," Ridley said, backing a step and growing greener at the sight.

"I think we must be going," Raven said with alacrity. "But another time, certainly, thank you, Judd. I'm sure I can persuade Miss Beryl to ride up again; she said there is nothing like such a view in Landringham."

"I'll come with them," Daria said stubbornly, "and bring my aunt's medicinal tea."

"I'm sure I will be grateful," Ridley managed, and backed quickly out the door, nodding at them wordlessly. The Sproules and Miss Beryl followed shortly after, Miranda Beryl wondering absently, as they walked out, why they had even bothered to dismount.

Judd took the tray back to the kitchen, where Mr. Pilchard was stirring a great stew of spring vegetables to go with the lamb on the spit.

"They didn't stay?" he asked Judd with surprise. "My walnut cake put them off?"

"No." Judd broke off a piece, tasted it with pleasure. "Your cake is wonderful. Mr. Dow, unfortunately, is feeling no better, and it was he whom they came to see."

"Ah. And here I just made up a tray for him, thinking he was recovering. Some hot roast chicken, a salad dressed in herbs and oil, leeks braised in sherry."

"Is that it?" Judd asked, eyeing dishes covered by a cloth on a tray. "I'll add a mug of ale to it and take it up to my father."

"Most likely he'd be disappointed by something so delicate," Mr. Pilchard objected, moving the tray off the table and out of reach. "I have some peppered chops cooking for him, and the roast potatoes he likes. I'll bring his supper up to him as soon as it's ready."

"You're probably right, Mr. Pilchard. And Mr. Dow might like the chicken later," he added, but dubiously, "after Hesper tends to him."

"Hesper?" Mr. Pilchard queried, flipping a chop.

"Hesper Wood. He asked to see her. Our local version of a wood witch. She knows everything there is to know about both the dangerous and the healing properties of anything that grows out of the ground."

"Ah."

"Even Dr. Grantham consults her." He took another bite of cake, then paid heed to the shouts and laughter rolling down the kitchen stairs. "I'd better go and help Mr. Quinn in the taproom."

He spent the evening ensconced behind the bar, except to escort Hesper Wood upstairs when she came, and back out again, when Mrs. Quinn said she was leaving.

He met her at the door; she told him, "I think he'll sleep peacefully now."

"What was it?"

"He said it was a kind of family ailment," she said only. "Something he inherited." She shook her head when Judd offered payment. "He'll pay me when he's well, I'm sure. Don't fret, Judd. He'll be all right now, as long as he is careful about what he eats."

"All right. Thank you, Hesper."

The long evening finally drew to a close. Visitors called for their horses to ride back to Aislinn House by lantern light; guests drifted to their rooms, or were carried by their friends. Judd left the mess for Mrs. Quinn in the morning and locked the taproom, feeling the weight of the long day and the brief previous night. He went upstairs, berating himself for not having sent a note to Gwyneth, a wildflower, a book, anything to tell her he had thought about her. Tomorrow, he told himself. Without fail.

He saw the light under his father's door and opened it, surprised. His father, put to bed by Mr. Quinn, rolled sleepily toward him.

"Judd?"

"Me. Your lamp is still burning. Mr. Quinn must have forgotten about it."

Dugold grunted. He lifted his face off his pillow then, an odd expression on it, maybe left by a dispersing dream. "Who was that, then?"

"Who?"

"Who brought my supper?"

"The cook, I suppose."

Dugold grunted again, dropped his face back onto his pillow. But his eyes stayed open, as though he saw something puzzling in the dark. "I couldn't tell. He sounded human enough. But when the door opened, I couldn't tell what was coming through. Something felt bright, burning maybe, and roiling like a wave, glittering yet full of shadows...Just beyond eyesight, so I could almost see it..."

"You were dreaming," Judd said gently, and turned down the lamp. "It was only Mr. Pilchard."

He remembered Dugold's odd description early the next morning, when he found Mrs. Quinn in the kitchen, crossly scorching porridge for her hungry family, and discovered with stark horror that his cook had vanished.

So, he found later that morning, had Ridley Dow.

Nineteen

When Ysabo went to feed the crows that morning, she found the tower door locked.

She stared at the unmovable iron latch in her hand. She wrenched at it frantically a few times; the door, thick wood bound in iron, did not even rattle in its frame. She could hear the crows gathering on top of the tower behind the door, their faint, harsh cries, as though they were calling for her.

Terror weltered through her, turning her fingers icy; she nearly lost her grip on the scrap bowl. In all her life, the door to the tower stairs had never been locked. She had no idea where to find a key.

She had no idea whom to tell.

Maeve? Aveline? They were sitting tranquilly in Maeve's chambers, shortening the dress for Ysabo's wedding. When the moon was full. Whenever that was. To a man whose name she was not exactly sure she knew. Who barely spoke to her. With whom she was expected to beget a child.

Who could feed the crows every morning for the rest of her life.

A cold tear rolled down her cheek, dropped into the scrap bowl. She looked down at it, the shreds and bones of last night's supper, bloody bits of meat, wilting salads, torn bread smeared with drippings and butter, fruit with the mark of someone's teeth in it. She was trembling, frightened nearly witless by the broken ritual, the disastrous unknown looming in her life if she did not feed the crows.

Deep in her, a thought surfaced, colder than the terror riming her bones.

Somebody had locked the door. So she couldn't feed the crows the unappealing leftovers of people's suppers. They probably wouldn't drop dead, if she didn't feed them. They probably wouldn't eat her instead. And even if they did, it was likely better than to be married to a knight whose heart, from what she could tell, was colder than her terror, and so tangled in the web of ritual he didn't have a thought in his head that hadn't been shaped by it.

Still shaking, she put the bowl down very quietly on the floor. The crows could find an open window if they were truly hungry. Anyway, they were birds. There was a great wood all around them. They wouldn't starve.

They'd think of something.

She turned stiffly, her steps as nearly soundless as she could make them as she walked away from the scrap bowl into the unknown.

The door didn't slam suddenly open behind her; the crows

didn't pursue her. She went down and around, down and around, making her way through empty walkways and inner halls, past the great hall with its noisy, clamoring, thoughtless knights. She couldn't go back to Maeve and Aveline, not sit there quietly and embroider, not hiding such a monstrous deed from them while they hemmed her wedding dress.

Why should she marry this knight? She didn't want to. Why not be condemned for two failed deeds as well as one? Or for three? Or five?

What if she didn't lock this door, unlock that, light this candle, leave the sword across the chair? What if she did everything backward, and at the wrong time?

So what if the roof fell in?

She felt another tear roll down her face, warmer this time. Grief was mingling with fear now, kindled by the loss of the only life she knew. It burned her throat, her heart. What if she destroyed her world?

What if she didn't?

She ignored the doors, the candles. She would leave the ancient sword in its scabbard. Let someone else take it out if it were truly needed. If not, let it gather dust. She went down, hours too early, as deeply as she could go, to the subterranean chambers where the water, if nothing else in the entire place, could at least find its way in and out of the house.

And so will I, she thought suddenly, fiercely. So will I.

She yielded to one point of the ritual: lighting a taper before she went underground. It was not the one she was accustomed to lighting. But it looked no different and burned just as equably; the lantern hanging beside the entrance to the rock-hewn steps accepted its fire.

The little boat with its mast and furled sail was moored

as always in the dark, slow water beneath Aislinn House. She studied it a moment. The water that welled up among the stones and ran down to the sea would carry it, but only as far as the grate running across the passage into the wood. But, she thought stubbornly. You are a boat. You are meant to follow water, not sit on it in perpetual gloom. Someone made you to go out into the world. You cannot pass beyond the grate unless it opens for you. So. It must open somehow. How?

On the boat a little flick just on the edge of the lantern light, quick and soundless as an eye blink, made her breath catch. She lifted the lantern higher, trying to see what had startled her. There was a very human murmur from the air. Then a figure took shape, sitting in the boat, darkly cloaked from hood to heel, holding a book open. A page had turned, she realized. And then she recognized the book.

She raised the lantern abruptly, recognized the face within the hood.

"Ridley," she whispered.

He looked astonished. "How did you see me when I was invisible?"

"I didn't. I saw the book."

He grunted, murmured puzzledly, "I thought it was invisible as well. Perhaps it has a mind of its own. What are you doing down here? It's not time—"

"For what?" she asked evenly. "Time for me to leave the lantern on the prow of the boat and go away again so that someone else can come and put out the light and hang the lantern back on its hook by the entrance so that I can come back again tomorrow and light it and leave it on the prow of the boat so that someone—Did you lock the door to the crows' tower?"

He thought about that; his face, stubbled and smudged with shadows, grew suddenly rueful. "I did. When I passed it earlier to get this book. I didn't want them attacking me again. I was going to return the book and unlock the door before you got there. But I lost myself in this book..." Something in her still, blanched face made his voice trail away. He rose quickly. "I'll unlock it now. It's a simple spell. There's time."

"Is there?" She shook her head, her eyes glazed with unshed tears. "Is there, Ridley Dow? You made me step beyond the ritual. I can't go backward. I can't stop thinking what I think, or wanting what I want. I think the crows are something more than crows, and what they want most is not their breakfast. I think the boat goes nowhere after I put the lantern in it. How can it? It is chained. Trapped by the grate. I want to know why. I want to know what you see in the book."

Gazing at her, he tried to say something, gave it up. He held out his hand. "Come and see."

She took it, stepped into the gently rocking boat and sat down beside him. The thick, heavy book, whose blank pages she had turned, one after another, every day since she could walk, had, in Ridley's hands, finally begun to speak.

It said colors; it said wonders, marvels drawn with ink and painted with such hues that melted into life, spilling across every page like a tide of ancient, forgotten treasure. There were words among the images, each letter a tiny work of art, each word, extravagantly decorated and totally incomprehensible.

"I think it's a spell book of some kind," Ridley said. "Maybe poetry as well. I'm not sure. It's all in a secret, or perhaps an ancient, language. But the book itself was spellbound, probably by Nemos Moore. That's why you saw only blank pages."

Ysabo touched a bird the color of dawn, perched among the golden leaves of an immense tree.

"It's so beautiful," she whispered. "All this time I never saw it. I turned empty page after empty page, never knowing . . . Why, Ridley?" She stared at him, her eyes wide, burning again, as though he might have an answer to her life. "Why?"

"I don't know," he answered softly. He turned a page, looking for answers there, maybe, then another. And then she stopped him, touching something familiar: a feast in a great hall, tables filled with knights and ladies, bright banners hanging above their heads. "Is that us?" she wondered. But no: the hall doors were open to reveal a meadow full of wildflowers, birds flying across a cloudless sky. And a crowned figure sat at the center of the table, an old man with hair like gray tree moss beside her. She turned another page, lingered there again, gazing at the dark water, sky the color of silver, trees loosing their last leaves. Upon a tiny island in the middle of the water, a silver shield lay like something lost, a torn pennant beside it.

"I know this," she whispered. "Why do I know it?"

"How could you?" Ridley asked with wonder. She lifted her eyes, looked at him, but saw Maeve and Aveline instead, embroidering the air with memories as they sewed.

"It's a place they described, Maeve and Aveline. As though they'd been there."

"How could they have?"

"I don't know." She turned another page, her fingers trembling. "I don't know. Here." She stopped at another image, of huge, worn stones in a wild wood, ancient trees around them tangled together like brambles. Queen Hydria was there, too, with an entourage of knights and nobles, and the strange old man in his long robe. "It was a place full of magic, Maeve said." Her voice shook. "She said she could feel it."

"But how?" Ridley's own voice vanished for a moment. "How could they have left this house?"

"I don't know, Ridley. When we sew together in the mornings, they talk about other times, other places, as though they remember them. As though they had other lives beyond Aislinn House. Or in this book, somehow . . . But if they are part of the ritual, they must have been born here, like I was."

Ridley's voice returned abruptly. "Can you ask them?"

"They wouldn't answer anything. They would only be furious with me for taking the book out of the tower, disrupting the ritual. That's all they would see. Not the strangeness of their lives, their memories, but the ritual."

"They may know who made the book."

"Never ask. That's what they have told me all my life. They don't answer even if they know."

Ridley was silent, his eyes on the painted stones, his mind elsewhere, Ysabo guessed. He said finally, "Princess Ysabo, is there a place you can stay safe and out of sight in this house while I work?"

"I don't know where to go to be safe," she answered, taking a bleak look at her life. "Can you raise the grate in the river at the wall, so that I could leave Aislinn House in this boat? I could wait for you beside the sea. The knights and the crows might not find me there."

"I doubt that you would find the sea through those woods,"

Ridley said grimly. "They're part of the magic. When the knights leave the house at midday, where do they really go? I've watched them. Wherever they go, it's into a different wood. Or a different time. They vanish the moment they ride away from the house."

She stared at him, chilled. "Then there truly is no way out of this house?"

"Unless you go through the stillroom pantry door into Emma's world. But I have no idea what would happen to you, even if you could. From this side, that door might just as easily open to nowhere as well."

She was silent, her thoughts threading their way through the maze of her life, coming up again and again against solid walls, locked doors, passages that spiraled endlessly and went nowhere. "Well, then," she whispered. "Well, then, Ridley Dow, we must find our own way out. You must undo what Nemos Moore did. You must unbind the spell."

"Yes."

"But what—Where do we begin?"

He was gazing at her, his lips parted, his eyes invisible behind reflections of light in his lenses. "You're sure," he said finally. "I could unlock the tower door, you could feed the crows, you could wait for me safely within your life."

She shook her head wearily, looking down at the shadowy stream flowing silently out, away, into. "I don't want to pretend anymore. Not even to the crows. Where should we go from here?"

"That bell," he said slowly, "has enough power in it to disturb perfectly comfortable lives as far away as Landringham. It is the single strangest, oldest, and most consistent link between two worlds. I want to find it. Do you have any idea where it is?"

"No."

"Who rings it?"

"No," she said again. "I never wondered about it. It's part of the ritual, part of our lives, a piece of the pattern of someone's day. Light this candle, lock that door, ring this bell."

He nodded. "I watched many pieces of the ritual. Most of them, like yours, were either absurd or hauntingly evocative, like the midday ceremony of the knights. I followed everyone I could, including Maeve and Aveline. No one led me to the bell. I spent much of yesterday trying to find that bell in books. Nemos Moore heard it; it's what drew him here. But if he saw it, he kept it hidden between the lines."

"How can we find between the lines?" she asked, her red brows crooked. "It isn't part of the ritual."

"No. It's not. That's the point..." His voice faded; he stared at her with absolute intensity, and without seeing her at all. When he spoke again, his voice had no sound. "That's where you are now. Between the lines."

"What?"

He saw her again, but slowly, as though he were struggling to waken from a powerful dream. "And that's where the bell is. Between the lines. It isn't part of the ritual at all. That's why I didn't see anyone ring it."

"But, Ridley, it is," she protested. "The bell calls me to the great hall to arrange the chairs, fill the cups. It summons others to the table. It is what we listen for, at the end of every day. It rings the sun down."

"It is hidden, disguised within the ritual. But it is not part of the ritual. It's like the book. When you see it as part of your ritual, it is blank. But if you look at it as it truly is—"

"It is full of treasures," she breathed. "Outside of the ritual, it is itself."

"And that's where the bell is. Outside of the ritual."

"Nobody in this house is outside of the ritual but you, Ridley Dow. And even if we could look for it, how would we find such a place?"

"You found it," he told her, "when you turned your back on the crows and came down here instead. It's the place where you are Ysabo. Where you live your life as you choose, where you ask questions and search for answers. Right now, you are outside. Between the lines of your daily patterns."

"Yes," she said, glancing again at the silken flow of water in the light, the stone arching above them. "I shouldn't be here at this time. But I still don't see a bell, inside or outside of the ritual, and if it truly is outside, then who outside is ringing it?"

He was silent again, staring at her again, as though if he looked hard enough, waited long enough, she might come up with an answer for him. But it was himself he searched.

"Oh," he whispered; she watched his eyes filling with wordless answers. "Oh, Ysabo, I think I know where it might be. What we might be looking for, trapped within the lines...Those were never blank pages you saw in this book. They were closed doors. And now, look: every one of them is open."

"Ridley—"

"Don't be afraid. Now we know where to begin."

"Ridley," she whispered, for her voice was gone, drained by the shape of whatever it was watching them in the dark just on the edge of their circle of light.

"You don't die easily, Mr. Dow," a dry, sinewy voice commented, and Ridley stood up so fast that the boat tipped wildly in the water, sent up a splash between wood and the stone it was chained to.

The man who stepped into the light was tall, lean, fair-haired, with eyes of a dark, brilliant blue; their alertness and attentiveness reminded Ysabo of Ridley. The stranger was also fashionably dressed, with the same rich and subtle details. His face, pale and lightly lined, was scarcely middle-aged. His eyes said differently. Ysabo, staring into them, thought they must be as old as the dark, still water beneath her feet.

He smiled briefly, aimed a bow her direction.

"Princess Ysabo. Surely you should not be down here at this time of the morning. I thought Maeve and Aveline had trained you better than this. You know that the moon will fall out of the sky and the sea run dry if you do not attend to the ritual."

"How do you know such things?" she demanded, prickling with wonder and sudden fear.

Ridley answered her abruptly. "Mr. Moren," he said, rocking with the boat. "Or should I call you Mr. Pilchard? Or are you finally admitting to the name of Nemos Moore?"

"Call me what you like," Nemos Moore said, shrugging. "You'll not need any of them much longer, Mr. Dow. You are truly the last person I would have expected to find here. The mild and scholarly and rather gormless young man adrift in the wake of Miranda Beryl's circle, hopelessly endeavoring to interest her, in the rare moments she found herself with nothing better to do than to speak to you, in the life cycle of toads. Yet here you are. I am forced to wonder why. I am forced to adjust my ideas of you. Clever enough to find your way here, fearless enough to breach these dangerous walls, powerful enough to stay alive this long...Why, Mr. Dow? What possessed you to come here?"

"The bell." He was quite still now; so was the boat, as motionless in the water as though something had seized it from beneath.

"Ah. A wonderful mystery for those willing to brave centuries of dusty tales."

"Your book."

"My book. Of course you would have run across it eventually in your studies. But how did you know it was mine?"

"You."

Nemos Moore's brows leaped up. "What could I possibly have done in Landringham that caught your myopic attention and persuaded you that Mr. Moren is Nemos Moore?"

"You reminded me of me." The sorcerer, rendered speechless, stared at him. Ysabo, her hands over her mouth, glimpsed a rippling, glittering, amorphous thing he wore like a shadow over his skin. "I was curious," Ridley went on, "about Nemos Moore's antecedents. Imagine my surprise when I found I recognized them in my own. Ancient relatives should have the grace and good manners to depart this life in an appropriate fashion, not make trouble across the centuries and leave cruel, spiteful distortions of magic for their descendants to clean up."

Nemos Moore found his voice finally. "Ah, I've had too much fun at it to give it up. Are we really related?"

"My great-great-great-great—"

"Surely not so many greats."

"Far too many," Ridley agreed.

"So that's where you got your gifts...And how you kept

them hidden from me." He was silent again, briefly, his eyes narrowed, seeing things in the air between them. "Is that what you really want, Mr. Dow? A chance to possess this ancient labyrinth of power and wealth? Surely you can't imagine you would win Miss Beryl's extremely flighty regard simply because you have solved the mystery of the house she is about to inherit? I doubt that she would understand anything at all about it, even if you opened a door and showed her what marvels exist in Aislinn House. She would assume it's all part of her own house party, her guests entertaining themselves."

"Do you think so?"

"I know so. Besides, I have my own plans for this house, as well as for Miss Beryl. I don't like to be thwarted, Mr. Dow. It makes me mean-spirited and spiteful. As you have seen. Haven't you?"

"Amply."

"So you should just go away. Leave Sealey Head, leave Landringham, leave the country. Will you do that, Mr. Dow?"

"You didn't offer me that option yesterday," Ridley said with a touch of asperity, "when you tried to kill me with your cooking."

"I didn't know we were related then, did I? For the sake of family ties, I might consider offering you some recompense to go away. Money? A share in my long and extraordinary experience of the magical arts? Perhaps, if I can learn to trust you, we might form some kind of a partnership. Such gifts you inherited from me shouldn't be wasted. And perhaps, over time, I could teach you to think like me." He paused. Ridley said nothing, did not move, did not, to Ysabo's eyes, seem even to be breathing. The sorcerer shrugged. "I could never understand a man who would not compromise when there is no other option. Good day, Mr. Dow."

Ridley flung up his hand instantly, murmuring. But the strange, darkly gleaming shadow around Nemos Moore had already flared. Light flashed through the chamber, turned the water to molten silver. Half-blinded, Ysabo threw her arm over her eyes. She heard Ridley cry out. The air rustled around her like satin, like dry leaves, like paper. She felt a hand clamp around her wrist just before she fell out of the world.

Twenty

G wyneth wrote:

The feast offered to the men of Sealey Head, Lord Aislinn, Sir Magnus Sproule, Mr. Blair, Mr. Cauley, their wives, and Lord Aislinn's daughter by the captain of the visiting ship was every bit as elegant as the strangers themselves. There were swans and peacocks stuffed with rice flavored with cinnamon and rose water and colored gold with saffron; there was roast boar stuffed with onions and chestnuts; there was a great roast of beef, bloody, peppered, and served with a sauce of its own juices. There were delicate bisques of wild mushrooms, of asparagus in cream; there were dishes of vegetables of every kind, even those like potatoes fried with apples, and colorful steamed squashes, that were not yet in season. There were cheeses that melted to cream in the mouth, and pungent cheeses that bit back; there was such an extravagance of fruit, such color and variety that must bring a blush to the cheek of the modest reader were we to describe it. And the array of cakes interspersed among the fruits seemed wondrous works of art more suitable for worship than for eating, especially the great sculpted tower of chocolate, cream, meringue, and raspberry sauce that rose majestically in the midst of them.

In all, a stupendous and gratifying supper for the long-suffering inhabitants of Sealey Head, who fell upon it with great gusto and cries of delight. And is it any wonder if, consuming such magnificent fare, they did not notice that not one dish contained any of the fruits of the sea? Not a fish, an oyster, a lobster was to be seen on the groaning board. Not the least shrimp, the humblest whelk. Can we blame them for their oversight in the midst of what they considered the epitome of plenty?

And, of course, all was served with unstinted and unending bottles of wine, champagne, port, and brandy. At the end of the meal, when surfeited ladies reached for one more grape or sweetmeat, and men cracked nuts together between their fingers, even then, no one wanted to leave. The visitors spoke so cordially, so eloquently of the far-flung ports, strange customs, astounding animals they had seen that they fairly mesmerized their guests. They, too, seemed reluctant to signal an end to the evening.

No one, later, remembered who made the first, idle mention of cards.

The idea was seized upon by all. No one knew how late it was; no one cared. What was there to get up for in the morning but the drudgery of daily life in Sealey Head? Even the captain admitted to a willingness to allow a certain slackness to the tasks of the morning. There was no tide they had to catch immediately. They had all been confined to the ship. Let the crew have the morning hours to swim, tend to their gear, entertain themselves.

The tables were cleared except for such necessities as nuts, choco-
lates, sugared ginger, grapes, and, of course, bottles. The ladies
declined, sat together on silken cushions, reveling in their indolence,
nibbling and gossiping. Lord Aislinn's daughter, Eloise, lay back in
silence and watched the wonderful faces of the visitors, their bright
eyes, and long, glossy hair. She was in love with all of them.

Her father dealt the first hand.

"Gwyneth!"

She started, her pen making a little lightning stroke of her last word. Aunt Phoebe's voice sounded a trifle high, even tense. And fairly loud as well: she must have come to the bottom of the attic stairs. Gwyneth put her pen down, blinking; she glanced out the gable window and was surprised by all the light. It should have been the middle of the night.

"Coming," she called, opening the door. It was still morning, she remembered, and wondered if she had forgotten to do something for her aunt. Phoebe waited for her to descend. She had something in her hand: a little bundle tied up in a ribbon. She did not look happy with it. She wore the particular expression, a mingling of disapprobation, regret, and resolution, that the twins had named her Duty Face.

"This came from Judd Cauley," she said, when Gwyneth reached the bottom of the stairs. She dangled the bundle by the ribbon with her fingertips. "To you."

"A book!" Gwyneth exclaimed with delight. "I wonder if it's that one of Mr. Dow's we talked about. *The Secret Education of Nemos Moore.* That sounds like it. Let me see what the note says." She tucked the book under her arm, and tried to ignore the wild iris that had been slipped beneath the ribbon.

"He sent you a flower," Aunt Phoebe pointed out.

"So he did," Gwyneth said, opening the note.

"I noticed at the party that there was a certain familiarity between you."

"Was there?" Gwyneth murmured, skimming the paragraph.

"He called you Gwyneth."

"Did he?"

"You called him Judd."

"Aunt Phoebe, we've known each other since we were born."

"I hope you have not been falsely encouraging him."

"Of course I haven't. Why would I—Oh, dear, Aunt Phoebe, Mr. Dow has vanished again." She lifted her eyes, stared, stricken, at her aunt. "And so has Judd's wonderful cook. See page eighty-two."

"I beg—"

"Eighty-two," she repeated, riffling pages in the book Judd had sent. "Mr. Pilchard was by all accounts a paragon in the kitchen. Poor Judd. I wonder what happened to him. Mr. Pilchard, I mean. Here we are, page eighty-two." She glanced over the page quickly. Some quality of the air changed; it seemed to grow darker, chillier. She reread the page more slowly.

"What does it say?" a voice asked impatiently. Her world shaped itself around her again: the morning, the note, the flower, her aunt standing in a patch of sunlight in front of her, waiting.

"Ah—" She struggled to contain the innocence in the written words without divulging the disturbances she had glimpsed between the lines. "It's a reference to Aislinn House.

Apparently, Judd thinks Mr. Dow has gone there again, perhaps to pay a visit to the man who wrote the book, who must be in Miss Beryl's entourage."

"Then we needn't worry about Mr. Dow," Aunt Phoebe said briskly. "You must send a note back to Mr. Cauley, thanking him for the book. I wouldn't mention the flower. It may have been an accident."

Gwyneth smiled in spite of herself. "And the ribbon, too. Mrs. Quinn, Judd's housekeeper, is always playing with them."

"There. You see? Everything explained."

"Indeed. That is one explanation," she answered mildly. "Another is that Judd sent me a flower. Nothing difficult about that, is there? And I'm sure that if I looked in the parlor, I could find something appropriately amazing to put it in, to match the rest of the bizarre furnishings in my writing room."

"But what of Mr. Dow!" her aunt expostulated, growing florid. "And what about Raven Sproule? You're only toying with Judd Cauley because Raven is temporarily infatuated with Miss Beryl, as was obvious at the—What is so funny?" she demanded, seriously annoyed, as Gwyneth, reddening herself, let loose a sound like a prodded hen.

"Oh, Aunt Phoebe, you've been reading too many romances. Of course I'm encouraging Judd Cauley. I like him better than any man I've ever met. He's kind and funny and we both love books and we're rooted in Sealey Head. And yes, I'm going to send a note immediately to him, thanking him for the book and the flower, and inviting him to tea as soon as he comes into town in search of another cook."

She went off to find a vase; Phoebe, she guessed from the sound of the library door pulled sharply open, went to find her brother.

Gwyneth had seen him cross the street an hour earlier, to his office in the warehouse. So she had some uninterrupted time to peruse the book Judd had sent. It was lively, disquieting, and indeed full of secrets. The writer had been drawn, like Ridley Dow after him, to Aislinn House in search of a source of great power, signaled by the ringing of a bell each day at sunset that reverberated across centuries of tales and writings. But did he find the bell? He didn't say. He dallied with one or two of the lovely inhabitants of the house; behind closed doors, he discovered astonishing marvels and colorful rituals. He fell in love. He learned a few things. He made a few adjustments. He left Aislinn House and Sealey Head to continue his adventures.

Judd had written: *He is an ancient relative of Ridley Dow's. Still alive after all this time, and returned to Sealey Head, it is my reluctant conclusion, in the guise of my cook, Mr. Pilchard. Now they are both gone. I suspect to Aislinn House. I must find a cook, then see what I can do to help Ridley. See page eighty-two. I have very grave misgivings about Nemos Moore.*

Gwyneth sat mulling over that. Where, she wondered, in the grim, quiet Aislinn House she had seen, in which the past was covered by dustsheets and an old woman lay dying, did they keep the marvels, the rituals, the magic? Under the floorboards? Within the walls? What was it that had drawn Nemos Moore back? And where?

And how far would Judd, after trying to explain things to the impenetrable Miss Beryl, get through the front door?

She gave up trying to imagine that scene and went back to

her story, to beguile away the time while she waited to hear from Judd.

For a time all went pleasantly well.

The visiting mariners lost a few coins; the guests from Sealey Head gained a few to line their threadbare pockets. All was convivial, amiable, gratifying. Bottles were passed; glasses continually filled. The ship scarcely moved; time and tide themselves might have been stalled, idled around the ship in response to the good wishes of those within.

The ladies drifted to sleep upon the cushions, woke to hear the game going on, went back to sleep. Lord Aislinn's daughter finally closed her eyes.

She had the most peculiar dream.

The candles around the gamers were dwindling. Great sheets of shadow loomed over them. The faces of the mariners remained unchanged, open, friendly; those of Sealey Head became most anxious, desperate. All the shiny piles of coin seemed to be in front of others. The guests asked for pens and slips of paper; these they were given graciously, with smiles. The games continued.

Candles sputtered, died, were replaced. Papers piled up amid the coins. The men of Sealey Head spoke very little; their words were heavy, toneless. Mr. Cauley made his final bet first: all he had.

"The Inn at Sealey Head."

It was duly written down. He signed the paper.

Cards were dealt.

Mr. Cauley staggered up from his chair, went into the shadows, and, in the way of dreams, nothing more was heard from him.

Mr. Blair, his face waxen in the candlelight, wagered his entire line of ships.

They went the way of Mr. Cauley's inn; Mr. Blair followed Mr. Cauley into the dark.

Sir Magnus Sproule, his own broad, rustic face defiant to the end, bet Sproule Manor and his lands upon his final hand.

When he rose, letting his cards flutter to the table, only Lord Aislinn was left.

He offered what, ostensibly, he still had. But the smiling visitors shook their heads. They seemed to know, in the way of dreams, that every field, every tree, every dusty book and bottle, every stone of Aislinn House belonged to his creditors.

"My lord?" Eloise heard. "My lord Aislinn?"

She opened her eyes.

Her father looked across the table at her.

"My daughter, Eloise, my heir," he wrote as his final wager, and the smiling mariners nodded briskly. Yes, yes, indeed... Their handsome faces turned toward her, their fine eyes, their lean, predatory jaws. She smiled back.

The cards were dealt.

Lord Aislinn sagged back in his chair, his eyes closed, his face bloodless. Eloise felt the only moment of pure happiness she would have in her brief life.

Someone opened a hatch above them. She felt the wild surge of water, heard the masts straining against the wind and realized, astounded, that they had sailed out of the harbor into open sea.

Then she saw the water bubbling up from underneath, around the unconcerned mariner's boots as they pocketed their gold, and the ladies around her stirred and gasped.

The water surged around them. Eloise screamed. As the ship sagged on its side and she slid across the room on a wave, she had one final glimpse, through the hatch, of the most beautiful sunset, ragged clouds of gold, purple, and rose engulfing the dying sun. They had played through the night and the entire day. And now the day was done.

The ship's bell tolled a final, solitary knell as the wild waves dragged it down into the sea.

Gwyneth heard from Judd sooner than she expected, even as she was puzzling over her ending and wondering why, tidy as it was, it did not satisfy. Perhaps she felt guilty about the unfortunate Eloise. She could see Pandora bouncing up from the sofa with a cry of indignation over that; she could see, above a palm frond, her father's raised eyebrow.

Well, she couldn't please everyone. And Crispin would certainly like the feast. It would be best, however, she thought a moment later, twirling her pen moodily in her hair, if she could manage to please herself.

"Miss Gwyneth!" It was Ivy, just outside the door. "You have a visitor." She gave a little grin as Gwyneth opened the door; she must have heard the discussion in the hallway, earlier. "Mr. Cauley."

Gwyneth took a step across the threshold and hesitated. "Tell him I'll only be a moment."

"Yes, miss."

She went back to her desk, gathered up her story, shook the papers straight, rolled them, and bound them with the ribbon from Judd's bundle. She paused for one more second, to touch the lovely iris in its truly hideous vase of tiny seasnail shells fastened with pitch onto teak. She felt the sudden lightness in her heart.

Judd, pacing the carpet in the hallway downstairs, wasn't smiling at all until he turned and saw her. Then his set expression softened; for just that moment, he looked as though he forgot why it was on his face at all.

"Gwyneth. You look so charming with that little scribble of ink on your cheek."

She sniffed. "And you smell like the sea. All windy and briny—have you been at the fish market?"

He nodded, frowning again. "I've been running errands all over town. Mrs. Quinn is back in the kitchen, and I'm hoping she'll drive all the guests away. I got your note. I wanted you to know that before—" He hesitated.

"Before what, Judd?"

"Well. Before I go to Aislinn House. To look for Ridley Dow. I have no idea how far I'll get. Or where—I just don't know. When I'll be back. I wanted to see you. To tell you that before I go."

"Indeed." Their faces were very close, she realized, both searching for something, maybe, memorizing lines, colors, the hollow of a throat, the slant of bone. She reached out, still gazing into his eyes, and slipped her story onto the hall table beside the door key and the mail. "To find the true secrets of Aislinn House, challenge the wicked sorcerer, and rescue Ridley Dow?"

"Something like that. If I can persuade Miss Beryl to let me in the door."

"Oh, good. I'm coming with you. There's something wrong with my version of the story."

He felt obliged to argue, despite the relief on his face. "But Gwyneth, it may be—What story?"

She slid her fingers under his elbow, tugged him toward the door. "Quickly, before the twins or Aunt Phoebe come down. I'll help you with the awkward parts, like getting us into the house; you can have the heroics. The ones I don't want, that is."

"We'll let Ridley have them."

"Good idea."

She opened the door. In the last hour of morning, with the sun pouring cheerfully into the streets, glinting and breaking on the wind-rippled harbor, they heard the single, unmistakable toll of the bell.

Twenty-one

Emma heard the bell down in the kitchen, where she was picking up the first of the breakfast trays for the guests. Granted, their hours were topsy-turvy; they turned night into day, morning into night, and noon into dawn, when they finally began to open their eyes and call for tea. But so far in her life, neither the sun nor the bell had ever deviated from schedule. They were inextricably bound, had been every day's end of her life. But she knew the sound of that bell, distant and melancholy, like she knew her mother's voice. She nearly dropped the tray when it spoke.

Something was wrong, she knew instantly. Very wrong, horribly wrong. Nobody else noticed; it meant nothing in their lives. She could only stand there with the tray in her hands, while Mrs. Haw fussed with the cloth over the toast, and muttered, "What I wouldn't give for a quiet house again. But we can't go backward in our lives, can we, any more than we can turn a ripe tomato green again, and Lady E will be the only one at peace around here when she goes, for no telling where the rest of us will end up then. There. Run up now, before the toast gets cold; they always send it back then."

Emma escaped. She went upstairs as quickly as she could, tapped at a bedroom door. She thrust the tray at the haughty young lady's maid who opened it and ran down the hall to Lady Eglantyne's bedchamber. The door opened to the bed-chamber, not, as she had hoped, to Ysabo's world.

Miranda Beryl was still there, another thing Emma had hoped. She turned her head quickly; their eyes met, and Emma knew that she, too, had heard.

So had Lady Eglantyne, apparently. She was shifting under her bedclothes, and actually spoke.

"Did you hear that?" Her voice was thin, spun so fine words drifted like cobweb. "Miranda?"

"Yes," she said. "I heard it."

"Why now? I just had my breakfast."

She knows, Emma thought with wonder. Lady Eglantyne knows, too.

Miranda rose, stood over the slight, perturbed figure beneath the lacy coverlet. She let her fingers fall gently on her great-aunt's wrist. "I'll find out," she promised. "Go to sleep."

"Be careful, my dear."

She watched Lady Eglantyne close her eyes, then gestured to Emma to follow her out.

"Emma," she said very softly. Behind the closed doors along the hallway, faint voices could be heard, laughter, complaints. "Did you open one of the doors for Ridley again?"

"No, miss. If he's in there, he found his own way. I never saw him come back into the house, either."

"Do you know where the bell is, in the other house? Did the princess ever talk about it?"

"No. I asked her about it; she only said it was part of the ritual. She never said where it is, or who rings it."

Miss Beryl stood silently, willowy and languid in her frothy morning gown. She gazed at something disturbing in a fall of light, a frown in her eyes. "If Ridley is there," she said finally, "Nemos Moore must have found him. Ridley said he wanted to cause trouble. I can't imagine what he did to change a pattern as inflexible as that bell. It's like the moon rising on the wrong side of the world. Emma, what have you to do this morning?"

"Feed your guests, miss," Emma said, envisioning trays backed up on the kitchen table and Mrs. Haw threatening to walk straight into the woods if anyone complained of cold eggs.

"Is that all? Never mind my guests. I need you to help me find Ridley."

"But, Mrs. Haw," Emma protested. "She'll have no one to take the breakfast trays up, and she'll have all the maids and valets coming to the kitchen raising their brows at her and speaking down their noses."

"What about my kitchen staff?"

"They only prepare, miss; they don't deliver. So they gave me to understand."

"H'm," was what Miss Beryl had to say, with particular emphasis, about that. "Find Mrs. Blakeley and send her to me. I'll have her give them something else to understand."

"Yes, miss." She hesitated. "Perhaps Mr. Dow is still at the inn."

"I doubt it," Miss Beryl said briefly. "I've seen nothing of Mr. Moren, either, this morning. I'll be in my room, changing into something with more authority and fewer frills. And a pair of boots in case I need to trample on Mr. Moren's feet again."

"Yes, miss," Emma said again, beginning to wonder, with some misgivings, what Miranda Beryl had in mind. But she turned away without explaining, and Emma went to the breakfast room, which nobody got up for, and where Mrs. Blakeley spent her mornings in the quiet, darning the moth holes in the table linens.

Emma delivered Miss Beryl's summons, reassured the housekeeper that it had nothing to do with Lady Eglantyne, and accompanied her at least as far as the staircase, when somebody banged the doorknocker. Mr. Fitch, who generally hovered in the library to pounce on the door, was nowhere in earshot. "You'd best answer it, Emma," Mrs. Blakeley said, as she went up. "He must be at the silver again."

Emma veered from the stairs and went to wrench open the door. To her astonishment, she found unexpected yet familiar faces, and together at that, she noted, without a Sproule around anywhere.

"Good morning, Miss Blair, Mr. Cauley," she said a trifle breathlessly. Both their mouths had opened; at the sight of Emma nothing came out. They seemed to have also expected anyone but her.

"Oh, Emma," Gwyneth breathed finally. "I'm so glad to see you. We've come looking for Ridley Dow."

"Yes, please, come in. I'll let Miss Beryl know you're here. I'm afraid I can't say about Mr. Dow. I suppose," she added without hope, "he's not at the inn?"

"No. Neither is my cook," Judd said tersely.

"Oh, Mr. Cauley." Emma put her fingers to her mouth. "I am sorry."

"That's hardly the worst of it."

But Gwyneth interrupted before he could add anything more interesting. "Do you know, Emma, I don't think we really need to trouble Miss Beryl at all. Perhaps you could just show us into the library, or some quiet place, where we could wait alone for Mr. Dow?"

Emma eyed her, mute with surprise, and then with sudden, improbable conjecture. "I think you should have your word with Miss Beryl."

"But we don't need to disturb—"

"She is already disturbed, and she'll want to see you. Come into the drawing room. Nobody will be down for another hour at least. She'll want to see you."

They followed her silently. She hoped, hurrying upstairs after she left them alone, that they wouldn't go wandering off on their own without her.

"Miss Blair and Mr. Cauley," she told Miranda Beryl, who appeared at her chamber door in sedate gray wool from throat to boot. She looked glacial at the idea of idle company. "I think," Emma added, "they might have noticed the bell. They came to search for Mr. Dow."

Miss Beryl's brows rose. She came out without a word, gesturing for Emma to follow her. She barely greeted her guests as they stood awkwardly at the cold fireplace; she asked abruptly, "Emma said she thinks you might have come because of the bell. Do you have any idea where Ridley Dow is?"

They stared at her, wordless again. Judd cleared his throat.

"No. And yes, we noticed the bell. I think—We're afraid he might be in a great deal of danger."

Miss Beryl nodded so sharply she nearly dropped a curl. "Yes. I'm afraid of that as well. Can you open doors, too?"

"Doors?" Gwyneth echoed faintly.

Miss Beryl sighed, dropped so gracefully into a chair she seemed to melt into it. "Sit down. Please. You came here to look for Mr. Dow. What kind of danger would you expect him to be in, here where there's nothing more threatening than boredom or an overboiled egg?"

Mr. Cauley drew breath, held it before he spoke. "None here," he said softly. "Not in this side of Aislinn House." He paused; Miranda Beryl was nodding again. "Then you know," he continued haltingly. "You know about the other Aislinn House?"

"Ridley told me. Emma opened doors to it. That's how Ridley found his way there the first time. This time, he might have found his own way in."

"Yes," Judd said, his hands tightening on the arms of his chair. "Something extraordinary must have happened in that Aislinn House to startle the bell into ringing at the wrong time of day."

"Ridley. You think Ridley happened."

"Yes." He added, seemingly at a tangent, "And my cook went missing from the inn this morning as well."

"Your cook," Miss Beryl said blankly.

"Mr. Pilchard."

"Mr. P—" She stopped, frowning at a dust mote. "Why do I know that name?"

Emma felt her nape hairs prickle. "The stranger, miss,"

she whispered. "He is the stranger in Sealey Head who would look to you like he belongs here."

"Mr. Pilchard," Miranda Beryl echoed faintly. "Your cook is Nemos Moore?"

"I think—I think so," Judd answered, looking dazed. "I believe he tried to poison Ridley yesterday, which is why he was so sick when you came. Fortunately, you sent for Hesper in time. Miss Beryl, how do you know about the bell, about the other Aislinn House? Ridley Dow spoke of you as someone with whom he was scarcely acquainted in Landringham. Nor did he wish more, it seemed."

She smiled suddenly, revealing a lovely, startling glimpse of the secret Miss Beryl. "So did I, Mr. Cauley. Speak of him that way, I mean. To keep Nemos Moore's eyes off him, and always on me. My friends here know Nemos Moore as the clever and wealthy Mr. Moren, who amuses himself in my company. To him, I'm the idle and fatuous heir of Aislinn House, which he regards quite possessively. To him, Mr. Dow has been only a rather earnest, scholarly young man who collects books and becomes excited about the most cobwebby topics, like ancient history and the habits of nightjars."

"And magic," Gwyneth interjected.

"And magic. Ridley learned years ago about the strange otherworld within Aislinn House. Of course he told me. We are—" She hesitated, while the faintest shade of rose warmed her skin. "We have always been close. And very secret. Nemos Moore is extremely jealous of his discovery of the world he found here, and is convinced that it rightly belongs to him. He has power over it; it is his perfect spell. I am heir only to its outward pillars and posts, a handful of sticks and floorboards. So he thinks: the rest belongs to him. He would marry me to keep it," she added with unexpected tartness. "Failing that, I don't know what he'd do. So far I've managed to persuade him that my total lack of interest is not in him but in the entire subject of marriage. I'm afraid that won't satisfy him once Aislinn House is truly mine."

"What a tale," Miss Blair breathed. "You and Ridley are both in danger from Nemos Moore, it seems. We must find Ridley Dow as soon as possible, help him in any way we can. But how? What should we do?"

"I could open a door," Emma suggested. "It worked before, when he was in trouble."

"Open a door," Gwyneth repeated, her brows peaked. "I don't understand. There's a special door into the other Aislinn House?"

"Any door in the house might open to the other Aislinn House," Emma explained, "to those who can see it. Most people never do. But I've found it behind nearly every door in this house, including the coal cellar and Lady Eglantyne's dressing room."

"So we can get into it that way," Gwyneth said, looking entranced. "Rescue Ridley, and—" She paused. "Well. Somehow. I wish I knew more about magic."

Judd glanced at her. "How much would it really help him, you mean, for us all to go blundering in armed with candlesticks and pokers?"

"The other Aislinn House can be frightening," Emma said. "I've never crossed into that world in my life, and I've been opening doors since I was tiny. I was never certain I'd find my way back. And there are things that you'd never think to be afraid of in this world. A great flock of crows nearly did Mr. Dow in, the first time. He barely made it back through the door. If I hadn't opened it, no telling, between the crows and the bad-tempered knights, what might have become of him."

"Not to mention the wicked sorcerer," Gwyneth murmured. "We can slam the door against birds, but would that work against Nemos Moore?"

Judd shifted restively, causing his chair to creak. "One way to find out," he reminded them. "We're not doing much to help, sitting here and scaring ourselves with what-ifs. From what you've said, Emma, an open door might actually help him. We could at least do that."

"It's a place to start," Miss Beryl agreed, rising quickly. "I have no idea what we can do against Nemos Moore, but I don't see why we should make things easier for him by doing nothing." She looked at Emma. "Which door?"

"The stillroom pantry," Emma answered promptly. "It worked before, and none of your guests would likely wander down there and see us."

None of the guests seemed to have bothered to get out of bed yet; no one was around at all, staff or visitor, to make a comment or ask a question as the little group followed Emma through the silent house. She didn't think to wonder if anyone might be already waiting in the stillroom itself. Opening the door, she realized that of course she should have known.

"Hesper!" Miss Beryl exclaimed, as the flighty-haired, barefoot woman slid off the table to greet them.

For once she had no smile for Emma, only a deepening of the worry in her eyes as she looked at her daughter.

"I guessed that this is where you might come." She cast

a glance askew at Miranda Beryl, acknowledged her uncertainly, "Miss Beryl."

"We all heard the bell ring at the wrong time of day," Miss Beryl explained, her eyes going to the closed pantry door.

"Even Lady Eglantyne noticed," Emma told her mother, who was still staring at Miranda Beryl.

"Did she? I've been wondering lately how much she knew. If that's why she is waiting."

"Waiting?" Miss Beryl queried, taking her eyes off the door.

"For the end of the story," Hesper explained. "I wondered if maybe she made a friend in the other Aislinn House, like Emma did, and she wants to see things put right before she dies."

"That could be part of it," Miss Beryl mused, pacing now, back and forth in front of the pantry door. "I know she worries about me and Ridley."

"Mr. Dow? And you?" The missing smile illumined her face; she exclaimed, "Well, that explains that, doesn't it, now?" Miranda Beryl looked at her without answering, except for the faint flush on her face, the wry smile. "That's why you sent me over to the inn so quickly to help him. And what now? Is your Mr. Dow in trouble again?"

"We thought we'd have Emma open a door and see," Judd explained.

"Good idea. Just seeing, that part, I mean."

"Well—"

"Of course you'd all have the good sense not to cross a threshold laid down by sorcery. Or rush into a spellbound world without a word to defend yourselves with."

"Of course we'd never do that," Judd said adamantly. "I mean, unless, of course, circumstances require."

"Are you going, too?" Gwyneth asked her shrewdly.

"I took a very strong dislike to Mr. Pilchard last night," Hesper answered roundly, "misusing good, green, living treasures like that. When I heard the bell ring, I put this and that together and wound up here, waiting for Emma. Let's see what you can do, girl."

Emma stepped forward, opened the stillroom pantry door.

A solid wall of stone blocked it from threshold to lintel: a message from the other Aislinn House.

"Keep Out," Miranda Beryl whispered. She moved abruptly, tried it with her boot: a fierce shove that in another world might have shifted a lesser stone.

Nothing budged. She turned finally, wordlessly, went to sit on the long wooden table, gazing at the door. One by one, they ranged themselves beside her and waited.

Twenty-two

Ysabo crouched on bare stone, staring at the bell.

It hung from nothing in the middle of the tiny room she and Ridley Dow had fallen into. The room had no door; it was a perfect cube, with a window in each wall, little more than gaps in the stones and open to the weather. One looked out over the sea, the others over the endless wood.

From the seaward side, she guessed, someone might watch the sun go down every evening, could ring the bell at exactly the moment the light vanished. If there had been a door to come and go by.

As they had tumbled into the room, the bell had rung. Ridley had fallen against it, the princess guessed. The sudden, loud, hollow clang was startling; it reverberated in the air like a word that should not have been spoken. It was an unlovely thing, its worn metal pocked, a jagged crack across it, the paint that had once gilded it bubbled and chipped from centuries of windblown rain, hot summer light simmering within the stones, the daily pound of the heavy clapper over years, decades, centuries.

"Where are we?" she had asked Ridley as they gathered themselves up. Even then, even before he had peeled himself off the floor, his eyes had been riveted on the bell.

"We're in the book," he said, and left her to contemplate the peculiar circumstances that made his answer perfectly comprehensible.

The next time she spoke, to wonder uneasily whether he might know how to get out of a doorless room, or, for that matter, a book, he didn't answer. He didn't seem to hear anything she said after that. He sat on the floor, leaning against the wall, staring up at the bell as though it spoke a secret, silent language only he could hear.

He looked spellbound.

I am trapped, she thought, in a stone cell with a man who can't hear my voice, who seems to be conversing silently with a bell. Should I have let him unlock the tower door and gone up to feed the crows instead?

It was past midday now; the sun was beginning its leisurely arc toward the sea, though no light spilled yet through any of the windows. What had Maeve and Aveline and the knights thought when no one came to hold the third cup at the noon-hour ritual? She couldn't imagine. The knights weren't used to thinking; perhaps they just made do without her. Or had they, already armed and suspicious, scattered through the house to find her, raging among barking dogs, shadowed by the crows?

On the whole, she decided, thinking of their mindless, angry eyes, their sharp swords, she felt much safer in this doorless place that they could never find.

The bell began to vibrate silently. A thumbnail of gilt flecked off of it. Ridley closed his eyes.

That much happened, then nothing, except the bell shimmering in midair. Ysabo watched it for a while; then she turned her head and watched Ridley.

Something was happening between the man and the bell.

Ridley straightened, as though the bell had slowly pulled him away from the wall. His eyes never left it. The bell seemed to pulse, throwing a golden shadow around itself that faded, then grew bright again. Then faded. Then grew bright. Ysabo pushed closer to the wall, trying to make herself small, trying to watch both at once. The air itself seemed to vibrate, a tension in it that crawled over her skin and made her want to hide within the stones.

Ridley caught his breath. Ysabo stared at him. He cried a word suddenly, his face illumined by the glow of the bell as light poured out of it in every direction. The bell cracked completely, metal torn from metal in an arc from rim to dome. The twin pieces thundered to the floor and re-formed in a dizzying swirl of shape and color. Ysabo flung her arms over her eyes but still saw it, glowing like the imprint of the sun behind her eyelids. Ridley made another sound, a garbled exclamation; whatever it was, he had gotten his voice back. Ysabo lifted one arm, peered at him. He was still staring raptly, so she lifted her other arm, cupped her hands above her eyes. The brilliant blur was slowing, sorting itself into long, long hair, a smoky mix of gray and black, a tall, lean-limbed body covered in gray silk and black wool, extraordinary eyes of blue-green teal, a pale, lined, fine-boned face somewhere between Aveline and ageless.

She gazed down at Ridley as intently as he had stared at the bell, until he spoke the word again, and Ysabo realized it was her name.

"Hydria."

Something snapped; the air sparked between them where a bond had broken.

The woman spoke, a boom like the sound of the sea and the bell together, and Ysabo covered her ears again.

"Where is he? I will tear his head from his shoulders and boil it for breakfast." Her eyes loosed Ridley abruptly; he sagged back against the stones, drawing breath deeply, his face glistening with sweat. She looked at Ysabo. "Who are you?"

"Ysabo," she answered, the only word, under the queen's fierce gaze, that she remembered.

"What are you doing here?"

"I came with Ridley Dow."

Queen Hydria moved suddenly, stepped forward to fold her long body down in front of Ysabo. "I know that face," she breathed, tracing Ysabo's jaw line with her forefinger. "It nearly broke my heart." She turned her gaze to Ridley again. "How," she asked with amazement, "did you find me?"

"It wasn't easy. I heard that bell ringing across the centuries and followed the sound of it. I had no idea what it was until I saw the magic in it. I looked into it, and saw you."

She closed her eyes, her face growing rigid, livid; Ysabo half expected the bell to sound again, Hydria's voice for so many years, her only word.

"No wonder it cracked," she whispered, and the queen opened her eyes, stared at Ysabo again.

"I felt such terrible sorrow, such loss, such fury, at that moment at the end of every day when the last light faded in the world. The bell was the sound of my heart, crying out to the world. Before Nemos Moore came, it was a joyous sound in my court. It summoned everyone to the evening feast, to music, laughter, companions. Before Nemos Moore came and broke our days into pieces, meaningless, joyless shards of tasks. Before he turned my knights into crows, before he replaced them with paper men from my wizard Blagdon's book. Before he turned half my world into paintings from that book, so that we could see the world and long for it, but no doors led out of Aislinn House into it, only into the flat worlds of ink and paint—"

"Why?" Ridley whispered. "Why did he do that?"

"Because he wanted power over me, my realm, and I refused him. Because I saw what he was: a little man with great power, who would toy with lives just because he could. I invited him into my court out of courtesy and curiosity. He told me that he was a scholar of the road, traveling to learn what he could. I never thought to ask what road he had found that led him into the rich, secret heart of Aislinn House."

"Your wizard. Blagdon. He made the book?"

She nodded. "He had great gifts himself, for magic, for painting and for poetry. All this Nemos Moore used—he trifled with those gifts, like a child tearing apart pages it doesn't understand—to transform something bright and happy into a place of meaningless patterns, strictures, fears. A place without doors, without dreams. All because he knew he could never belong in my court. Blagdon was very old, almost as old as the house itself. He did what he could against Nemos

Moore. But in the end, I was trapped within the bell. I don't know what happened to Blagdon."

Ridley had grown silent, in a way that Ysabo recognized; he was gazing into the queen's eyes but not seeing her, seeing inward, backward. "I wonder..." he murmured finally and stopped, then began again. "That boat..."

"What boat?"

His eyes came alive again; a smile rose and sank beneath the surface of his face. "Can you get us out of here?"

"How?" she demanded. "There is no door. I have no idea where we are."

"You had the power to speak to the world when you were spellbound," he reminded her. "Nemos Moore is in your house again. If you want him, I'll help you."

"Oh, yes." Ysabo saw the shimmering around the queen that had trembled around the bell. "I want him."

She turned abruptly, walked into the stones. They tore as though they were paper. Ysabo heard Ridley's breath shake. He pushed himself to his feet, held out his hand to her.

They stepped through stone into the wood beyond Aislinn House.

Hydria had already left a black rip between the trees, which were oddly silent and smelled of nothing. They followed quickly, stepped into a great hall full of painted knights drinking from cups held by three women. The tear that Hydria had left was through the sunlight falling into the open doors of the hall. The next rip in the paper world was through a flock of crows.

And then into shadow, walls of stone, dark water flowing silently through the underground cave. Ysabo could smell the water, the dusty, ancient air, feel the chill of a place that sunlight never found.

They were out of the book and in the boat. It was still moored by its chain and the stake hammered into stone. The lantern on its prow was lit. Nemos Moore stood within the light.

"Ah," he said softly. "You found your way, Mr. Dow." He nodded to Hydria. "My lady. Ladies. How does it feel to take a simple breath of air after so many years? Wonderful, I would think. Is it?"

He was no longer the elegant, clever, middle-aged man Ysabo had seen before. He was now young and lithe, with long hair and a genial expression not unlike Ridley's: the traveling scholar, she guessed, whom Hydria would remember welcoming so innocently into her house.

She recognized him, and she didn't waste time talking to him. She moved in the boat as unflinchingly as she had moved through the pages of the wizard's book. With one kick she sent the lantern flying to strike and spatter oil all over Nemos Moore before it hit the stone and shattered.

Flames shot up his clothes. He shouted, cursing, and flung himself into the water. The intense, oblivious expression had appeared again on Ridley's face. He didn't hear Nemos Moore's next shout, which sent rocks rattling down among them; he didn't seem to see the danger Hydria put herself in, trying to push the sorcerer back under the water with her foot. He grabbed at her, cursing again, and she lost her balance, tumbled to the bottom of the boat, which rocked wildly and nearly tossed Ridley overboard.

Something was happening to the boat. It was softening, dwindling, changing shape. Ysabo, feeling it turn under her feet, gasped and grabbed the chain to keep them close to the shore. It came up lightly in her hands; she stared with horror at the empty end of it. The boat drifted toward the middle of the river, passing Nemos Moore, shoulder deep in water as he reached the shore. He pulled himself up on the stones and turned.

He said Ridley's name. It came out in gusts of color, gouts of glittering shadow that fell over Ridley like rain. He stopped moving, looking vaguely surprised by something he didn't expect. Nemos Moore said Hydria's name. She, too, grew still beneath the rain of her name, though her desperate, furious face recognized the spell. Nemos Moore looked at Ysabo.

She moved before he said her name, whipping the chain across the water, sending it curling around his knees. She wrenched at it. Then the boat turned like a live thing under her feet, and flung her backward into the water.

When she surfaced again, coughing and clutching the motionless, floating bodies that had slid in with her, she saw a tall old man with hair like moss and skin like melted wax standing in the water. He held the wizard's book open with his hands. His eyes were locked on Nemos Moore, who was back in the water, shouting something at the chain around his knees.

The old man slammed the book shut, and Nemos vanished.

He ran his hand over it, murmuring. A seal flowed over the closed pages, hiding them, binding the book together from cover to cover. Ridley and Hydria came to life abruptly, floundering until they caught their footing, their heads turning this way and that, searching for the missing Nemos Moore. They found the wizard instead.

"Blagdon!" Hydria exclaimed, her wet hands over her mouth. "You're still alive!"

"My thanks to that young man," he answered.

"Yes, mine, too," she answered tightly. "He saved my life. But where's the other one? Nemos Moore?"

The old man smiled, a sweet, oddly content expression for someone who had been chained in water for a very long time and still hadn't found his way out.

"I closed the book on him."

THE change in the great house was subtle but immediate. Ysabo noticed it first after they left the underground chamber, tracking wet footprints on the stones, and were met by solicitous servants who did not elude their eyes, but sought them, offering towels and a fire, dry clothes. They seemed to recognize everyone but Ridley Dow, the stranger whom they welcomed with courtesy and good cheer, offering him, as Hydria commanded, the best of everything.

He declined with thanks and went off somewhere with the wizard instead.

They escorted Ysabo to her chambers, which seemed to be exactly where they had always been in a house whose bustlings were at once domestic and unfamiliar. As they passed through the great hall to the stairs, someone flung open the broad doors through which the knights rode at midday. But the knights seemed to be elsewhere; the hall, except for musicians and elderly courtiers playing chess, was oddly peaceful. Nothing came in the door but light and wind, the soughing of the trees, the surprising sounds, beyond the courtyard walls, of a blacksmith's hammer, the bellow of some barnyard animal.

It was as though several different times had merged, like ripples in water crossing one another, changing shape, forming a new pattern. One of the ripples had to do with the wizard's book; another with the spellbound house and those who had been born and lived and died within that dark time while the queen and the wizard had been imprisoned; a third had to do with Queen Hydria's house as it had been, generous, rich, happy, before Nemos Moore had found his way into it. Nothing had been lost, Ysabo realized slowly and with wonder, except a thoroughly wicked sorcerer, who existed now only in the pages of a book.

The servants delivered her into the hands of her ladies, who took such delight in her return that they rendered her nearly speechless. They exclaimed over her wet clothes and seemed to think she had fallen into a stream while riding in the wood. Their smiling eyes suggested some romantic import to the mythical ride, part of which she must surely have enjoyed.

Ysabo found it easiest just to agree with everything they said.

A pair of them escorted her to Maeve's chambers; as usual, Aveline was with her.

The ripples of time had flowed a bit differently through their memories. They welcomed Ysabo with relief; she was not sure how long she had been trapped in the bell chamber, but apparently long enough for them to worry.

"We haven't seen you all day," Aveline said. "No one could find you. Were you with Zondros?"

"Zondros." Belatedly, she remembered a knight with ivory

hair and black brows; she wondered if he still existed, or if he had turned back into a painting in Blagdon's book. "Oh. Mostly I—ah—I was immersed in a book."

They took it with remarkable calm, this shattering of ritual. "We missed you," Aveline murmured, smoothing Ysabo's drying hair. There was no sign in the room of the wedding dress; it must have gone the way of the paper knights, she realized with relief.

The door opened; a lady murmured, "Queen Hydria."

Maeve and Aveline stared at one another. Maeve dropped her embroidery; they both rose hastily, and curtsied to the tall queen, whose gray and black hair swirled now into a braided pile on her head, whose exquisite green gown and blue mantle matched her teal eyes. She wore a crescent of gold in her hair, jewels on her fingers, in her shoes.

She smiled at them. They gazed at her silently, memories coming and going in their eyes. Was she a dream? Their faces wondered. Were they the dream? Whose story had they all been in?

Aveline spoke first, huskily. "My lady. You have been gone—No, we have—Where have we all been all this time? And how old have we gotten to be?"

"You remember," Hydria said gently, with a sigh of relief. "Please. Sit with me. We can get to know one another."

"Did we ever?" Maeve asked confusedly. "Or are you a story that Nemos Moore told us long ago?"

"Perhaps. I have been spellbound, like this house, for a very long time. Years past my counting. You both know Nemos Moore?"

"He came to visit us now and then," Maeve answered. "Mostly when Aveline was small, and I was young. He took us out—I think he did—I remember roads, rain, adventures...Or was it only stories?"

"It may have been only stories," Hydria said. "But his stories had a way of seeming very real. I think you are still in your own time. I am as old as I was when he bound me into the bell, but I came back into your time. Those who were spellbound with me, servants, courtiers, knights, remember me. Those, like you, who were born to the ritual and bound by it, know me as a name. A memory of Aislinn House. One of the tales that Nemos Moore found in Blagdon's book and brought to life."

"The ritual." Aveline had picked up Maeve's embroidery; she sat with it in her hand, absolutely still, looking back. "There was a ritual once. I remember it. Pieces of it. A long time ago. Wasn't it?"

"Not worth remembering," Hydria said with an edge in her voice. "My wizard Blagdon has made me a new bell," she added, "with a beautiful sound. The other was weathered and cracked; it had a toll like all the sorrows in the world. This one speaks a bubble of gold. You will hear it this evening. I am giving a feast in honor of his work."

"Blagdon," Maeve murmured politely, looking as though she were struggling to remember. Her face brightened. "He wrote poetry, didn't he? And painted with inks. Delicate scenes of Aislinn House when it was ancient. Nemos Moore—" She checked herself, seeming to feel a chill in the air. "Someone," she amended vaguely, "showed me his book. Beautiful, it was."

Later, after Hydria had gone, she looked helplessly at Aveline. "I must be getting old," she said. "I can't remember anymore who's alive or dead."

"We'll find out at supper tonight," Aveline assured her, and looked at Ysabo. "You will be there?"

"Yes, Aveline."

"Good," she sighed. "As long as I see you, I know where I am in this house. I still have all my memories of you."

The knights came to supper as always. Their faces had changed, Ysabo thought. They smiled; they spoke to the women as well as to one another; they touched their wives. They weren't mindlessly noisy, like a flock of crows, intent on only one another and their food, saying nothing that hadn't been said a thousand times before, as though even their conversation had been ritual. One among them, Ysabo noticed, had long pale hair and black brows. He looked at her several times down the long table as though he knew her. His eyes were gray. Once he gave her a sweet, intense smile that astonished her.

Ridley Dow had not appeared for supper, nor had Blagdon. Ysabo suspected they were together somewhere, sharing their unusual knowledge and experiences. She hoped she would see him to thank him before he returned to the other Aislinn House. She found the queen's eyes on her once. Hydria, holding her gaze, raised her cup and inclined her head.

"To Ysabo," she said, without explaining why. Her court raised their cups and cheered without knowing exactly why and drank to Ysabo, who finally understood exactly why.

Twenty-three

The bell tolled the sun down, as always, and Ridley walked out of the stillroom pantry door.

It was a different bell, Judd thought: a deep, sweet, mellow toll that had forgotten all its sorrows. And a different Ridley, rumpled, unshorn, carrying a fat bright book under his arm and smiling peacefully as he saw who waited for him. He went to Miranda Beryl, who was sitting with Judd on the table; he set the book down and took her hands.

"All's well," he said, and kissed her fingers. She freed her hands, put her arms around his neck, held him tightly. Judd heard her long, slow sigh.

"So many years of secrecy," she said, raising her head to meet his eyes. "Ridley, we won't know how to behave among people. Is Nemos Moore—Is he truly—"

"Gone, yes." He tapped the book. "In here. And the wizard who trapped him there taught me the spell in case my wicked ancestor finds his way out between the lines. The wizard's powers are astonishing. He said I could come back whenever I like to learn from him."

"Nemos Moore is in that book?" Miranda and Judd exclaimed together.

"Yes. A paper sorcerer, he is now." He smiled over her shoulder at Judd. "Come to rescue me, did you?"

"Well, of course. Along with Emma and Hesper."

"Invaluable women."

"Gwyneth was here, too, most of the afternoon, until her aunt sent a message to the inn and found out that Judd had come here," Miranda said. "She requested rather adamantly that her niece return home for tea. We were prepared to take the other Aislinn House by storm, except that the house refused to let us in."

"I'm so very, very glad it did. Nemos Moore was an evil, dangerous old man; his cooking alone would have killed me if you hadn't sent Hesper in time. He would have had no mercy for any of you, either."

"I am so sorry," Judd said ruefully.

"How could you have known? He was under my nose, and I didn't recognize him. Anyway, he was a wonderful cook." He cocked a sympathetic brow at Judd. "I suppose we're back to Mrs. Quinn."

"Indeed not," Miranda answered. "I lent him Mrs. Haw. My guests spend most of their time there anyway; she was wasted here, and most unhappy."

"What a marvelous idea!"

"Wasn't it?" Judd agreed, smiling.

"Ridley."

"Yes, my dear one?"

"You were going to explain to us how you rescued Aislinn House from Nemos Moore and changed the voice of that bell."

"Yes, it does sound completely different, doesn't it?" He paused; they waited. "Well. It's complicated." He hesitated again. "Very."

The door opened; Emma put her head in. "Excuse me," she said, and saw Ridley. She put her hands over her mouth. "Oh, you're back. Oh, Mr. Dow, is everything—"

"Yes."

"I knew it," she whispered behind her hands. "I knew it when I heard that bell. That everything was right again. And so did Lady Eglantyne."

Miranda opened her mouth; nothing came out for a moment. "Were you with her?" she asked abruptly.

"Yes, miss. My mother is still at her bedside. We all heard the bell. Lady Eglantyne just said, 'Good.' Then she closed her eyes and—and went. Shall I send for Dr. Grantham?"

"Yes, please, Emma."

"I am sorry, miss."

"So am I," Miranda murmured. She was silent a moment, touching her fingertips quickly to her eyes. She dropped her hand, continued steadily, "And tell Mrs. Blakeley and Mr. Fitch. Tell them not to worry. They will still have their places in this house for as long as they choose."

"I will." Emma lingered, a line across her brow. "She must have opened a few doors in her life, to understand what happened."

Miranda nodded, blinking. "She understood a great deal.

271

Much of it always between the lines in our letters. Where Nemos Moore never thought to look."

Emma's eyes moved to Ridley. "Ysabo?" she asked softly.

He nodded reassuringly. "I don't know what we would have done without her. She helped us all with enormous courage. She can tell you everything when you find her again."

"Thank you, Mr. Dow. I'm very glad to see you safe."

"So am I, Emma. So am I."

Judd left him to wait for Dr. Grantham and to tend to the domestic details of death with the new lady of Aislinn House. Miranda offered him a horse, which he accepted gratefully, wondering, as he rode home in the lingering spring dusk, what he would find in the way of chaos among his own staff and the new cook, all left to deal with the rambunctious guests by themselves. But the scene seemed much as usual when he arrived: gambling in the taproom, Mr. Quinn calling orders down the stairs, wonderful smells wafting up them.

"I took your father his supper," Mr. Quinn told him. "He's been asking for you. He seemed a bit worried. I took the liberty of mentioning Miss Blair; that calmed him down."

"How did you—?"

"Small town, Mr. Cauley, small world." He produced a rolled-up manuscript with a wildflower wilting underneath its ribbon. "She sent this up to you."

Judd read Gwyneth's story later to his father, when the inn quieted, and they could drink a beer together. Dugold listened without a word, giving it far more careful attention than he had to Nemos Moore's adventures.

At the end of it, he grinned. "Now there's a tale you might believe in! She made all that up? Are we sure?"

"That some previous Lord Aislinn didn't gamble away his daughter to some ruthless sea folk? Not to mention one of your ancestors gambling away our inn."

"It rings true," Dugold said stubbornly, and Judd smiled.

"It does indeed. We'll ask her."

Ridley came back late; they stayed up even later, while Ridley told another story of the bell, so complex, so full of mystery and magic that Judd found it as unbelievable as the secret Aislinn House. But there it was.

The next day, he was summoned to tea in a note from Gwyneth, by order of her aunt. He brought the manuscript with him, to the delight of the twins, who met him at the door and wrested it out of his hands.

"She sent it to you before she even read it to us," Crispin grumbled. "We had to wait for the ending."

Pandora was regarding him with a disconcerting intensity, as though trying to understand what exactly had possessed her older sister. She smiled sweetly at him in a manner he found vaguely ominous.

"Will I do?" he asked her finally.

"I suppose, if she must. Anyway, you're much better than the bird. Aunt Phoebe is wonderfully annoyed."

But Phoebe seemed resigned when he ventured with trepidation into the overstuffed parlor. She greeted him graciously, and poured him tea with only the faintest of sighs. Raven and Daria were already there, along with Ridley Dow, who had been at Aislinn House most of the day. Judd was surprised to see him.

Gwyneth came to him, slipped a hand under his elbow, and smiled at him. The simple, trusting gesture took his breath away; his teacup rattled on the saucer.

"Gwyneth," he said softly, with a great deal of satisfaction.

"Judd?"

"Nothing. Just that. I wanted to say your name."

She smiled again. "Did you like my story?"

"Yes, very much. My father is convinced that it must be true, though how the Cauleys got their inn back from the wicked sea folk, he couldn't say. Perhaps that should be your next story."

"I don't know . . . I'm unsure about my ending."

"Why? What don't you—"

But Phoebe interrupted them, raising her voice. "Gwyneth. Mr. Cauley. Mr. Dow says he has a piece of news he came especially to tell us first."

"Oh, what is it, Mr. Dow?" Daria asked eagerly. "Have you fallen in love with Sealey Head? Are you going to take up residence?"

"Part of the year at least," Ridley answered. He paused, searching for words, it seemed, in the face of the Sproules' anticipations. He continued finally, gently, "Miss Beryl and I have been secretly engaged for over a year. We didn't want to announce it during the sad time of Lady Eglantyne's illness. Now that it is over, we can be open about our decisions. Miss Beryl has become quite fond of Sealey Head and plans to keep Aislinn House as a peaceful haven from the noise and crush of Landringham."

Daria interrupted, her voice so high it fairly squeaked. "You're getting married?"

"To Miss Beryl?" Raven said incredulously. "But you never—you hardly seemed to—"

"We couldn't speak of it," Ridley said apologetically. "For

various reasons. It is my dearest hope that you can share our happiness."

There was a thump: Aunt Phoebe sitting down hard on the rocker. "Why, Mr. Dow!" she exclaimed. "I never imagined—you seem so unlikely!"

Gwyneth gave a hiccup of laughter, caught it behind her hand. Phoebe flushed bright red. Ridley only chuckled.

"I understand."

"I beg your—"

"No, no, Miss Blair. Perhaps it's more that Miss Beryl has seemed unlikely. When you know her better, and I hope you do, you'll understand why she might choose a bookish, bespectacled scholar with uncivilized habits and inexplicable interests." He cast another apologetic glance at Judd. "Since we plan to marry in Sealey Head at the end of the summer, I'm afraid you must put up with those of our noisy friends who have also been enchanted by Sealey Head."

"So much for spending the summer reading your books. My father will be pleased."

"The end of summer," Daria murmured, her stunned expression easing a little. "That's ages away. Anything could change by then."

"Yes," Raven said, with a little sideways glance at Gwyneth.

"Yes," Aunt Phoebe agreed.

Gwyneth drew a step closer to Judd, told them both firmly, "No."

They heard a sudden shout from Pandora, two closed doors away in the library. It brought Phoebe to her feet.

"What ails the child?"

"Oh, dear," Gwyneth said ruefully. "She must have read the end of my story."

Judd put his teacup down and squared his shoulders. "That reminds me ... Is your father at home?"

Phoebe sighed again, audibly. "Mr. Blair is in the library, Judd. I'm sure he'll be happy to see you."

Judd found Toland Blair and Mr. Trent there, with the twins, one disgruntled, the other grinning. The two men, immersed in the final pages of Gwyneth's story, nodded absently to him.

"I can't believe she killed poor Eloise," Pandora muttered, sitting on the sofa with her arms crossed.

"I think it's brilliant," Crispin said cheerfully.

"I think it's diabolical," Mr. Blair murmured. "Have you read this, Judd?"

"Yes, sir."

"And you still want to marry her?" He glanced up, smiled at the expression on Judd's face. "If my daughter is pleased with you, so am I. Maybe you can persuade her to change her ending, show us all some mercy."

"Oh, could you?" Pandora was on her feet suddenly, clinging to Judd's arm. "I think if my sister can please herself, she might allow Eloise to do the same."

"I wonder if any of it is true?" Mr. Trent said, looking over his spectacles at Judd. "Do you know?"

Judd hesitated, found the most ambiguous answer the most accurate. "No."

"I'll have to look into my histories."

"I do think she could come up with another ending," Pandora insisted stubbornly. "One where they all live happily ever after and the sea people become their friends."

Crispin groaned. Pandora flung herself back on the sofa to expostulate. Judd left them in dispute and went into the hall, where he found Gwyneth waiting for him.

"He was most reluctant to give up his beloved daughter," Judd told her, "but could not deny her what she seemed, so peculiarly, to want."

"Don't be silly," she said, taking his arm. "He's relieved that anybody at all would want a woman with such a deranged imagination and abnormal sensibilities. I just bade Mr. Dow good night; he has gone back to Aislinn House for the evening. Raven is under the table playing with Dulcie; Aunt Phoebe and Daria are making dire predictions about the romance between Miss Beryl and Mr. Dow. It will end, they think, around midsummer. Miss Beryl will flee to Landringham in complete, crashing boredom, complaining that she cannot get Mr. Dow's attention for the book that's always under his nose. Mr. Dow will contemplate throwing himself over Sealey Head into the sea, but will eventually allow himself to be consoled by Miss Sproule . . ."

"And you and I?"

"Will watch the sun go down every evening from the Inn at Sealey Head, and listen to the bell."

"Will you ever write the true story?" he asked her.

"Of course I will, when you and Ridley get around to telling it to me," she said, leading him out the door and down the road toward the headland bathed in light from the lowering sun. "But no one will ever believe it."